ST. MARTIN'S

MINOTAUR

MYSTERIES

Linda Barnes

the B
IG
DIG

St. Martin's Paperbacks

THE BIG DIG

Library of Congress Catalog Card Number: 2002068353

ISBN: 0-312-98969-5

Printed in the United States of America

St. Martin's Press hardcover edition / October 2002
St. Martin's Paperbacks edition / August 2003

St. Martin's Paperbacks are published by St. Martin's Press, 175 Fifth Avenue, New York, NY 10010.

10 9 8 7 6 5 4 3 2 1

In memory of Ellie Donner

Acknowledgments

The Central Artery/Third Harbor Tunnel project is real and currently slated for completion circa 2005 at a cost that will probably exceed $15 billion. This novel, however, is a work of fiction. There is no Site A1520, no Horgan Construction Company, and none of the characters invented for these pages exists in real life.

I would like to thank the men and women of the Dig who answered my questions, among them, Ann Davis, Andy Paven, and Tony Brown. Thanks to Richard Dimino of the Artery Business Committee. The Boston *Globe* and the Boston *Herald* have devoted columns of informative print to the subject of the Dig, and so has *Boston Magazine*. I'd also like to credit the Big Dig's Web site, one of the finest on the Internet, and three books: Dan McNichol's *The Big Dig*, with photographs by Andy Ryan; *The Big Dig: Reshaping an American City*, by Peter Vanderwarker; and *Building Big*, by David Macaulay, for helping me grasp a few of the complex building techniques used in the project. Thanks also to Eddie Jacobs, Nancy Hawthorne, Luis Tovar, Jennifer Magnolfi, Monica Tovar, Steve Appelblatt, Richard Barnes, Brian DeFiore, Michael Denneny, Kelley Ragland, and Gina Maccoby.

CHAPTER 1

I used to work with Happy Eddie Conklin when I was a cop. He had a gruff voice, a blunt, dogged manner, and while he was "freakin' old enough to be my father," as he reminded me often enough, he never treated me like a child. When he asked me to meet him at Ocean Wealth in Chinatown, I accepted for two reasons: they serve pungent, spicy squid to die for, and I knew he'd cover the lunch as a business expense.

After a minor heart attack, cushioned by eighty-percent disability, he'd moved on to join a national security firm. I'd bailed at the same time, *sans* pension, and driven a cab nights while I got the Carlyle Detective Agency off the ground. My name is Carlyle—Carlotta Carlyle—and I've been an independent operator for more years than I hung on as a cop. I run a solo shop, pilot a cab between cases, and don't stress my first name because it's seldom seen as a plus in the business.

Eddie, now head of Foundation Security's Boston office, was early, wearing a gray suit that did its best to make him look ten pounds lighter, seated at a table barely big enough to handle two plates and a teapot. He rose, clasping my hand in both of his, yanking me into an embrace.

"Business, I tell ya, fantastic. Boomin' don't come close. Lack of trust in this town, geez, it's amazin'. Due diligence alone, bodyguardin' alone—I could run my own freakin' police department, ya know? Ya like this place? Ya want something to start?"

He relayed my order of hot and sour soup to the hovering waiter and demanded "egg rolls, spring rolls, whatever ya call 'em," as well. "Bring that sweet sauce, ya know? The duck kind."

I poured steaming tea into small white cups.

Eddie looked prosperous, from his blue silk tie to his tasseled slip-ons. His gray hair was short, his jaw freshly shaven. He glanced around to discourage eavesdroppers at neighboring tables, lowered his voice half a notch. "So how's your boy, Mooney?"

Some rumors have a longer half-life than nuclear waste. Lieutenant Detective Joseph Mooney, head of Boston Homicide, is another former colleague. We're friends, no more, never so much as a misguided one-night stand, but the grapevine says otherwise. If Eddie was planning to use me to cozy up to Moon, all I'd get out of lunch would be calories.

"Think it's gonna snow later?" I asked.

Eddie gave me a look. "Ya got yourself shot up, I hear."

"I'm fine."

"Good. Glad to hear it."

He was studying my face like he'd never seen green eyes, a pointy chin, or flaming hair before. Made me wonder whether I looked drawn or pale. I widened my smile, hoped the extra wattage would substitute for blusher.

I wasn't fine, to tell the truth. I had raised red scars on my left thigh from a through-and-through bullet wound. I couldn't play my usual three-days-a-week game of killer volleyball, and the exercises the physical therapist demanded ranged from painful to torturous. Yesterday the jerk had mentioned that my leg might always ache in bad weather. Considering I live in one of the slush and muck capitals of the planet, his words hit like a death sentence.

The tea was too hot to taste, so I set my cup down on a paper placemat bordered by Chinese signs of the zodiac. "So, business is good," I said, aiming Eddie back to professional ground.

He sniffed his tea suspiciously, searched the table for a nonexistent sugar bowl. "I got regular jobs up the wazzoo and a lot of special shit, too. The presidential debate at UMass? I handled that, the local stuff. They had G-men for the vice president, FBI, Justice. A few more red-carpet deals like that, I could retire rich."

I tried my tea again. "You got the ex-presidents when they speak at Faneuil Hall?"

"Damn, that's comin' up, right?"

"Patriots' Day." April nineteenth is Patriots' Day in Boston, always has been, always will be. They've tried to turn it into another one of those Monday holidays, but it rankles. Nobody celebrates the Fourth of July on the closest Monday.

"I don't think so." Eddie nodded gravely like I'd just offered him the job. "I got my plate too full, which is why I'm here. I'm interested in spreading a little largesse your way."

Largesse. You can go years without hearing anyone say that word. It plinked against my eardrums like a rattle of gold coins.

"The Dig." He mouthed the word rather than speaking it, very hush-hush.

When you say "the Dig" around here, you don't need to elaborate. The Dig is the Big Dig, formally known as the Central Artery/Third Harbor Tunnel Project. It's the biggest urban construction project in the history of the modern world, no less, a mega-dollar boondoggle to some, a brilliant and farsighted plan for Boston's transportation future to others. Read it either way in the newspapers, hear it praised and damned daily on talk radio.

The Central Artery/Third Harbor Tunnel project is all about running 161 lane miles of highway through a 7.5-mile-long corridor. Easy enough, except that instead of racing through some featureless desert, the corridor slices straight through the heart of one of the nation's oldest, most congested cities. Add the news that half those highway miles are located in tunnels and include four major highway interchanges. Plus there's a landmark bridge over the Charles River and an under-Boston-Harbor tunnel for good luck.

To weary natives, it seems like it's been going on forever, but really, here in the year of our lord, 2000, the Dig is just hitting its stride, moving into the heaviest period of construction, with four thousand construction workers planting three million dollars a day deep into the ground.

"There's stuff going on." Eddie kept the whisper low. "Graft. Fraud."

"No shit." I widened my eyes. "Gambling in the backroom?"

"Huh?"

A guy Conklin's age, especially an ex-detective, ought to know his vintage Bogie movies better. I bit the inside of my cheek. Really, the very idea that a project okayed by the federal government in 1987 at a price tag of two point six billion, and currently playing at fourteen billion bucks and counting, might have graft and fraud associated with its execution . . . I was shocked, simply shocked.

Eddie leaned his head close. Foundation Security had been hired by the Inspector General of the Commonwealth after a series of scathing reports lambasting the IG's failure at ferreting out Dig fraud. As Eddie told it, the IG wasn't sure which of his guys were on the take, so he'd opted to bring in fresh blood. Eddie and his ops had already uncovered a few irregularities. Nothing major, but the TV broadcasters had eaten them up—and the IG's office had finally grabbed some positive headlines.

Would I be interested in joining his team, on a temporary basis that might lead to something more than temporary?

Before my lunch with Happy Eddie, I'd been juggling medical bills, grocery bills, property tax payments—deciding whether, and then when, to loot my little sister's college fund. I'd been nursing a bum leg, dunning deadbeat clients, paying full rates for physical therapy. In short, I was more than ready to consider the delights of a regular paycheck plus health benefits. I gulped tea and wondered whether I could deal with the concept of having a boss again, or whether I'd lost the knack of working well with others.

Happy Eddie Conklin's safe, secure, and possibly long-term job looked pretty damned good to me. *Geshmak iz der fish oyfyemens tish.* That's the Yiddish for what my mother's mother might have said about the situation: "Tasty is the fish on someone else's dish."

And so, eight weeks ago, after polishing off Kung Pao prawns and pungent, spicy squid, I'd signed on the dotted line. Foundation Security, for their part, provided two weeks basic training. There had been initial skepticism among Eddie's colleagues as to whether a six-foot-one redheaded woman could move from site to site undercover. Before my final training session I'd invested in a box of Lady Clairol, Ash Brown, worn my newly mousy hair in an upswept do, and added a pair of clear spectacles. When the instructor gazed at me blankly as I entered the room, and politely inquired whether he could help, I passed with flying colors.

I thought I knew the Dig when I started, but what I knew was myth and legend. I knew that depressing the Central Artery was the notion of a young MIT-trained engineer, Fred Salvucci, who later became Governor Dukakis's transportation secretary; that it was his dream, and some said his revenge for his grandmother's Brighton home, bulldozed almost forty years ago because it lay in the path of Massachusetts Turnpike Authority Chairman William Callahan's ill-planned Turnpike extension. I knew that Salvucci's idea had been initially derided, that then-state rep Barney Frank had reputedly said it would be cheaper to elevate the entire city than sink the artery. I knew driving through and around the Dig. I knew confusing signs and miles of blue-and-yellow barriers. I knew endless delays and complex detours. I knew the sound of travelers, cabbing into the city from Logan Airport, catching their breath at the mouth of the Ted Williams Tunnel, gasping at the forest of giant cranes that loomed over the South Bay.

I didn't know the icy bite of wind on construction sites, or the stubborn grit that stayed under my nails, or the sticky blue clay that clung to my boots. I didn't know union rules and OSHA standards and how a hard-hat limits vision and when to wear earplugs to prevent hearing loss.

I didn't know shit, and I still didn't, not after a mere six weeks on two sites. But I had a better idea of what I didn't know, and I was developing a fine disdain for clueless civilians who didn't even know that the blue-and-yellow barriers went by the name "kit-of-parts."

I hadn't mined gold on either of my previous sites. The rumored drugs at the pit where I'd toiled as a laborer traced to a single user, not an established ring. A brief truck-driving gig hadn't revealed the promised gas-siphoning scam. Oh, I could have made a case against a couple of petty scroungers, but really, was it worth it? Seemed to me the big guys, the heavy-duty grafters, were walking tall while I kept an eye out for twopenny-nail theft.

Maybe my third site would be different. The job was.

CHAPTER 2

Keyboarding, filing, and answering the damn phone. They were easier on my sore leg than hauling pipe, gentler on my tailbone than driving a 'dozer, but they came with their own set of problems. Secretarial chores meant dressing neatly, obeying orders, and smiling till my cheeks ached.

"This ain't no South Bay, ya know, no effin' wonder of the world." Harv O'Day, the site super, tried and failed to sound modest. A wiry little guy in his thirties, what he didn't know about the Dig you could probably stick in the corner of one of his cool gray eyes. "At the Bay, they have to freeze the goddam dirt, it's so soft, and tunneljack the highway under the railroad tracks. At South Station, the sandhogs go down a hundred and twenty feet, and they have to worry about the subway overhead, and the trains. Nothin' like that around here."

It was warm and stuffy in the double-wide trailer that housed the field office of Horgan Construction. The Horgans, Gerry and Liz, husband and wife, ran a local company with major political pull. They camped in the private office behind the thin wooden door to the right. I shared the central section with two desks, four filing cabinets, a chatty coworker named Marian, a Dell computer, and a ton of filed and to-be-filed paperwork. To the left, O'Day ruled an area no larger than a phone booth, watching workers punch timecards, studying specs and schedules, filling out requisition forms.

On a counter along the back wall, a microwave oven sat next to a sink. The tiny bathroom looked good compared to the outdoor Portolets.

Marian, twenty-four, cute, and curvy, had already informed me that Gerry Horgan was her dream boss, referred to his wife as "the big cheese," and hinted that the Horgans' only child, a "total darling," was neglected by her workaholic mom. She'd termed O'Day a confirmed bachelor with a sniff that said she might have taken a run in that direction. She said my keyboarding skills needed improvement.

The trailer crouched in the shadow of the doomed elevated interstate, AKA the Central Artery, close to where it met Commercial Avenue. The adjacent site, Site A1520, was—according to O'Day—a relative piece of cake, a top-down job that included rerouting utilities, constructing slurry walls, cutting away the steel and concrete columns supporting the elevated highway, and replacing them with temporary supports built on top of the slurry walls. Then came tunneling between the walls, removing the dirt through openings in the roof deck called glory holes, and the actual construction of roadway and interchanges. All this underneath a major highway that had to remain open to

190,000 or so cars a day. One Dig boss compared it to performing open-heart surgery while the patient played tournament tennis.

We were near the end of the digging phase, getting ready for massive infusions of concrete—enough, O'Day said, to build a sidewalk three feet wide, four inches thick, all the way to San Francisco and back three times. The paperwork to prove it was stacked helter-skelter on my desk.

The trailer door banged and I thought, here we go again, another laborer to inspect the new talent. My first day on the job I'd worn a short skirt, provoking gazes so intent I'd been worried someone would spot my bullet-wound right through my tights. I'm not saying the traffic in and out of the trailer was all about me. By no means. First of all, everybody tramped in and out, engineers, supervisors, consultants for this, consultants for that. Second, it was damned cold outside, and third, Miss Marian Farrell, my co-gofer, dressed like a men's mag covergirl. She also kept a box of chocolate-covered cherries nestled next to a pile of condoms in the lower left-hand drawer of her desk, and glanced in my direction more often than I liked ever since she'd found me "looking for a paper clip" in her blameless top drawer.

I'd been searching for computer passwords. A lot of people write them down, in case they forget.

O'Day headed back to his desk as the door slammed behind a man whose watery blue eyes didn't go with his tough-guy face. He cradled his hard hat in the crook of his arm, marched over to Marian's desk, and announced, "I wanna see Mrs. Horgan," without so much as a glance in my direction.

"You have an appointment, Kevin? I didn't notice you on the schedule—"

"Oh, she'll see me, okay."

Marian shot him a glance, and he dropped one eyelid into a wink, a good-looking guy who knew it, strolling into the trailer like he owned it. Some of the workers seemed shy indoors, scraping their boots before entering, ducking their heads like they felt too tall for the ceiling. Kevin's boots were caked with mud.

The office door opened and Liz Horgan stepped out, smoothing a slim navy suit. The man's eyes lit up.

She couldn't have been much older than me, mid-thirties tops. Her oval face was the kind that looks different from different angles, her silky blonde hair long enough to yank back in a ponytail. A nitpicker might have said her lips were too full. Too many expressions played over her features too quickly for me to read them. At first I thought she was pleased to see the man named Kevin, then displeased.

All she said was, "Oh." The sound stretched and hung in the air.

"Why don't we—" Kevin began.

"I'm just leaving," she said at the same time.

The inner door reopened and Gerry Horgan emerged, head down as usual, a short bull of a man, with heavy shoulders and a barrel chest. He halted at the sight of his wife and Kevin, and it suddenly seemed as if too many people were crowded into our little trailer.

Horgan was third-generation construction. Old man Horgan, builder of City Hall, was dead and his son,

Leonard, builder of hospitals and office towers, was tucked away on corporate boards, confident the business was in good hands. And why not? Gerry was a double eagle, meaning he'd graduated from Boston College High and Boston College, like a lot of area movers and shakers. Liz was an architect and an engineer as well as a looker, and a full partner in Horgan Construction. The gossip mill said she owed her partnership to the feds; on a big project like this they held plum contracts open for minority and woman-owned businesses.

"Meeting's gonna start without you, Liz." Horgan's voice boomed in the small space.

"I'm going, Gerry. On my way." She patted her skirt nervously and flashed a distracted smile in my direction before hurrying out the door. It could have been aimed at Kevin, but it warmed like sunshine and I had the feeling that of all the trailer's inmates, she was most likely to remember my name. For this job it was Carla. Carla Evans.

"Help you with something?" Horgan's voice hadn't lost its edge. It held Fournier in place.

"Never mind."

"Why did you want to see Liz?"

Fournier shifted his hard hat. "Look, I heard they're going to twenty-four/seven next door."

"So?"

"Well, a lot of us are wondering when we're gonna go twenty-four/seven."

"You'll know when I tell ya."

"They're saying the other guys'll be moving on to other sites—"

"Our guys will still be working while the guys next door are sitting around with their thumbs up their asses."

"Or maybe those guys'll be working new sites, and when we're ready, the new work'll be gone."

I noticed that Harv O'Day had left his cluttered desk and was standing behind a filing cabinet. Man moved like a cat, on springy, noiseless feet. He took two more silent steps and entered the fray.

"Hey, a guy has problems with the schedule, he goes through channels, Fournier. And I'm the channel. You talk to me when—"

"Horgan asked me—"

"And what *Mr.* Horgan says goes, you know that."

"Just next door they're going to twenty-four."

Horgan said, "We'll go to twenty-four when we need to. How'd it go today?"

"Today's good. But you can't count on weather like today."

"You can't count on weather, period."

"Right, so I figure we should go twenty-four while it's clear. I was talking to Mrs. H, and she seemed like she agreed with me, so I thought I'd—"

"Fournier, maybe you don't hear so good." O'Day was getting red in the face. "Look, Gerry, I'll handle this." He clapped Fournier on the shoulder, turned him around, and hustled the larger man out the door. Their voices trailed off, arguing but with less vigor. O'Day was going to win and he knew it.

Horgan didn't return to his office. He stood frozen, fixed, as though he couldn't quite remember where he was. Marian leaned on her elbow, accentuating the cleavage in her deep V, and stared up at the dream boss with big eyes. Something going on there.

Something going on, all right. The tension in the trailer was so thick I could almost grab it like a rope. I hadn't been on the job long, but already it reminded me of other poisonous workplaces, of the squad room when reprimands were in the air, when wrong choices had been made, when a big case was going nowhere, nowhere, nowhere.

Eddie had instructed me to report, acclimatize myself, get familiar with the operation and personnel. He'd given me nothing else, not a name, not a clue as to what had caught the Inspector General's eye.

"Gerry," Marian said softly, "is Tess doing okay?"

"What?" Horgan sounded perplexed, as though he'd been woken abruptly.

Krissi was the neglected child, a super-smart thirteen-year-old, according to Marian. Tess was a new one on me.

"We had such a great time together," she went on enthusiastically, not noticing Horgan's increasing irritation. "At least, I thought—"

The dream boss cut her off. "Did I ask you to get me the specs on the finish work for the Channel tunnel?"

"I don't think so."

"Sure I did. Jesus, Marian, try to stay on top of things, okay? I'm sure I—Hell, hold my calls for awhile. And get me those specs ASAP." He disappeared into the inner office.

Marian shifted her posture, bit her cherry-red lower lip. "What are you lookin' at?" she asked me.

I hit the keyboard, but I kept wondering why Kevin Fournier really wanted to see Mrs. H. The intensity in his gaze, the catch in his voice hadn't been provoked by any scheduling anxiety. No way.

CHAPTER 3

I posted OSHA regulations, double-checked invoice figures, fielded insurance information requests from inquiring hard hats. Since I didn't know whether I was documenting substandard building techniques or counting fewer workers than were carried on the payroll, I concentrated on the computer system, memorizing what I could while the phone rang non-stop. Marian did most of the answering, polite and well-informed, an oasis of calm, and my opinion of her competence soared. I was studying the make and model of the trailer's alarm system when she invited me to join her for lunch. Nothing beats office gossip, so I said sure, I was practically starving.

With half an hour and all of downtown to choose from, I'd have headed back to Chinatown like a homing pigeon. But I wanted Marian to be my new best friend, so I let her pick a lunch spot, and wound up slogging through the food court at nearby Quincy Market elbow-to-elbow with a scrum of tourists. Marian was partial to Regina's pizza slices, which was a better outcome than the single-lettuce-leaf salad for which I'd braced myself. She grabbed two slices of sausage and cheese, ordered a diet cola to wash it down. There was a wait for anchovy, so I made do with pepperoni and mushroom.

"Mostly, the hard hats don't come here; more guys from offices." She gave a passing man in a three-piece suit the glad eye while settling at a crowded table in the rotunda. "The guys at the site bring sack lunches, eat sitting on the ground."

More comfortable than this joint, I thought grimly, moving aside undiscarded trash and wedging my backless chair between a group of teenagers arguing over who was going to pay for dessert and a hostile husband and wife.

"You seeing somebody?"

"Huh?" I managed through a mouthful of pizza.

"You got a boyfriend? You don't wear a ring."

I let her interrogate me for awhile, had some fun making up my life as I went along. I kept fairly close to reality, the best lies being nearest the truth. I got sympathy points for my brief marriage, the weird respect that young unmarried women have for women who've already been there, done that. As soon as I could, I turned the conversational tide back to Marian's life and woes, clucking over the fiancé who'd developed cold feet at the last minute, skyrocketing Boston rents, and other single-girl-in-the-city blues.

She'd started working for Gerry Horgan right out of school, learning the ropes from the fearsome Miss Farlock, a demon with no apparent first name. Miss Farlock hadn't resigned, she'd simply died at her desk, the only way Gerry could get rid of her since she'd been Daddy's secretary and came with the company. Since Miss Farlock's demise, there'd been a bunch of unsatisfactory hires and temporary fill-ins. Marian sure hoped I'd work out.

She had started as a Dig enthusiast, she told me, proud to be a part of it. The project was great, historic even, and although it got cold and drafty in the trailer, she'd been gung-ho, because the Dig was great for business. Now she wasn't sure, what with all the delays and cost over-runs. Gerry and Liz kept giving orders, then contradicting them. Really, O'Day was a saint the way he coped. I tried to get specifics, but she wanted to detail more personal stories, like the time the iron-workers banged on the trailer wall when she wore this red dress, and she'd been so embarrassed that she hadn't worn that dress to work ever again, and really, maybe, it was just a shade too tight for her. Did I think she needed to diet?

I reassured her, then added, "Don't get down on yourself just because Horgan gave you a hard time. You didn't warn me he had such a short fuse."

"He doesn't, really."

"Who's Tess? An old girlfriend?" She'd drawn a harsh rebuff for even mentioning the name to the boss.

"Nothing like that. Tess is Gerry's dog." Marian pressed her lips together in a thin, anxious line.

"He brings his dog to work?" I wondered whether it was a guard dog, and whether it stayed behind after the work crews had gone.

"No, it's just I used to sometimes take care of his dog. It's not like he made me walk it or buy dogfood or anything. Gerry would never ask me to do stuff like that. Liz, now—"

"She makes you run errands?"

"Well, she's not that bad." The admission was made grudgingly. "Every once in a while she'll ask me to take something out to this ritzy school. Krissi, their kid, is practically a boarder. Honestly, you'd think a mother could take an hour off to see her kid."

She told me that Tess was the *cutest* dog, a yellow lab, really *adorable*. It was daughter Krissi's dog, really, and Krissi was adorable too.

I smiled and chewed. The pepperoni was oily and spicy, and I was considering going back for another slice when she abruptly asked if I could keep a secret.

I felt like I ought to cross my heart and hope to die; she looked that young, gazing at me earnestly from under miles-long eyelashes.

"Sure," I said. "Try me."

"I may have *done something* to Tess."

She'd been baby-sitting the pup one day, a Sunday she thought it was, a day off, anyway. Tess had been fine at the apartment, even though they couldn't horse around much because she wasn't supposed to have a pet, and the prissy old fart on the second floor would be sure to tell the landlord if he heard barking. It wasn't till after she'd brought the dog back to the Horgans that she'd realized the needle was missing.

"Needle?"

"I was gonna sew a button on my coat."

Visions of syringes and drugs faded. *A sewing needle.* It's not that I hang with druggies; it's an ex-cop thing. Or maybe it's an anti-housework thing. I haven't sewn a stitch in so many years I doubt I'd remember how to start. In high school, the homemaking teacher recommended I take shop.

"I had it threaded and knotted," Marian went on, "and then the phone rang and I must have put it down. After I took Tess home, I really looked for it, but I absolutely couldn't find it. So, big deal, I thought, but then Gerry didn't bring the dog around anymore, and when I asked, he sort of brushed me off, and next thing I heard, the dog's at the vet. I mean, what if she ate it? A needle and thread?"

"They have X-ray machines."

She went on like she hadn't heard me. "Do you think I ought to tell Gerry? I mean, it's so dumb. I tried calling the stupid vet, and he wouldn't tell me anything, wanted to know *who I was*. I thought about calling back, pretending to be Liz, but I could never pull it off. And I mean, what if Tess just has some dog thing, like worms or something. I don't want Gerry to think I'm like careless or—"

"I could pull it off," I said.

"You? You mean, call the vet?"

"If you want me to."

"You would? That would be so great, but what if they, like, *know* Liz, what if they'd, like, recognize her voice?"

"I'm good with voices. I could probably do a decent Liz."

"Would you?"

I was about to say yes, but two men in jeans and heavy boots were making their way through the crowd, waving and smiling in our direction. "You know those guys?"

Marian rolled her eyes, ran her tongue over her lips, and quickly asked if she had anything stuck between her teeth. Her improved posture and gleaming smile seemed to be automatic responses, some sort of reaction to testosterone.

Waves of it flooded off the cuter one. Dark and curly-haired, he greeted Marian with a "Hey" and a lingering pat on the back. The other one jerked his neck in a silent nod. He was tall and stringy with a pronounced Adam's apple and too little chin. The crowd of dessert-eating teens decided to clear out and the guys sank into their abandoned seats, kicking back from the table to insure legroom.

"Pizza good?" Curly-hair extended his hand in my direction. "I'm Joey. Mason. This is Hector. You the new girl?"

I nodded, lowering my eyes, accepting "girl" so the new secretary wouldn't get a rep as an uppity snot.

"I'm a mason. What I do, not my name. You one a the Hingham Evanses?"

"How'd you know my name?"

"Gets around, Carla, names, stuff like that. I knew a guy from Hingham name a Evans. Police commissioner's an Evans. Irish, right?"

That's Boston. People hear your name, they've got to place you and label you, and around here, Irish and Italian are the major categories.

"I grew up in Detroit," I said, which usually puts a stop to it.

"It's all Arab there now, Detroit, right?" With that,

Joey, amateur sociologist, bit into a hot dog. He kept shooting Hector sidelong glances and I thought I had them placed and labeled. Shy Hector was sweet on Marian, or at least got a kick out of staring down her shirt, and Joey, his buddy, was bringing him by to get a better look.

"You on break?" Marian's eyes narrowed suspiciously.

"Why we're here, most a the cement trucks, they're not here. Another fuck-up, ya should 'scuse me."

"Shit." Marian immediately started collecting paper plates and napkins.

"Trucks stuck at some other site, ya know, and nobody knows if they're on the way or what. So Hector and I figure we'll grab a couple hot dogs, watch the babes."

"Winter," I said. "You're not gonna see much."

"Hah," said Hector, his biggest contribution thus far.

"I'm gonna go, Carla. Gerry might want me to make calls."

"Marian, you're way too good to him." Joey hid a smile behind a Coke can. "Whyn't ya stay a while, Carla?"

"Heh," Hector said.

"I'll stick with Marian."

She flashed me a smile as I helped her jam trash into an overstuffed can. We made good time over the cobblestones, no more than two minutes from the rotunda to the barriers and the chain-link fence.

Wonder of the world it may have been, but to me it looked like a huge hole in the ground, a gaping horizontal wound bridged by decking, stuffed with scaffolding, trucks, and mysterious machinery, bristling with pipes and hoses. One guy was pushing a broom around the hard-packed earth at the bottom of the massive trench. The rest were milling aimlessly, leaning against corrugated metal storage sheds, sitting on piles of iron bars. At union wages, they were an expensive bunch of bench-warmers.

Horgan was up top, yelling at a driver sitting high in the cab of a red truck with NORRELLI AND CO. painted in white letters on the door. The boss waved his arms angrily, pointed and shouted. The truck driver had the world's weariest expression on his heavily lined face, as though he'd heard every argument a hundred times and nothing could faze him, certainly not a red-faced construction company boss. He shrugged as though it were an effort.

Horgan's hands were curling into fists, uncurling, curling again, and I wasn't sure he wasn't about to reach for the door handle and take a poke at the driver. O'Day was nearby, yakking into a cell phone. I didn't recognize any of the hard hats. Those that weren't down in the trench were keeping well back, eyeing the scene like it was on television.

Marian made a beeline for her dream boss. I hung back, not eager to make myself conspicuous. Just because I didn't recognize any of the laborers, didn't mean there was no one on-site who wouldn't recognize me. Not that there are a bunch of jailbirds on union construction crews, but I'd be kidding myself if I thought there was no crossover, no risk of being made as a former cop, especially if I stepped up and defused a situation that looked like it might turn violent.

O'Day stuck his cell phone back in his tool belt. "Norrelli's kid says we're definitely on for tomorrow. He's real sorry about today."

"Fuckin' bet he is."

"Leave it, Gerry."

"And let the whole damn crew sit?"

"We'll pour first thing tomorrow."

"We're ready now!"

"Mr. Horgan? Maybe you could help me take a look at the man-loading charts." Marian's voice was as smooth as milk and twice as soothing. "They'll need revision, and when we transferred them onto the new system, I'm not sure I got the procedure straight."

I could almost see Horgan's blood pressure recede. He smiled down at her automatically, and it was then that I noticed his wife. She'd changed from suit to jeans and a heavy sweatshirt. Wearing a hard hat and vest, she melted into the crowd. I gave a quick glance at the workers closest to her, but Kevin Fournier wasn't among them. If I'd had a camera I'd have taken her picture. I've never seen anyone look so alone in a crowd, so lost, so scared.

CHAPTER 4

When I tried to reach Eddie after quitting time at three o'clock to get the lowdown on the Horgan assignment, I was told he was in a meeting, temporarily unreachable, might as well have been on the moon. So I left a message on his voice mail, and went to school.

No, I am not taking keyboarding classes. I go to school, my local high school, Cambridge Rindge and Latin, to pick up my little sister, Paolina, for the simple reason that she's been grounded for rotten grades and worse behavior, and can't be trusted to go home alone.

Her home is not my home. She lives with her mother and three younger brothers in a tiny house in Watertown. I lend her a "legal" Cambridge address, so she can continue to attend the school she began as a freshman and loves for the social life instead of the academics. I'm the school mom, mainly because Marta, Paolina's mother, speaks little English and could care less whether her daughter gets an education in anything beyond mascara application. More often than not, when I get off work, I go over to Rindge, enter a room where my little sister is supposed to be sweating algebra homework or playing drums with the jazz band, and find her gone.

Often she and two or three boys have stepped out for a stroll. I have talked to her about her reputation, about what guys want and what she'll get, but she is almost fifteen, and nothing I say penetrates her multiply pierced ears.

She was studying for a change, but gave it up as soon as she saw me, turning sullen, pouting her lower lip, and announcing that she had no intention of going home. She and Amelia and Juan and maybe some other kids were gonna maybe rent a couple movies, go over to somebody's house, and watch them.

"Right. Somebody whose parents are home?" My eyebrows slid halfway up my forehead in disbelief. As far as I can tell, Paolina's buddies have parents who work night and day, and are conspicuous only by their absence.

"Who cares?"

"Guess."

She simmered while I signed her out with the supervisor. She's already broken so many promises, squandered so many opportunities, proved herself so untrustworthy that she's on probation, a couple steps removed from expulsion. Outside, on the way to the parking slot I'd snared on Broadway, I got an earful about why she *absolutely couldn't* go home. Marta treated her worse than a slave and would exit as soon as she entered, leaving her with dishes to wash, a meal to cook, three slobby younger brothers to watch, and it fucking wasn't fucking fair.

I almost told her to watch her mouth, but these days I pick my battles, and I'm no language saint. Besides, it's not what comes out of her mouth that's got me worried. Her grades have got me worried. She's smart, but she won't turn in her homework. Her clothes have got me worried. Today's chosen outfit was low-slung pants, tied well below the waist, and most of a hot-pink shirt. Her attitude has got me worried, her belief that today is the only day, that now is the only time, that every immediate itch needs to get immediately scratched. Her survival has got me worried. Sometimes I think the only way I'll pull her through this crappy adolescence without her getting addicted, pregnant, or— considering the kids she hangs with—knifed, is to rent a moated castle, throw her in, and raise the drawbridge. As if I could.

"When are you gonna get a cooler car?" She slid into the passenger seat of my aged red Toyota with disdain.

"Let me make a phone call, okay? I need to wrap up something from work."

Since I didn't have the benefit of Happy Eddie's guidance, I figured I'd better continue to ingratiate myself with Marian. I hadn't wanted to risk phoning the vet from the trailer, with the constant threat of Liz walking in on me, so Marian had scrawled the number on a yellow Post-it. I took my cell out of my backpack and punched buttons, closing my eyes, raising my voice to a higher register.

Busy signal again, dammit.

The constant aggravating beep could mean the phone was malfunctioning. It could mean the practice was overwhelmed with barking and mewling customers, the help incompetent. I could give up, tell Marian I'd drawn a blank, but I didn't like the idea. I wanted Marian to know I delivered on promises. I wanted her to owe me.

My stubborn streak runs a mile wide and is probably my best private-eye trait. I'm not the most patient person in the world, God knows, but if I find the faintest trail, I will stick to it to the end. I also have more than my share of curiosity, and Horgan's evasiveness about the dog didn't make sense. If the dog was sick, why not tell Marian? If the dog was dead . . . well, maybe he didn't want her to blame herself. Maybe he really was a dream boss.

Marian had written the vet's name as well as his number. Paolina waited in the car, glowering, while I ran into a drugstore and checked the Yellow Pages. No, she hadn't copied Dr. Aronoff's number incorrectly. Not only that, his office was temptingly close, on Pearl Street in Central Square. I walked back to the car, my tongue caught between my teeth, pondering options. Paolina wasn't thrilled with the idea of a visit to a vet, but I told her it was either that or straight home. I had to do it for my new job. She said anything but home, so I dialed Marta.

No more than an hour late, she insisted in urgent Spanish. She needed to go out. Paolina would stay with the boys.

I hung up, asked Paolina if she had homework.

"Nothing important."

I took Broadway to Inman, made a left at Mass Ave.

"No way I'd dye my hair or dress like that, not for any crummy job."

She's trying to pick a fight, I told myself, *and she's doing a good job.* I drove, staying between the white lines, listening to imaginary music while Paolina searched the radio for stations she knew I couldn't stand.

Sometimes I think about deserting her, forgetting we ever met. She's been my little sister since she was seven; she's not blood kin. When I was a cop, a volunteer from Big Sisters sold me on the idea of mentoring a neighborhood kid. When I met Paolina, seven and smart, with a bad family situation and an ocean of potential, I was more than sold. I was enchanted.

I tried to revive the image of that staunch seven-year-old as I searched for on-street parking, traveling slowly enough to earn a blaring honk from a passing Buick. I gave it up and headed for the municipal lot behind Blockbuster Video. "We can get ice cream at Toscanini's after," I promised Paolina. Ice cream usually brought the seven-year-old back for a short-term visit.

The vet's office was further down Pearl Street than I'd figured, a small storefront halfway to Putnam Ave. When I opened the door a bell jangled and the waiting room inhabitants collectively glanced my way. If I had that kind of crowd in my waiting room, I might turn off the ringer on the phone, too. The bell set off a wild round of barking. Two pugs tried to leap off an elderly woman's lap, disturbing a huge mutt who lay in the center of the seating area, imitating a rug. A schnauzer was busily humping the corner coatrack. A man cradled a metal cage on his lap. I couldn't see what was inside, and wasn't sure I wanted to.

The reception desk was in an alcove, a tiny desk, a laptop, a silent phone, all under the care of a motherly woman with soft brown curls, a saggy face, and pink cheeks, possibly due to the overheated room. I wondered if the thing in the metal cage was the reason for the heat.

An elegant woman in a gray suit and impeccable pumps stood near the receptionist, entirely out of place in the shabby office, shaking an angry and insistent finger. She wasn't tall, but she was thin and imperious enough to give the impression of height.

The receptionist spoke wearily, "Now, Miss, I've told you and told you, I haven't seen her. I *do* know who you mean, and yes, she *did* come in, but not on Friday—"

"It's in her book. I can show you."

"I'm sorry. It doesn't matter what it says in her book. I can't—"

"Well, when did you—"

I made a noise in my throat.

"Can I help you?" The receptionist turned to me with relief.

"I'll wait," the elegant woman said defiantly.

"I don't know what for," the receptionist muttered under her breath.

Paolina, who'd veered off to take a look at the denizen of the metal cage, now stood at my side, bridging the gap between me and the well-dressed woman. Prada bag, Italian shoes. I did a little calculating and almost whistled. You don't often see a couple thousand dollars' worth of clothing on the hoof, not in Cambridge-port.

"What can I do for you, Miss?" the receptionist prompted.

"Horgan," I said firmly, deciding on the spot that if Liz didn't have time for her kid she probably didn't ferry the dog to and from the vet. I'd taken the precaution of raising the register of my voice so it wouldn't seem totally different. I also hadn't given a first name; I could be Liz's sister-in-law, if this woman turned out to be utterly familiar with Liz Horgan in person. "I wonder if I could have a quick word with the doctor about Tess."

It was simply an opening gambit. No way she'd let me see the doc, not with a full waiting room. Paolina shot me a glance out of the corner of her eye, but she knows never to correct me about matters of name, address, or occupation when I'm on a job.

"Oh, Tess, such a lovely dog." The receptionist might not know Liz, but either the mention of Horgan and Tess together had rung a bell, or all dogs were lovely. A buzzer sounded, and she consulted a list on her desk.

"Miss Tepper, Ruffy and Tuffy can go right into Room Three."

The pugs moved and the thin woman said, "If the doctor has a moment, maybe I could ask *him* if—"

"Really, it would be a waste of time. I *told* you she wasn't here." The receptionist checked Miss Tepper off her list, consulted her watch, and beamed to show me I was not the object of her bad temper.

By feigning confusion over a bill, I learned that Tess was not currently at the vet, and hadn't been a patient for at least two months, beyond which the harried woman would have to check records stored elsewhere. Mission accomplished. I could relieve Marian's mind, and surely she'd continue to confide in such a cooperative coworker.

Tess was overdue for a checkup, the receptionist told me. Either she'd skipped an appointment or there had been a mix-up. The schnauzer knocked the coatrack down and the mutt yipped his congratulations. I thanked her and said I'd be sure to schedule Tess's checkup soon. When I turned, Paolina wasn't there.

Shit! In Central Square, one of her prime stomping grounds. She could be in the cut-rate makeup store or the ninety-nine-cent shop or hiding in the narrow aisles of Pearl Art. The Food Co-op has front, back, and side exits, a felon's delight. She might be halfway to a friend's house, ready to join the video-watching, dope smoking, and sex play. I'd have to track her down, or go to the cops, who'd already hauled her back a couple of times, sharing a few jokes at my expense. I'd have to call Marta . . .

She was barely ten yards from the door, deep in conversation with the elegantly dressed woman. I blew out a breath and watched the steam rise in the frigid air.

"Miss Carlyle," the woman said when I approached, "your sister says you might be able to help me."

"With what?" I may not have sounded gracious.

"It's okay, Carlotta, I've seen her around." Paolina was smug. "At school. She's, like, one of the do-gooders, drop-inners, ya know. Would I, like, get a finder's fee? If you take the job?"

"Huh?"

"Let me explain—" the woman began.

"I already have a job, Paolina."

"But this is totally up your alley." Behind her back, so I could see and the well-dressed woman couldn't, my sister rubbed her thumb across her fingers, the universal code for cash.

"Your sister says you're a police officer, Miss Carlyle."

"Hey, no, you got it wrong. She's a private investigator now, finds missing people all the time. Miss, uh, Endicott, right? is looking for a friend of hers. Miss Endicott, this is Carlotta Carlyle, my sister—a big deal private eye. You've probably heard of her." Paolina spoke rapid-fire, like she was selling a used car.

"Please," the woman said. "Please, it would be such a relief to talk to someone who could tell me what I ought to do. Couldn't you just listen?"

"I'm sorry," I said.

"But you are a private investigator?"

"Yes."

"You have done missing persons work?"

"Yes."

"Please. Can't we just talk?"

"I'm trying to explain. I already have a job."

"Whatever you charge an hour, I'll double it. Triple it. An hour of your time. Please." She wore a heavy gold chain around her neck, a Rolex on her wrist.

Missing persons cases are more my line than construction fraud. Plus it's been a long time since I've heard a trace of admiration, let alone respect, in my little sister's voice. I didn't think it would take long or lead anywhere. Sometimes a person just needs to talk things out, to hear her own thoughts, put them in order.

"Come on," Paolina urged. "Somebody has to find people if they disappear. You'd look for *me* if I was missing, even if I ran away. Wouldn't you?"

"You're not—"

"I'm not planning to run." She looked me straight in the eye, but I couldn't say whether she was telling the truth or not. Years of experience listening to cons try to scam themselves out of holding cells, and none of my lie-detector skills work with my little sister.

I gave Dana Endicott my card and agreed to meet her at my office in an hour. She didn't want to wait, but I'd promised Paolina ice cream, and I try to keep my promises.

CHAPTER 5

My office is my house; my house is my office. My Great-aunt Bea left me a three-storey Victorian within walking distance of Harvard Square that does double duty with room to spare. The mortgage is history, all paid off and a good thing, too, because the sky-high property tax more than makes up for it. My last case, the one in which I got shot, took its toll, but the structural damage from the fire has finally been repaired. I repainted the interior walls myself.

I decided to give Miss Prada-bag half an hour, then change into sweats and head over to the gym. I was pouring myself a Pepsi when the bell rang.

Three rings means the doorbell is for Roz, my third-floor tenant, housekeeper, and sometime assistant, a post-punk artist with alien hair, a pierced left nostril, and tattoos in unusual places. When I heard no encore to the single bleat, I put down my glass and reversed my steps.

The woman made no comment as I ushered her down the single step from foyer to living room. I like to think she didn't notice the sparse decor, but she was probably too well-bred to mention it. I wasn't too well-bred to take a guess at her age. Thirty, give or take five years, with beautiful skin, the kind that's never been outdoors without sunscreen and a wide-brimmed hat.

The living room used to have a velvet sofa, a high-backed rocking chair, an Oriental rug—all courtesy of Aunt Bea—but I haven't gotten around to replacing them. My big rolltop desk was ruined as well, but at least I have a substitute, even if it is a slab of oak that started life as a door. With black legs under one side and a filing cabinet under the other, it's serviceable, not elegant. For a client chair, there's a canvas butterfly job on loan from my bedroom.

I invited her to sit.

"I appreciate your time." She sank gratefully into the chair and then I waited while she opened her mouth, closed it, clasped her hands, and finally came out with, "Your sister is charming." Earlier I'd noticed her clothes. Now I observed the small neat features in the perfectly oval face, the glossy brown hair, the sprinkle of freckles across the otherwise patrician nose.

"She can be."

"Such lovely eyes." Her voice, which was probably pleasant enough when she had control of it, sounded high and tight, almost tinny. "I know I said an hour of your time, but, well, I made a few calls. My attorney speaks well of you."

I lifted an eyebrow.

"Arthur Goldman says you're honest and you don't give up easily."

I knew Goldman. I wasn't sure about his honesty,

but what the hell, he was a lawyer so it didn't count. If he was her lawyer, she numbered her bundle by the millions, not the hundred thousands.

"I want to hire you."

"To find the person you were asking about at the vet's office?"

Light glinted off three heavy rings, none of them on the telltale third finger of her left hand. "Listen, I'm not a fool. I'm not given to dramatic displays. I went to the police first, but the officer seemed to think it was none of my business. I really don't know where to begin—"

"It's Miss Endicott, isn't it?"

"I'm sorry." She plunged her hand into the side pocket of her bag, leaned forward, and handed me her card. Thick and creamy, with raised dark print, it said *Dana Renee Endicott*, and hadn't come from the cut-rate printer with whom I do business. It gave a Beacon Street address, a local phone number, and nothing so vulgar as a place of business. "Call me Dana. Please." She tried to reposition her slender body comfortably in the sprawling chair and I made a note to replace it sooner rather than later.

"So, who's missing, Dana?"

"A young woman. Veronica James."

If I'd been considering taking the case, I'd have scrawled notes on a yellow legal pad. I wasn't, so I simply listened. "And she is?"

"I suppose Veejay has been my tenant for almost two years, although I don't think of myself as a landlord. I live on upper Beacon, one of those old brownstones. It's been in my family for—oh, generations. It's

too big for me, but I haven't wanted to split it up—
and sometimes through charity work, I meet potential
tenants—roomers, you might call them. At times, the
place is almost a halfway house, but right now, there's
only Veronica. And the dogs."

Slivers of upper Beacon Street brownstones, converted to condos, go for seven figures, often eight. An
Endicott with her own upper Beacon Street manse de-
fined what Bostonians mean when they say "old
money." Coupled with the "charity work" reference,
the pricey attorney, and the kind of clothes I can't afford at rock-bottom reductions in Filene's Basement,
chances were I'd fulfilled a fantasy and encountered a
living, breathing philanthropist.

"I met Veronica at a fund-raiser," she said. "We
talked, the way you do at those things, and it turned
out she was looking for a place downtown. I trusted
her on sight, and I don't do that with many people."

Did I look more trustworthy with brown hair rather
than red, wearing secretarial garb instead of sweats or
jeans? She was silent for so long I thought I'd have to
prompt her. I didn't want to; I like to hear the way
people talk, silences and all.

"Maybe I ought to begin with Friday." I stayed quiet,
not wanting to disrupt the pictures behind her faraway
brown eyes. "On Friday, I saw her just as I was coming
home. She was holding a duffel bag and wearing her
backpack, I think, and she waved, and told me she was
going to visit her parents, and that she'd be back Sunday night. She knew I was supposed to travel on Monday, knew I was counting on her to take care of the
dogs."

It was Tuesday; if we were talking about last Friday, five days had elapsed.

"I have three dogs, two golden retrievers and a chocolate Lab, and Veronica's Norwegian elkhound, Tandy, makes four. That's why I know something's wrong. Veronica would *never* have abandoned Tandy."

Five days in a Beacon Street brownstone with three canine pals didn't sound like abandonment to me.

She said, "If Veejay's going away for the weekend, or if I plan to be out of town—I travel quite a bit; I sit on several boards—often I'll lend her a car. She doesn't have her own, but she does drive, and I have a Jeep and a car. I was planning to use the Audi, so I offered her the Jeep."

"She took it?"

"I *offered* it."

I nodded and said nothing, but I was thinking that the cops must have gotten a charge out of that one.

"I haven't seen or spoken to her since. I had to cancel my trip to Baltimore. I tried to file a missing-persons report, and I know what the policeman said is true—she's a grown-up; she can go where she likes—and I don't begrudge her the Jeep, but she *would have called*. And she would *never* have left Tandy behind." The woman bit her lip and went silent.

I waited, but this time she'd turned to stone and I had to prompt. "Is there anything else?"

"Several things. I called her parents. I'm—I *snooped,*" she said emphatically. "I don't feel good about it. I—Veronica left her date book—there are addresses in it, and phone numbers."

"Smart move," I said reassuringly. "Exactly what I would have done. Called her parents."

"She hadn't been there."

"Changed her mind?"

"Hadn't been expected." Dana stared down at her manicured nails. "I know. You're thinking that if she lied about where she was going, she might have lied about how long she'd be gone."

I was thinking that she might be having such a good time, she'd lost track of it.

"Her parents . . . Her mother. I don't know. She seemed so odd, so vague. I couldn't connect with her at all."

I nodded.

"And then, well, I checked Veronica's appointments. She didn't write much down, and then a lot of it I didn't understand. But she did have an appointment with Aronoff last Friday. I guess she didn't show up."

"But you saw her *after* that."

"Well, yes, but this whole week was blank, and I thought she might have said something, talked to someone, mentioned her plans—You can see I'm floundering here."

"Does Veronica have a boyfriend?" I asked.

Dana shrugged.

"Does she date a lot?"

"If you mean is she out all hours, I don't keep tabs on her. But she impressed me as a steady, reliable person."

Who disappears with vehicles not her own. I should have stopped asking questions, fobbed her off with a bland reassurance, or sent her to somebody else, but I was curious. If I hadn't been working for Eddie, I'd have been downright intrigued. "Do her parents live far away?"

"It could have been an impromptu visit, a sudden decision to go see them, is that what you mean? They're north of the city. Near Lowell. Tewksbury, I think. Do you think she might have had some kind of accident? It's not an old Jeep, but it's broken down before. She doesn't have a cell phone."

There's not a lot of deserted highway between here and the New Hampshire border. If she'd driven into a ditch someone would have noticed. Still, there are ponds, frozen ponds this time of the year. They're bleak and cold and sometimes call out to the would-be suicide.

"Was she depressed?" I asked.

"God, no. I don't think so. Do you think I ought to call hospitals? I mean, she might have gotten into an accident. She could be hurt. I—I'm usually *competent*. I handle crises; I don't fall apart. And now I don't know what to do. I've tried the police. What am I supposed to do? Put her picture on a milk bottle? Hang posters on trees as if she were a lost pet?"

"Slow down. Take a deep breath."

She made a visible effort to pull herself together. "I'll pay you to find her, whatever it costs, whatever it costs and more. A bonus. Anything. I'm worried that something terrible has happened, something vile."

"How old is she?"

"Twenty-one."

I remember twenty-one. Working on a divorce, my parents dead. My soon-to-be-ex-husband probably gave up wondering where I spent my nights. Wasted on cocaine, he probably never noticed I was gone.

The rich woman's tenant could be off on a one-night stand that turned into a dirty weekend that blossomed into a full-fledged affair. If so, she wouldn't thank anyone for reminding her that she had obligations in the real world. The tenant could have stolen the landlady's car. The cops might not encourage a missing persons beef on a woman who'd taken off under her own steam with packed bags, but they'd file a stolen car report quickly enough.

On the other hand, unlikely things happen. Maybe this Veejay, this Veronica James, was the rare street-crime victim, snatched at random, luckier than most in that she knew someone willing to start the machinery in motion, an angel eager to foot the bill.

If I'd been planning to take the case, I'd have filled pages of my legal pad with information about Veronica James, from her middle name to her current job, her hobbies, her friends. As it was, I started wondering whether I could handle this case and Eddie's stuff as well. The thing about working for Eddie, I had fairly regular hours, and early ones, too. I don't need much sleep. It was tempting. The woman looked good for some serious dough.

"Want my honest opinion?" The phone rang before I got a chance to find out whether she did or not. If I'd been working for her, I'd have let the machine pick up. But I already had a job, so I answered and got an earful of Happy Eddie. I gestured excuses to the elegant woman in the butterfly chair, and carried the receiver into the kitchen for a little privacy.

"So, Eddie, what am I looking for?"

"It's kinda routine."

"Come on. I haven't been with you long enough to do routine. Nothing around the Dig looks routine to me."

He hesitated, more uneasy with this assignment than he'd been with the others, more uneasy and less forthcoming.

"Eddie," I said. "Give."

"Look, you oughtta know, I ain't neutral on this one. I've known Gerry Horgan mosta his life, knew his dad. By me, the Horgans are the kinda people give builders a good name. I think what the IG's got hold of here is some jerk tryin' to black their eye, ya know? Jealousy. Business shit. Who knows? They're up for new contracts, so some asshole tries to screw them over on the hotline."

Back when the inspector general was getting terrible press, his office initiated a special Dig-fraud hotline for the general public, made a big fuss about it. You call; we investigate.

"Caller says stuff's walking off the Horgan site," Eddie went on.

"Petty theft? That wouldn't necessarily involve the principals."

"It would make them look bad, like they don't know what's going on under their noses."

"No ID, I suppose?"

"Didn't leave a number. But he said he might call back."

Designed to encourage whistle-blowers, the hotline also enables anonymous cranks. Rewards are offered for information leading to arrests. No names required, but most callers give an identifying seven-digit number they'll need to repeat if and when the time comes to collect. Sometimes no identifying number is given. The IG likes to think such callers operate from the noblest motives. Me, I wondered whether the Horgans had done any firing lately.

"It's a complaint and we gotta follow up," Eddie said.

"And Horgan just happened to need a secretary? He fire his? She make the complaint?"

"Caller's definitely a guy."

"So much for that."

"Carlotta?" Eddie sucked in a deep breath. "I was wonderin'. Maybe you could help me out here."

There was something in his voice that made me lean against the kitchen counter and brace myself.

"This ain't about the Horgans. It's more a general thing you could maybe find out for me. Ya know, where there's heavy construction, there's rumors. About, ya know, the mob, about, like, uh, mob involvement."

Here it comes, I thought, and suddenly I knew with cool certainty why the bastard had hired me. Because I used to be with a guy named Sam Gianelli. *Used to.* And the Gianelli name is so identified with the Boston mob that the fact that my lover—ex-lover—Sam Gianelli, youngest son of mob underboss Anthony Gianelli, has *never* been a player, never been a North End soldier, is something nobody, but nobody believes.

"You could maybe just keep your ears open," Eddie muttered.

I punched the button to cut the connection, took a deep breath, drank a glass of cold water. Then I went back to my living-room office and enthusiastically accepted Dana Endicott's case. If Eddie hadn't pissed me off I might not have taken it. But I figured it this way: He didn't tell me everything when he hired me. Okay. So I wouldn't tell him everything, either. And a little high-priced moonlighting would go a long way toward dispelling my anger. I've never been a Mafia moll and I don't like being taken for one.

CHAPTER 6

The missing woman and I had something in common: We both worked two jobs. Veronica James did days at a sort of pet camp, nights at a bar-restaurant combo called Raquela's. By the time I'd finished quizzing Dana Endicott, filling twenty-eight pages with facts and queries, it was past seven, and my rumbling stomach influenced my decision to start the search with Veronica's night job. Raquela's served food.

Dana had been late for a dinner engagement, so my first impulse—to examine the tenant's room—hadn't panned out. Another time, she assured me, signing a very substantial check as a retainer. I had her card; I should call and schedule an appointment.

Arthur Goldman, the lawyer, still at his desk, verified that Dana Endicott was indeed a client and a good one, too. Her parents had been clients, before they'd moved to New York, and her grandparents, he believed, had been clients of his mentor at the firm. In other words, the check wouldn't bounce. I filled out a deposit slip, stopped at the bank on my way to dinner.

Not only are missing persons cases more my speed than construction fraud, smoke-filled bars are more my idea of places to investigate than early-morning building sites. Raquela's was long and narrow, dimly lit, with a mahogany bar slicing it narrower, running the length of the room. Leather swivel bar stools with high backs sprouted from the wooden floor on metal poles. I chose a seat toward the rear, where I could keep an eye on the tables reflected in the long mirror behind the bar.

I'd never visited the place as a customer. Too much of a pickup joint, with its trendy waterfront location. Wrong kind of sound, piped-in Sinatra and swing instead of live blues. I inhaled secondhand smoke and sipped overpriced beer. The clientele, mostly white, with lots of lawyers, to judge by the conservative suits, looked well-off, pleasantly buzzed on a mix of alcohol and affluence. I checked out the dating couples at the small tables, marvelling at the age differential, the youthfulness, feigned or otherwise, of the women as opposed to the men. I wondered how many of the ladies hailed from nearby colleges, how many had been ordered from escort services the way you'd order a lamb chop off the menu. One large group, more male than female, at a corner booth had the weary cheerfulness of an after-office drinks session that had stretched into dinner and more drinks. I marked a couple of women on bar stools as pros, trolling for out-of-town conventioneers. I thought maybe I'd booked one of them when I was a cop. Same narrow eyes, but the brassy wig gave her a different look. I was glad I'd dressed down.

Slacks and sweater, minimal gold jewelry. I didn't want to be mistaken for a pro.

The only TV was a small one over the bar, tuned to CNN. Not enough screens to attract a sports crowd. I found myself wondering if Sam Gianelli ever strolled over from his Charles River Park apartment. Not that I was actually hoping he'd walk in and give me the kind of lazy smile that tingled up my backbone. It was simply that he'd be good cover; a date is always good cover. Couples fit in a bar, blend into the background. A single at a bar is either interested in losing that designation or in getting quietly and thoroughly drunk.

I have considerable bar experience. My ex and I hung at a series of Irish pubs, but I expanded my repertoire after he left. For a while, I barhopped with a vengeance, picking up a different man each night, bringing him home. I was lucky, I insisted on protection, and I got over it. And then there was Sam and I haven't gotten over him, although I haven't seen him in some time. I can still dial his number from memory, but damned if I wanted to do it in response to a business query from Eddie Conklin. I ordered another beer, tugged at a strand of my wrong-colored hair.

You can divide missing persons cases into categories. Start with the absentminded frequent flyer who forgets to tell the wife about the conference in Dubuque. Then consider missing stockholders and no-show heirs, usually sought by attorneys rather than anxious family members. Those are bread-and-butter cases for PIs like me. I also handle adoptees searching for birth parents and birth parents searching for a long-surrendered child. The common denominator in the above is that the missing person has no idea they're classified AWOL. They take no evasive action.

Those who intentionally disappear make for dicier trade. Loan skips spend and run, and professional skip tracers make a good living tracking them through the bureaucratic labyrinths of banks and utility companies. Teenage runaways are another special group; I keep an updated list of runaway shelters and hotlines to help track them. Custodial kidnappings turn small children into divorce-settlement pawns. Those who disappear intentionally are harder to find; they live on alert, change their names, alter their habits.

The missing woman, Veronica, Veejay, didn't fit neatly into any of my categories. On the face of it, she'd gone off voluntarily. On the other hand, she'd left her dog.

My cat is an independent operator. He goes his way; I go mine. As long as the water dish is full and an occasional can of Fancy Feast appears, T.C.'s fine, and I strongly suspect he could fend for himself if I forgot all about him. According to Dana Endicott, Tandy, Veronica's Norwegian elkhound, required both vigorous walking and elaborate grooming. I sipped beer, hardly noticing its taste.

I'd called area hospitals before leaving the house, not that I thought I'd locate Veronica that way, since amnesiacs with no identification only inhabit the world of daytime soaps, but because I knew I'd feel dumb if I ignored the possibility and she turned up in a coma at the General. I'd also dialed the morgue, because I'm thorough and because I know a guy who works there. No 5'6", thin, dark-haired woman was lying unidentified in an emergency room or unclaimed in a refrigerated drawer.

The beer slid down easily. The waiters wore unisex uniforms of tight black jeans, white tees—the women's version low-cut—small white aprons with pockets for checks and change. They seemed efficient, except for one who looked increasingly desperate as the night wore on. I tagged her as Veronica's replacement.

The bartender, in his fifties, with a narrow, lined face, wore a neatly trimmed beard. None of his motions seemed hurried, but he got things done with such lack of fuss and quick economical movements that if he quit, they'd have to hire two to replace him. The regulars called him Carl, and enough of them asked how business was that I decided he wouldn't quit since he was probably an owner. When I ordered my next round, I asked whether Veronica would be in later. Veejay.

"You a friend?"

"Friend of a friend."

"Tell your friend to tell Veejay she better gimme a call. I don't hear from her, she's toast. I mean, what am I supposed to do, run the bar *and* wait the tables?"

"Heidi here?" It was a name Dana had tossed out. Sometimes Veejay mentioned her.

"Heidi's always here."

She wasn't your typical Heidi. No tall strapping blonde with crisscrossed braids, yodeling away in lederhosen. Small, dark, and the only characteristic she shared with the girls' book heroine I remembered was rosy cheeks. Carl pointed her out and I watched her work until I knew which tables she served. When a couple paid up and left, I took their place.

The menu, as trendy as the location, featured Chilean sea bass and Tuscan steak, neither of which I felt like eating, not even on a rich client's dime. I ordered a burger, which they offered with my choice of cheese, although Velveeta was not an option. Heidi asked if anyone was going to join me and I said I'd hoped Veejay would, but she hadn't shown up.

"You okay on the beer?"

When it came, the burger was big and meaty and unhealthy and I loved it. A pile of fried onion rings mounded the plate. I requested ketchup, and when Heidi wound her way back through the closely spaced tables, I said, "Veejay talked about you."

"Say anything nasty?"

"No."

"Okay, then."

"You know when she's due in?"

She shrugged. "Overdue is what she is."

"If you've got a minute, I'll buy you a beer."

Her lips formed a smile. "Why not?"

The "minute" didn't come for forty-five, by which time I'd eaten every onion ring, greasy and salty. I'd watched the shifting traffic patterns at the bar, and I knew that the man at the table behind me was contemplating a fishing trip with his wife's best friend, and pooh-poohing the buddy who warned him his wife would surely find out. I was wondering how long the buddy would hold out before informing the wife when Heidi yanked a chair and sank into it, flexing her booted feet.

I could have told the truth, that I'd been hired to find Veejay, but the beers were buzzing through my bloodstream, and it seemed easier to continue my tale of casual friendship. We traded "Do you know so-and-so's" before I returned to my pal's no-show status.

"Soon as she walks in, Carl's gonna fire Elvira's ass." Heidi spoke with a satisfaction that boded ill for Elvira.

"Did Veejay work Friday night? I could have made a mistake; maybe she said to meet her Friday."

"She wasn't here. Grabbed the whole weekend, trading shifts and begging, which pissed Carl off plenty. He sure hates to see anybody get a weekend."

"Why?"

"Maybe 'cause he hasn't had one since the flood. And then when she didn't show Monday, well, that seemed to prove his point. Elvira's covering, but she can't keep orders straight worth a damn. I mean, look at her tables; everybody glaring."

Heidi didn't know how Veejay had heard about the waitressing job. She thought she'd worked there maybe a year, maybe a little less. Kept to herself, didn't have any real friends on the staff. The longer we spoke, the more obvious it became; while the two women may have talked, they hadn't shared secrets. Heidi knew more about Veejay's dog than she did about her friends.

"She like waitressing?" I asked.

"Hey, what she likes is what we all like. The money. Prices aren't exactly cheap, and the tips are good. Conventioneers, lawyers showing off for their clients. These guys don't stiff you. Even the lunch business is good."

"Veejay work lunch?"

"Nah. Carl's always trying to land her full-time, but she likes that dog stuff she does. If they paid more, she'd quit here fast enough."

"Maybe the dog place gave her a raise."

"She's not some dimwit just wouldn't show up. She'd tell Carl." *Veejay isn't the type to disappear with no notice.* It was good to have Dana Endicott's opinion seconded.

"I can't figure it," I agreed. "Unless she met a new guy." I nodded in the direction of a waiter with a well-muscled build and pale gold hair.

"Walter? No way. Strictly off-limits. Married and religious both. Definitely not."

"One of the others?"

"Well, we got old Carl, and gorgeous Walter, and two Freds, tall and short. And Marty." She seemed to consider the possibilities with relish before shaking her head.

"A customer?" I asked.

"No way."

I raised an eyebrow. "Guys don't hit on the help?"

"Oh, yeah, you think when you get this job, yeah, boy, lots of guys, lots of hits, but who looks at the waitress, huh? The winners come in with heavy dates, and they're so focused they can't even remember who took their order. The rowdies, the guys looking to get drunk, who wants 'em? Veejay had this bunch Thursday night, thought we'd have to call the cops."

"Regulars?"

"Carl showed 'em the door. Didn't need cops."

When I wondered aloud whether Veejay had known the rowdies, Heidi said she didn't think so, hurriedly thanked me for the drink, and said she had to get back on the job. I glanced in the mirror to see if Carl had given her a signal. The brassy-haired woman was no longer seated at a bar stool, but if she paid Carl a percentage, she might have tipped him about my former occupation. Not much goes on in a joint that a good bartender doesn't notice.

I stayed at the table till the check came, watching the waiters do their semi-invisible dance, wondering if there existed a more anonymous occupation in the world than waiting tables. Several of the help had the hopeful air of college students, part-timers on their way to better things. A couple, including Elvira, had the desperate demeanor of people who needed the job, maybe kids at home, a spouse in jail. Heidi had a strong Townie accent, but seemed smart enough. Was this the best gig she could land? Did she see it as more glamorous, less restricting than an office job?

The hostess wore stiletto heels and a glittery top—evidence, my little sister would think, that she had a *great* job. Paolina's mother, Marta, would encourage that belief. Meet men, wear sexy clothes, what more could you want? *I met a man in a bar.* How many times I'd heard those words, preface to some dismal tale, while booking some sad-eyed woman. *I met a man in a bar.*

I paid the check, tipping big and sliding one of my cards, the kind that don't say PI, in with the cash. Then I made my way back to the bar, where Carl seemed neither suspicious nor talkative. I slipped him a card as well, told him to tell Veejay I was sorry I'd missed her; she should give me a call. I asked about Thursday night's rowdies, but he barely reacted, and what did it matter? Even if they'd waited outside till closing time, harrassed Veejay in some way, it wouldn't be significant. My client had seen her tenant on Friday, alive and well. And Veejay hadn't waited tables Friday night.

If she'd come here Friday night, if the rowdies had been waiting . . . Well, at least I'd have an idea, a place to start. There are places in the harbor where stolen cars go to die, and every once in a while, when the cops pop the trunk, a body's inside. But Veejay had left Beacon Street driving Dana Endicott's Jeep. She wouldn't bring a car down here, not when she worked two jobs and could walk or take the T, save twenty bucks in parking fees.

I brooded about the dark waters not half a block from Raquela's, nursed another beer. I left when the guy on the next bar stool started to remind me of Sam, a sure sign I'd had too much to drink and would regret my next move.

CHAPTER 7

Fourteen billion bucks to perfect a concrete path from suburbs to airport, streamline auto travel to and from the financial district, and here I was, waiting eighteen minutes on an overcrowded T platform the next morning before the train arrived. Onboard, heat blazed in the front car while passengers in the rear cars shivered. Jammed nose to elbow, clinging to metal poles, commuters stared glumly at grafitti-covered walls.

At Government Center, I escaped and headed east. Over the bleak, windswept plaza, down the steps, the salt tang hinting at the closeness of the sea. Cars streamed down Congress Street till the light forced them to give way to the pedestrian tide. A man held up a sign in front of Faneuil Hall, a protester, maybe, or a tout for a tour bus. Faneuil Hall, Cradle of Liberty, is a major stop on the Freedom Trail, the redbrick path that leads from the Boston Common to the site of the Boston Massacre, and the area was full of tourists even on a chilly April morning. A school group marched behind a flag-toting teacher who expounded briskly on

Sam Adams, Paul Revere, and the Sons of Liberty. They had to pass practically single-file in front of the Hall because of the concrete Jersey barriers that walled it off from the street.

They've got barriers at the airport now, and in front of the White House, I hear, the result of and hopefully the antidote to the Oklahoma City bombing. Anywhere a lunatic can drive a bomb-rigged truck, the concrete abutments rise. Most of the tourists didn't seem to mind the added security, but then most would rather visit the generic shops in Quincy Market than climb to the second floor of Faneuil Hall, view the old meeting room, listen for the echoes of long-dead rabble-rousers. I noticed more cops than usual, but maybe that was because Eddie had mentioned the increased security for the Patriot's Day gathering.

I replayed Eddie's phone call in time with my footsteps. *Routine. Stuff walking off the Horgan site.* Was Eddie trying to tell me I shouldn't go out of my way to find the answers? Had Eddie changed since he'd left the force? Was he assuming I'd changed too, subscribed to some new, private-enterprise concept of truth as whatever the client wanted, whatever the boss assigned?

Maybe Eddie simply figured that as a field-office secretary, I'd never have time to discover the truth. In between the data entry, file retrieval, and inspection of change orders that made up my morning, I had plenty of time to sneeze if I skipped the tissue. And when my first break came, the ever-present Marian was ever-present.

I told her about my trip to Dr. Aronoff's office,

found her suitably impressed by my enterprise and grateful for the news. No problems with the Horgan family pet; she could forget about her needle causing irreparable damage. I didn't mention that she'd done me a favor, helped me land a rich client. Instead I engaged her on the subject of security, starting with whether it was safe to leave valuables in the trailer.

Keep your purse locked in your desk drawer. Guys are always walking in and out, and who wants to take a chance?

And what should I do if I forgot something on-site? What time were the gates locked at night?

Depends on the schedule. Just wait till morning.

"They don't have guard dogs or anything?"

They didn't. I shrugged into my coat, went outside, and gawked at a passing construction vehicle with wheels bigger than my car. Then I took an inspection stroll by the high chain-link fence. No razor-wire, top or bottom. Signs proclaimed this a hard hat site and assured me that safety pays. Uneven ground made crawling underneath the fence possible in several places, and at least one area, tucked behind a storage shed, was neatly shielded from passing traffic. At night, with light only from distant street lamps and caged, sparsely hung work lights, illegal entry would be a snap.

And then what? You can't pass a boom crane under a fence.

I'd tried to get Marian going on equipment theft, but either she was unaware of any or had been warned against discussing it. I planned to rifle the insurance files as soon as I got an unobserved moment. If equipment had been stolen, the Horgans would have filed claims.

Moving deeper into the shadow of the overhead highway, I skirted stacks of rebar, sacks of cement, coils of heavy cable. Behind a corrugated storage unit, I found a spot where I could stare down into the excavation, watch the crews toil, their breath frosting the air. Listening to the whoosh of overhead traffic, I considered the tons of steel supporting the old highway; I knew that used steel beams had "walked off" a nearby site.

On the whole, I wished my assignment were in the trench instead of the trailer. Oh, I'd had my problems on other sites; I'd been awkward and slow at first, even though I'd worked construction in my teens, side-by-side with my off-duty-cop dad. Some of the hard hats assumed I'd earned my union card by sleeping with a shop steward, some assumed I was a stone dyke. A few leered and one yelled "woman on the site," as a warning to clean up the fuckin' language. It didn't bother me. I hadn't stayed long enough on either site for anyone to know me as *me,* or even as the me I pretended to be. I was a woman the same way they were micks or paisans, the way Gianelli was Mafia. But whoever they were, wherever they came from, they were building something that would change the city, something that would last—a graded curve, a twisting off-ramp, an underground highway their grandchildren would travel and admire.

"Incredible, huh?"

My head turned so quickly my neck almost snapped. The distant thud of a pile-driver, the sputter of jack-hammers had prevented me from hearing the tall black man's footsteps. His teeth gleamed in the shadow and his eyebrows almost met over a jutting nose. Part American Indian, I thought. He looked like he'd been carved out of dark stone.

"What are you looking at?" he asked.

"Can you smoke here?" Whenever I don't want to answer a question, it's my policy to ask one of my own. I'd been considering smoking ever since the bar, thinking about reviving a bad habit. Marian smoked; I could smell it on her clothes. We could bond during cigarette breaks.

"Nope. Too close to the acetylene. I'm Leland Walsh, by the way. Foreman. Haven't seen you around."

"Laborer?"

"More than just grunts and dirt jockeys here. I'm a carpenter. Local Thirty-three. You?" He wore a heavy flannel shirt and a zipped hooded sweatshirt beneath his orange safety vest. His voice was unaccented, maybe just a touch of broad Midwestern A.

"Carla. Secretary."

"Heard there was somebody new in the trailer." He gestured toward the trench. "So, what do you think?"

Steel reinforcement bars protruded from concrete slurry walls. Gizmos, gadgets, machines I couldn't name, were scattered and piled on dirt beneath the beams and girders that temporarily held up the old highway. I knew time would wave its wand and the trench would be transformed into a hidden high-tech superhighway. City planners spoke of reclaimed land, fountains, gardens, an open-air theater. There would be bright daylight where we stood, no trace of the old elevated eyesore, not even a shadow.

"Hell of an expensive hole," I said. "With a hell of a lot left to do."

"You've got no idea what *was* down here, what we had to dig through. Utilities, gas, electric. Water. Sewer lines. Big damn sewer tunnels. Steam, in high-pressure pipes. Everything had to be rerouted, changed, with no interruption in service."

"So that's why it costs so much."

"Just wait." His teeth were white and even.

"Till it's more expensive? When's that gonna be? Tomorrow?"

"Wait till it's done. Nobody's gonna give a good goddam how much it cost then. You like working here?"

"Haven't had a chance to find out yet," I said. "How's the work going? I heard a couple guys say they'll need a miracle or overtime to stay on schedule. What do you think?"

He pressed his lips together. "Well, number one: I think a lot of guys talk too much. Number two: I think some of the crews need to work harder. Not my crews, of course. My crews are full of terrific guys. Like me, for instance."

I didn't get to find out where that line might lead, because we were interrupted. Liz Horgan wore a heavy black coat, and her high-heeled boots sank into the dirt.

"Carla, isn't it? Can I talk to you for a minute?"

"Sure," I said easily, moving away from the foreman, joining her in an alcove between two storage units, wondering if she were going to admonish me for taking too long a break. "I've been meaning to come see you, really introduce myself. Saw the picture of your daughter on your desk. What a great-looking kid. I've got a little sister maybe a couple years older." I caught a glint of desperation in her eye and paused.

"Can I ask you a favor?"

"Sure." She hadn't heard a word I'd said. Her face hadn't even registered pleasure when I'd complimented her daughter. Maybe Marian was right. She didn't care.

When she tried a smile, lines cross-hatched the corners of her eyes. "It's really nothing." Her voice petered out, leaving me wondering what on earth she could be planning to ask.

"Your meeting go okay yesterday?" I said to help her along.

"Oh. Oh, yes. The meeting. That's it. I had another one this morning, a political thing, a breakfast deal, and that's what I wanted to ask. I'd go myself, but I'm not wearing the right—And I'm running late—"

"What can I do?"

"I want to get a message to the man who came into the trailer yesterday. Kevin Fournier. Do you think you'd recognize him? He ought to be down in the trench, near the Gradall, that monster truck behind the bulldozer."

The man with the watery blue eyes.

"Could you give him a message? From my husband? Just tell him three o'clock."

"No problem." There'd been the faintest hesitation before she said "from my husband." Maybe she'd realized how the words would sound coming from her—like an assignation.

"Oh, yeah, there is." I wondered whether the black man had been spying on me or on Liz Horgan. He sounded faintly amused.

"Leland," she said softly. "If I'd seen you, I'd have asked you to—"

"Kevin's not here today. I dunno where he is, maybe off sick."

"Are you sure?"

"Yeah."

I said, "I'll grab a hard hat and go down anyway, just in case he—"

"No," Liz Horgan said. "If Leland says he's not there, he's not there." Her voice was so flat, I couldn't tell whether she was relieved or increasingly worried. She might have been talking to herself.

"I've been meaning to ask." The dark man stepped forward and I noted his wide sloping shoulders. "You find the key to that storage shed, Ms. Horgan?"

"Not yet."

"I'll talk to O'Day about getting another one made, ordered from the company, whatever."

"Let me talk to Harv, Leland. No need for you to bother. Everything going okay today?"

"No more rats, if that's what you mean."

Before I could inquire about rats, which might mean rodents and might mean informers, Liz slipped her arm into mine. "Let's go inside," she said with a shiver. "It's freezing out here. I hope you're adjusting okay, Carla. Any problems, just come to me." Her tired smile and easy friendliness made me feel uncomfortably like a spy. *Another kind of rat.*

I worked undercover as a cop, but it was a while

ago, and I never forgot who I was and to whom my allegiance belonged. I knew cops who'd gone over, who'd bonded with crooks, who'd forgotten where the line fell between us and them. The line seemed blurry on this site; I didn't have the sense that I was infiltrating a criminal organization. I felt like I was deceiving a kind woman, deliberately giving a false name to a good-looking man.

We ascended the wooden steps to the trailer, Liz Horgan's smile pasted in place like a mask. I closed the door before Walsh could ask for my phone number, or I could ask for his.

By two-thirty I strongly suspected that no insurance claims records were filed in the outer office. Investigating the inner office looked impossible until luck stuck in an oar. First, Marian left early to deliver some papers to a consultant at Bechtel. Then, a guy in a hard hat hustled in, muttering about groundwater. He mentioned rats as well. I didn't catch a lot of other words, but those two were sufficient to march O'Day and both Horgans outside double-time.

My primary target was the tall filing cabinet in the corner of the inner office, but I spent three minutes at Liz's desk, searching for a desk calendar, an appointment book, something that would give me a fix on a planned three o'clock meeting. I couldn't find anything, decided to move on. I yanked out the upper file drawer, flipped quickly through the folders: Equipment rental, Equipment purchase . . . I scrawled down the names of insurers. Eddie's ops could scam them, get them to check their claims records . . .

The phone rang. At first I thought it was the desk

phone, ringing through from the outer office console, but as I approached, I realized the noise was coming from Liz Horgan's top drawer. Most Dig workers rely on cell phones. Liz had forgotten to transfer hers to her purse. I put out a hand to see if the drawer in which it rang was locked.

I have perfect pitch. It's a gift, but there's not much call for it, unless you're a piano tuner or a Vegas impersonator. When the drawer opened smoothly, I lifted the phone, pressed the button, and said hello, raising my pitch to Liz Horgan's level. I thought I'd be speaking to Kevin Fournier, hoped he'd tell me something I wanted to know.

At first I heard nothing, just a smooth murmur like the noise of the sea. Then, a faint crackle, then a voice. No word of greeting, but someone speaking, faintly, far away, droning into the phone, reading, or chanting.

"The Central Artery southbound ramp to the Leverett Circle Connector Bridge, Exit Twenty-six-A, will be closed weeknights tonight through Saturday morning, nine P.M. through five A.M. The Storrow Drive ramp to the bridge will remain open through Thursday." The voice sounded hesitant and unsure. Unlike a recorded announcement, it stumbled over words.

"Hello?" I repeated.

The voice continued, uninflected. "The Central Artery northbound ramp to Causeway Street, Exit Twenty-five will be closed Thursday and Friday nights, eleven P.M. through five-thirty A.M. The I-Ninety-three northbound ramp to the Tobin Bridge, Exit Twenty-seven, will be—"

"Who is this?" I asked.

A quiet click, then silence.

CHAPTER 8

At quitting time, I left the trailer, walked to Quincy Market, and lost myself in the crowd. Near the chocolate-chip-cookie kiosk, with no obvious Dig workers in sight, I hauled out my cell and called Foundation Security. Eddie had told me to ask for Spike, to feel free to use him to run down information, much as I employ my tenant, Roz, when I'm working a case. She's a computer freak and a phone freak, and as long as I don't use her in person, no one can see her tattoos, piercings, or oddly dyed hair. Spike knew my name, was expecting my call. I rattled off the names of the insurance companies, asked him to check the claims, gave him my cell and home numbers. He sounded competent, and I wondered whether he was secretly as weird as Roz, if he was ever tempted to freelance, or if he preferred the steady paycheck, the regular hours.

I wondered if I was wasting taxpayer money investigating the Horgans. Stuff walking off the site wasn't exactly a capital crime, unless Eddie suspected that they were ordering more than they ought to be, resell-

ing equipment, either on the black market or to unsus-
pecting colleagues. He seemed to be holding something
back. Maybe I ought to pay Roz to check out the relationship between Eddie and old man Horgan.

I blew out a sigh and shook my head. No wonder
I'd rather work for myself. I know I can trust myself,
except when it comes to men. Lots of attractive men
on a construction site, rugged and well-built like this
Leland Walsh. Hard to tell whether Walsh was overly
curious about me or not. Could take his job as foreman
seriously, think of himself as some kind of friendly
welcomer for newcomers. And then there was Kevin
Fournier. I didn't have a fix on him. Was he attracted
to Liz Horgan? Or attracted to Liz Horgan's power? I
stared at my cell phone, decided it was time to make
the transition to my night job even though it was barely
three-thirty in the afternoon.

Some investigators swear by Johnnie Walker Black,
but I never send Claire Harper, my favorite source at
the Registry of Motor Vehicles, a bottle of scotch for
Christmas. I send a dozen long-stemmed roses on Val-
entine's Day instead. Claire, a shy, middle-aged clerk
who'd have been termed a spinster in my grandmother's day, gets a lot of mileage from those stems,
and she always remembers my name.

She put me on hold for three minutes, but for the
Registry, that's nothing. When she got back on the line,
she confirmed the facts I'd written on my legal pad.
Veronica James owned no vehicles registered in the
state. Dana Renee Endicott owned a black 1997 Jeep
Grand Cherokee and a brand-new dove-gray Audi A6
Quattro sedan. I made sure of the license plate number

of the Jeep, got the vehicle identification number as well.

"Parking violations?" In Boston, with its residential-parking-only zones, the Registry can be the fastest way to locate runaways with cars. They park in the city and zap, they've got a ticket.

"Sorry."

"How recent is your info?"

"If they tagged the Jeep after Sunday, I won't have it yet."

So much for automation and efficiency at the Registry. I told Claire I'd call again, punched Dana Endicott's number into the phone, hit Send. I could take the train to Beacon Street, or walk, which might be faster. I felt the need to inspect items belonging to the missing woman, to observe her space. Did she have prints or posters on the walls? Flowered pink sheets or black satin? Did her closet hold raggy jeans or leather pants? Did she wear perfume, shave her legs? I wanted to know what she'd taken with her, what she'd left behind. I'd never seen the woman and she seemed an insubstantial ghost, hinted at by strangers.

A recording told me that Miss Endicott was not available. I left a message asking her to return my call as soon as possible. Damn. I didn't even have a photograph.

I double-checked to make sure I had the correct address for Veronica's day job, decided a phone call would be unnecessary. Someone would be on the premises of Charles River Dog Care, located on Western Avenue in Allston. Dogs need care; dogs aren't cats.

You can't get to Allston directly via the T. You need

to transfer to a bus, and if you think the trains have gone to hell, the buses have descended to a lower level. Last time I took one, two guys swearing in Portuguese started a brawl, bleeding on their fellow commuters until a third passenger bellowed and pulled a .38. I decided to save the aggravation, take the T home, and switch to my car.

Charles River Dog Care, with a big red sign in the window, shared a block with two shabby auto repair shops and a fast-food mart. The parking lot was behind the building, down a long narrow drive. It held an old brown Volvo station wagon and a former school bus, painted sky blue. No sign of Dana's Jeep. The entrance to the low brick structure was also in back, cheerfully painted, red letters and cartoonish paw prints on the glass panels of the inner door. I didn't need to press a buzzer or knock. The minute I approached, raucous barking filled the air.

"What?" The man wore gray overalls that looked like hospital scrubs. He stuck his nose out of a narrow crack.

"I'd like to see the owner, please. I'm not selling anything."

"You gotta dog?"

"Tell him it's about Veejay. Veronica James."

"You that Dana woman?"

"No."

"I'll see if he's gotta minute."

I would have thanked him, but he'd already shut the door in my face. Just as I was starting to wonder how long I was going to listen to dogs howl, Gray Scrubs returned, smiling to show me he hadn't dawdled on purpose.

"Dogs won't bother you," he said, swinging the door wide.

Dogs don't bother me. I have a slight preference for independently arrogant felines, but as long as dogs don't slobber all over me, I think they're great.

The business occupied an area that looked like it might once have housed a dance studio, a large wood-panelled room down a flight of stairs, with a partitioned corner big enough to hold a threadbare couch and a couple of sprung armchairs. It didn't smell like a dance studio. It smelled like essence of wet dog. Dogs there were, terriers, and Labs, and golden retrievers. Wire cages lined three walls, not small cages either, more like zoo enclosures. I stopped counting at twenty-seven waggly tongues only because I'd crossed the large room and was entering the small office beyond.

It was tiny, sparsely furnished with a metal desk, a couple of chairs, and a lone file cabinet. The nameplate on the desk said Rogers Walters, both names plural. A man sprang to his feet when I entered. His welcoming smile dimmed when he confirmed that I was not a prospective client. '

"I'd like to ask you a few questions about Veronica James."

"Really? On whose authority?" Walters wore brown wool slacks, a beige checked shirt, nothing fancy, but probably the dogs didn't mind, and it was a step above the outfit worn by his employee, more suitable for meeting the public. A thick sweater, covered with dog hair, hung over the back of his chair.

I hadn't decided on an approach. I try not to, until I see what I'm up against. "She works here, right?" I offered him my most charming smile.

"And you are?" His voice stayed crisp and chilly, and I wondered whether my smile was more effective when I was a redhead. I noted his erect posture and spartan surroundings. He could have been a former cop from the calculating look in his eyes, and I decided that deception was not the way to go. I handed him a card that stated my true occupation. I don't use them all that often, but sometimes they seem like the ticket.

"Private investigator?" His mouth twisted as though he were tasting something unpleasant. "Well, Miss Carlyle, what's this about?"

"Veronica does work for you?"

"I haven't seen her this week."

"Heard from her?"

He shook his head.

"Her friends are worried about her."

"You mean I'm not the only one she's gone AWOL on?" He was maybe thirty-five, hair starting to thin, parted at the side and yanked across his forehead.

"When did you see her last?"

"Friday. When she didn't make it in Monday, I figured she was sick. Inconvenient. I had to fill in, do her work. She didn't call. Inconsiderate. A friend of hers did, later. Or was that her sister, looking for her?" He scratched the back of his neck before sinking into his chair. "Gave her name. Dana something?"

He didn't invite me to sit. "Her landlady."

"Ran out on the rent?"

"Nothing like that."

"Okay, it's just she's—it's not like she's wanted by the police or anything?"

"I'm not with the police." I tried the smile again, got no answering warmth. "You weren't concerned or alarmed when she didn't come in?"

"No, but I can't say I expected her to stay long. I'll be frank about it. I don't pay enough." A dog yelped in the distance and I heard the outside door open and close. "Only reason Veronica stayed was the dogs. She's great with dogs. Clients beg for her—can Veejay pick up the dog, spend time with the dog, school the dog. We do complete day care, pickup, exercise, grooming, the whole package. I'll tell you, if she walked in the door right now, apology or no apology, good excuse or no excuse, I hate to say it, but I'd take her back, no questions asked. I don't know how I'm going to find somebody else, terrific with animals, willing to work." He stared at me with hopeful eyes, as though I might suddenly break down and confess a desire to care for other people's pets. When I didn't, he said, "Is that all?"

"Did she get along with her coworkers as well as she got along with the dogs?"

He seemed puzzled by the question. "Well, there's just Harold and me, and Erica, part-time. She—Veejay—never made trouble. Small place like this, I'd have heard about it."

"No fights, no arguments?" Gray Scrubs must be Harold.

"No."

He wouldn't let me see her employment file—confidential—but allowed a peek at her job application.

She'd filled it in slightly less than a year ago. Her address, social security number, next of kin matched those I already had. Nothing different, nothing out of the ordinary.

Walters lowered his voice. "Most likely thing, she met some guy and—you know, she's shacked up with him somewhere. She'll turn up. Of course, that's probably not what you like to tell your clients."

I ignored his assumption that I was trying to run up my fee, since PI's need to cultivate thick skins, and convinced him to run through Veejay's last day with me. She'd worked a regular eight to four shift on Friday, going out with the van in the morning, picking up charges for the day. Twenty-four dogs, give or take a couple, but Veronica and the driver—Harold usually drove—could handle them because the van was specially equipped and the dogs knew the drill.

"Any breaks in her routine lately? Unexplained absences?"

"No."

"Any evidence she took drugs? Drank?"

"I don't put up with that sort of thing. Look, I don't have a lot of time right now. I haven't been able to replace her, and I have work to do." He stood, a none-too-subtle hint that he considered the interview over.

"Maybe she mentioned her plans to one of your clients."

"I doubt it."

"I'd like to be able to ask them myself."

"Look, I run a service for busy people. It's not cheap and there are others who offer pretty much the same thing. I'm not going to annoy my clients by giving their names to a private investigator."

"I'd be discreet. I wouldn't mention you."

"Veronica works for me. They'd know. Forget it." He held my gaze.

"I'd like to speak to your other workers."

"Is that necessary?"

"It won't take long."

He stalked to the door. "Harold!"

The man with the gray coveralls appeared, and before I could say a word, Walters demanded, "Did Veronica tell you she wasn't coming in this week?"

"No."

"There." He folded his arms, and the gesture seemed to say, *that's that, get out.*

"And your part-time employee—"

"Erica."

"I'd like to ask her."

"She'll just say the same as me." Harold had a narrow face, a big squashy nose. "Veejay left on Friday, same as always. We were both surprised she didn't show up."

"She have any special friends among the owners?"

He shook his head. "Nah, she liked the dogs."

"Ever see her with a boyfriend?"

"Nah."

"And now," Walters said firmly, "we have a schedule to keep, like the military. A time to run the dogs along the Charles—plenty of fresh air and exercise here—a time to feed them, a time to get them on the bus. It's loading time. Why don't you see the lady out, Harold?"

I hadn't seen Veronica's room yet, hadn't spoken to her parents. I'd probably never need Charles River Dog Care's client list, but it seemed to me that Walters guarded it too zealously. As we climbed the steps, I tried my smile on Harold. "You probably keep track of all the places you go to pick up the dogs."

"Boss gives me a list."

"I'll bet you could make me a copy."

He didn't say yes and he didn't say no, but his steps slowed, and when we got to the landing, he didn't open the door immediately.

"It would be worth money," I said.

"How much?"

"Fifty bucks. On receipt."

My card disappeared into his pocket.

CHAPTER 9

I considered driving to Dana Endicott's brownstone and banging the door, in case she was home but not answering the phone, debated the wisdom of harassing a wealthy client while pondering the hostile parking situation in her neighborhood—tow zones, fifteen-minute meters, resident-only parking. My leg throbbed, probably because of the worsening weather, but possibly due to guilt. I hadn't been to the gym in three days.

I drove to Gold's—plenty of parking in the lot—raced a stationary bike for half an hour, did prescribed leg lifts and extensions, grunted through ˙hamstring strengtheners. The regime relieved the guilt, but didn't improve the weather.

It was wet and nasty when I emerged, horizontal gusts of rain rendering my umbrella useless. I rarely cook, but on nights like this nothing beats chili, so I stopped for ingredients at the Star. The recipe varies, but cans of Ro-tel diced tomatoes and green chiles are usually in the mix, along with a couple of huge Spanish onions, ground meat, and plenty of garlic. I showered as soon as I got home, got into comfy sweats, then chopped, stirred, and tasted, downing a beer to counter the spices. I felt good about work, something I hadn't done for awhile. I prefer working for myself—that had something to do with it—but for some reason, a line from a Tennessee Williams play kept slipping into my head, the one about the father who worked for the phone company and fell in love with long distance.

I could easily fall in love with missing persons. If I ever get to the point where I can pick and choose, specialize, concentrate, I'll take a missing persons case every time. I like studying what isn't there, envisioning the hole in the doughnut. It's like observing air currents, disturbances caused by the absence of a body in space. I couldn't yet see Veejay, not even in my mind's eye, but I was starting to feel the eddies of her absence, from the unskilled Elvira covering her tables, to the business owner doing the work of his employee, to the landlady with an empty room and a missing car.

Missing people move me more than missing construction equipment, no doubt about it. Was meeting rich Dana Endicott a sign that I should go back to working for myself? I considered my finances. My bankbook needed more than a single boost. Paolina and college, I reminded myself. Paolina's got money of her own, from her absentee druglord dad, but I'd spent a lot of it recently, getting her out of public housing on the theory that she'd never make it as far as college if she stayed.

I ate steaming chili, listening to the thump of icy rain against the windows. I thought about calling Sam

Gianelli, asking whether Norrelli Construction was a familiar name, how he was, was he married, what kind of money was the mob screwing out of the Dig. I'd had about a beer too many, I concluded. I played guitar, went to bed.

Morning. I dressed in the dark, decided to concoct a sack lunch featuring leftover chili. I didn't want to cement a lunch habit with Marian, and it seemed to me that the workers might be prompted to chit-chat about theft over lunch, once such traditional matters as who should play center field for the Red Sox dried up. Then, wouldn't you know it, I couldn't find the thermos. I knew I had one, red plastic with a wide mouth. The idea of eating cold chili sitting on the cold ground was definitely unappealing.

By the time I found the thermos I was running late. I missed a train, the snow turned to slush—you get the idea—but when I rushed into the field office, primed with excuses, I found it deserted. I poked my head into the inner office, saw no one. Marian's purse was visible in her half-opened desk drawer, but there was no evidence that either of the Horgans had been in, and O'Day was missing, too. I made a quick inventory of items on the Horgans' desks. The photo smiled. The laptop was absent. A glossy brochure from the Artery Business Committee lay on top of a payroll form. I gave a quick tug at the top drawer of Gerry's desk. It didn't budge, but Liz's opened easily. Her cell phone was gone.

The lights were on, the alarm disengaged. I went back into the outer office, checked my watch against the clock on the microwave. Yesterday, in the same trailer at the same hour, I'd heard engines whine, jack-hammers sputter and jitter. Now, only the rush of distant traffic, speeding by. I parted the curtain over the stingy window, stood fixed for a moment, then grabbed a hard hat. It took seconds to kick off my shoes, stick my feet into heavy boots, shrug into my coat. I ran outside, taking the three cement steps in a leap.

Yesterday, the site was a hive of activity wherever you looked, each person working at his own rhythm, each person part of a group that moved to a different beat. Now the site had little movement, a single focus. Knots of hard hats stood near the glory holes that pierced the decking, staring down into the pit, their breath rising in a cloud. I headed for the west scaffold steps and found myself blocked by the crowd.

"Shit, looks bad."

"Is he moving?"

"Where's the fuckin' EMTs?"

Three had died on the Dig since Governor Weld smashed a bottle of champagne to begin work in December of '91. One had been badly injured. Construction machinery was heavy and ornery, conditions hard and wintry. Acetylene torches burned, footing was treacherous. Still, workers were careful, safety officers wary. Thousands had died building the Panama Canal, hundreds on the Golden Gate Bridge. The Dig was a model site with an enviable record.

An ambulance pulled to a whip-tailed halt, lights flashing. A man standing near the east scaffold semaphored his arms, yelled, "Bring a gurney!"

I tucked myself into the crowd, edged closer to the

nearest glory hole. No one descended the staircase and I wondered if it were blocked.

A man said, "The way Horgan's reaming out Charlie, you figure something went wrong with the scaffold?"

"Charlie checks those fuckers every morning."

The EMTs were having trouble lowering their gear down the scaffolding. Hands grabbed it, eased it down. There was grumbling about how long the rescue was taking. There'd been drills, hadn't these guys been paying attention? One site, they had to haul a man out in a clamshell bucket, by crane. This was fucking nothing, and look at the time it was taking!

"Yeah, well, he ain't movin'."

"Could be paralyzed."

"Yeah, look on the fucking bright side."

Out of the corner of my eye I caught Gerry Horgan, red-faced, shoving toward the ambulance, Liz behind him, breathing hard. The paramedics, aided by random workers, were lifting the stretcher, passing it hand to hand. A man was fastened to the gurney with orange straps. I tried to see his face but it stayed hidden behind heads, shoulders, hard hats. The gurney surfaced, and a name surged through the crowd, group to group, like a rushing breeze. Kevin Fournier.

Watery blue eyes in the trailer. An urgent need to see Liz Horgan. I made tracks for the ambulance, too.

The orange-clad paramedics were moving fast, rigging oxygen lines. The victim was strapped to a spinal board. I caught a glimpse of his head, partially wrapped in a sweatshirt hood, dark with blood. *He ought to be bleeding more,* I thought. Gushing blood, from a wound like that.

O'Day, the site super, stood at Horgan's left. He looked like he wanted to strike out, smash something. Liz Horgan clutched her husband's hand, but he shook her off, pursuing the paramedics, yelling into a walkie-talkie. Liz touched O'Day's shoulder, then started after Horgan. She looked as though she were about to be sick.

"Can I help?" I cut her off at an angle of the fence. "Are you okay?"

She stared at me blankly.

"Carla," I said.

"It'll be okay," she said, more to herself than to me. "It'll be okay." Her teeth were chattering. She took a step, staggered, grabbed the fence to stay upright.

Her husband was suddenly next to me. "You! Get her out of here! Get her some water or something, up at the trailer. Go on, Liz. Leave it to me. It's gonna be okay, Liz."

"How?" she said softly. "How? With this—"

"We'll go to twenty-four/seven if we have to. We'll do what we have to do."

"We'll hire a night watchman." Her voice was so low I barely made out the words. "We'll hire him. Promise."

"Okay. Jesus Christ, okay." His head was turned away from me; I couldn't see his expression, but he sounded reluctant.

She touched his shoulder. "Promise, Gerry."

"Okay, okay, Liz. I'll take care of it."

"Promise," she insisted.

"Get her a blanket, too," Horgan told me.

I wanted to abandon her, find a way into the trench, examine footsteps, bloodstains, but such actions on the part of a secretary would be noted, questioned. Instead I ushered Mrs. H. into the trailer, my arm protectively circling her shoulders. She asked for aspirin. Her hand, when it touched mine, felt icy.

She kept aspirin in her bottom desk drawer, she told me. I found it, grabbed a sweater off a hook in lieu of a blanket, wrapped the garment around her shaking shoulders. Her teeth were chattering so hard it took five minutes before she could manage the aspirin. If she hadn't been there I'd have called Eddie. I no longer had any desire to quit my day job. I'd seen Kevin Fournier as he lay on the gurney. I thought he was probably dead, or dying.

A dead man is a missing person, too.

CHAPTER 10

Through the window of the trailer I saw Horgan jump into the back of the ambulance with the injured man and a female EMT. Mass General was closest. I'd spent time there with my bullet wound. Mrs. Horgan, still shivering, clutched my hand and asked me to fetch Leland Walsh. I couldn't find him, but used the break to alert Eddie via cell phone. I tried to get close enough to the accident site to take a few discreet photographs, but the scaffold staircase was guarded by grim orange-vested hard hats. Later Marian told me Walsh had gone to the hospital, too.

Work didn't stop for long. The east scaffold staircase remained closed, but the west staircase reopened quickly. Some grumbled about forging on so soon after a coworker had been lifted motionless from the trench, but no one walked off the job. Everyone knew that the project was a huge-bellied beast, that delay was costly. Marian rang project headquarters, assured me that they'd run with the ball, notifying insurers, OSHA, the Turnpike Authority. Marian and I started to assemble photocopies of weekly safety-inspection charts. The phone started ringing and didn't stop: reporters; OSHA; the chief safety officer. Charlie Perez, the site safety officer, argued fiercely with Harv O'Day. In the midst of chaos, Liz Horgan, recovered and working, sent over coffee and Danish for the trailer staff, and even Marian was touched and grateful.

"Accident" was the only term I heard when I ate lunch on the cold ground with a bunch of laborers. Rotten fucking luck. So far behind, and now this. Getting to be a bad luck site. I tried to guide the conversation toward Kevin Fournier, what he'd been like, who his friends were, but the group drifted into awkward silence. No one wanted to speak ill of Kevin, which meant they weren't optimistic about his recovery. Some of the workers had seen his injuries from a closer vantage point than I had, but no one, it seemed, had seen him fall. There was no rousing chorus of what-a-great-guy-Kevin-was. No one claimed to be a friend, to know his family. He wasn't married, I gathered from remarks about numerous, hot-looking girlfriends. Good football player, somebody said. Liked a bet.

I half-expected Eddie to show up. When he didn't, I rang him again and arranged an evening meeting. Marian had trouble getting through to the hospital, figured hard hats were flooding the line with cell calls. She sent me to spread the word that she'd act as liasion, phoning every half hour, letting people know if Fournier's condition changed. It was initially described as grave, which meant he'd gotten there alive. It didn't improve during the long afternoon. It couldn't have worsened; in hospital-speak there was no term more perilous than grave.

I left at three o'clock, quitting time for secretaries, frustrated but feeling that there was nothing else I could do. I wasn't Fournier's next-of-kin; I couldn't waltz into his hospital room and check out his injuries up close. I wasn't a city official who could slap a "stop work" order on the site, or a bigshot Dig manager who could demand an immediate investigation. I wasn't a cop working an attempted homicide, and I wasn't a solo operative either. Eddie had warned me to stay undercover and keep my nose clean. Still, I might not have torn myself away if I hadn't had a second job, a scheduled appointment.

It should have involved viewing Veronica James's room, but it didn't. Dana Endicott, in New York on unexpected business, had left neither a key nor a firm date for her return, simply a message on my answering machine. The delay annoyed me; I don't like to skip steps. I wondered what the rich landlady had done with the dogs, whether she'd entrusted them to Rogers Walters and Charles River Dog Care.

I didn't go home to change, didn't have time. I stopped to fill the gas tank, stuck a Robert Johnson CD in the deck, and tried to let the thumping bass of the Delta blues soothe my mind. Driving usually helps me unwind, but images from the Dig tensed my fingers on the steering wheel—the swaying gurney in the shadowy light, the man who'd removed his hard hat and crossed himself as the injured man was carried by, the tense faces of the workers at lunch. *Why had no one seen Fournier fall, heard him cry out?*

• • •

Tewksbury, Veronica James's childhood home, twenty-two miles from Boston, used to be poor folks' farm country, but few of the old spreads remain and much of the rocky ground is occupied by treeless subdivisions. The Jameses lived near the town center, a cross-roads with a village green and a steepled clapboard church, in a Cape-style house with a saggy porch and weathered gray paint. I didn't see a doorbell so I knocked.

The woman who opened the door had no sparkle left in her brown eyes. She stared at me as though I were about to deliver bad news. I gave my name instead, reminded her that we'd spoken on the phone.

"We don't *have* to talk to you. You're not the police."

"That's right. May I come in?" The low-ceilinged foyer smelled of mothballs. There was noise coming from somewhere, chirpy little jingles from a distant TV.

"Well, Jack—that's my husband—he's in the back room. It's kind of a mess. He's been off sick, but then, you wouldn't know that."

Vague. Dana Endicott had described her phone conversation with Veronica's mother as vague and uninformative. "I don't mind about the mess."

She shrugged and stepped aside. The vestibule emptied into a front room with an aged, overstuffed plaid couch. There were doilies on the sofa arms and chair backs, a cross-bound Jesus on the wall. The room into which she led me was an add-on larger than the living room, and the fifty inches of gleaming color screen at one end looked more like a religious shrine than the front-room Jesus did. Two fat armchairs were positioned like movie seats, a snack table between them. The man in the righthand chair was watching *Jeopardy* and the volume was loud.

Veronica's dad was easily twenty years older than her mom. Pale and puffy, he looked like the act of raising a potato chip to his lips was his idea of vigorous exercise. His chair was in the reclining position, elevating veiny feet encased in furry slippers.

"Company, Jack," the woman yelled over the TV blare.

"What? Who's that?"

"That Carlyle woman come to ask about Veronica."

He regarded me with irritation and reached for the remote. If he could have pressed a button to make me disappear instead of the game show host, I'd have dissolved in a puff of smoke.

"The hell you want?"

"You get good sound on that set," I said admiringly.

He sniffed a little, nodded. Sixties, salt-and-pepper hair, grizzled patch on his chin, not quite a goatee, but trying. "You wanna talk, then sit down, the both of you. Go on now, Helen. Why you standing up so I have to gawk?" He craned his head at me. "I hurt my back. Makes me goddam irritable."

Helen hovered till I lowered myself onto a small settee. Then she took her place in her big armchair.

"What's all the fuss about Ronni anyway?" the man said. "She's over twenty-one. It's a free country, last time I looked."

"Certainly is," I agreed. "I just want to make sure I get a balanced viewpoint, include your input about your daughter."

"I have *four* daughters, four, grown and gone. Two married, one at Fitchburg State—sophomore this year—besides Ronni. Plus four grandchildren." He waved an arm at the framed photos on the side wall, relentlessly posed high school graduation shots mingled with Sears kiddie candids of the grandchildren. The frames were identical dime-store brass, and there were rectangular spots on the wallpaper that spoke of rearrangement as more grandkids came along. "Now our Elsie's here at least three times a week, always stays for supper. Helen looks after the boys while she shops."

"Can you point out Veronica for me?"

"One in the low-cut blouse," he said disapprovingly.

The mother made a noise. "I told her to wear something with a nice collar, but she said all the girls were wearing those V-neck things."

Veronica, on the lower right, wore her hair sleek and dark, parted to the left, hanging artlessly around a thin face. Her eyes, too big for her face, were dark as well. They stared somewhere over the photographer's left shoulder. While I studied the photo, Mrs. James prattled on about Veronica's high school wardrobe, how she always wore black or white, while Mrs. James preferred pretty colors, just like her oldest, Elsie, did.

"Hell." Mr. James's outburst stopped her cold. "Hell's just the first part of my wife's name—it's not like I'm swearing all the time." He gave me a look that said I ought to appreciate his subtle humor, so I contorted my face in what I hoped was the right kind of grin. "Let's get this over with. What do you want to know about Veronica?"

"I take it she doesn't visit as often as Elsie."

Helen James looked up from picking invisible lint off her skirt. "Once, maybe twice a month."

"Is she regular about visits?"

"Not really. She comes around birthdays, anniversaries."

"Last weekend, the weekend her landlady expected her to stay here, was that somebody's birthday?"

Her eyebrows were brown, but her hair was platinum, straw dry, badly bleached. She shook her head. "No. Our Elsie's oldest boy had a big party three weeks ago. Six years old. Lovely party. Had a magician and all, made those cute animal balloons."

"Was Veronica at the party?"

"Yes, but she hardly stayed."

"And you weren't expecting her at all last weekend."

"Well, the girls know they can always come home. Our door's always open. Once there was trouble with her husband, and our daughter moved—"

"Hel, that's none of her business."

"Jack, I'm only saying Ronni knows she can come home without arranging for it in advance."

"Well, it's nice for *me* to know ahead of time," he said. "Not like it's a hotel."

"When did Veronica leave home? Go off on her own?" I glanced at Helen, but it was Jack who answered.

"Out of high school one day, out the door the next. Big city girl in a two-bit town. Says she has to live somewhere she can see a new movie every night. Now, our Elsie lived right here all the way through college."

I was starting to hate Elsie. I'd already decided on *her* photo, the one with the stuck-up nose and superior sneer.

"Jayme lived here till she married, too, but little Jackie, she wanted to try the dorm this year. Jackie's our youngest." He sounded fond of Jackie.

"Which daughter is Veronica?"

Helen said, "You know, I always thought she'd study hard, be a vet. She's a smart one, she is, but it's always animals with her. Momma, can I bring home the hamster, the rabbit, whatever they're keeping at the school."

"Hel, this lady doesn't care a fig about those damn animals."

"Jack, reason that woman's all upset is Ronni left her dog."

"Yeah, well, she can afford to feed the damn thing. What's the difference, three mutts or four? She's a damned busybody is what she is. I mean, think about it. Veronica's a pretty girl. I'm not saying she's an angel, maybe she's a little wild. She goes out, and that woman wants me to report her missing? Hell, I'm lodge brothers with half the police officers in town. Half the girls in town are shacked up with some man not their husband. I'm not shocked by it anymore, even if I do think some of them ought to be horsewhipped. If you raise a child right, they'll turn out right, that's what I always say." His face was reddening.

Here's what I always say: If you believe that bullshit bromide about child raising, you pretend nothing's wrong even when it is wrong. Because your daughter's conduct reflects on you. I dropped the idea of asking the Jameses to file a missing persons report and, staring at Jack James's mottled cheeks, decided I wouldn't even mention the Jeep. Man might have a heart attack in his Barcalounger if he thought a daughter of his was suspected of car theft.

"Helen, goddam it." He touched a button on the side of his chair and his massive body jerked upright. "Why's this woman wasting my time, anyhow? You told her about that phone call, didn't you? Honest, Helen, I don't know what's wrong with you sometimes."

His wife bit her lip, stared down at her lap. "Well, I didn't talk to Ronni."

"Did she phone while you were out?" I asked. "Leave a message?" If they hadn't erased it, I'd make a copy. "Did she say where she was?"

"Well, just this morning, what happened is, a man name of Peter called, said she was fine, not to worry. Asked me to call her landlord. So I did, left a message."

"Peter?" I repeated. "Peter who?"

"I'm sorry, I don't remember the last name. He gave it, though, very polite. Nice friendly voice, like a talk show host. I thought it was gonna be some come-on for a bank, maybe I won some contest. I always send in those contest forms, gives me something to look forward to. He said I could save him some bother, make the phone call, like he was at a pay phone or something. You know how they eat up your change."

"Did he say the landlord or the landlady?"

"I don't know. Don't recall."

"Did this Peter say why Veronica didn't want to say hello, make her own phone calls?"

"Oh, he was just doing her a favor." Helen picked at her skirt some more. "I hope I didn't do wrong. When I called Miss Endicott, I left a message, saying I heard from Ronni, and not to worry."

"But you didn't. Hear from her."

"Well, not in so many words."

"You calling my wife a liar?" Mr. James said loudly. "That's it. We've answered enough of your questions."

"I'm certainly not calling anyone a liar," I said smoothly, "and I appreciate your time. This Peter, do you remember your daughter mentioning him? Did she work with him, go to school with him?"

"We don't know her Boston friends," Helen ventured. "I don't remember any Peter from her high school crowd."

"Gal didn't have any high school crowd. Ronni's a loner. Not like Elsie. Elsie was a cheerleader her junior year. She—"

"Ronni sang with the choir," Helen said defensively. "That was her crowd, the choir kids."

"And look what they dragged into the choir," her husband said angrily. "That's why she never met any decent boys."

"*She met Rick.*"

"Who's Rick?" I said.

"Her goddam husband," Jack said in a disgusted voice. "Hel, you would have to go and mention the bastard. *Was* her husband, the asshole."

I'd run a document search on Veronica James, first thing. No record of a marriage, or a divorce. Dana Endicott hadn't mentioned a marriage. Jack James hit the remote and the television boomed full volume. I tried to ask another question. A grinning model piloted a silver SUV about a hundred miles an hour down a rain-slicked road to a deafening rock-and-roll beat. James glared at me, shouted good-bye, turned his full attention to the set.

As she ushered me into the hall, Helen James glanced at me shamefacedly. "Ronni and Rick, they were never really married. He knows. Not by the church and not by the law, but she lived with him and all, so he calls Rick her ex-husband."

Standing in the tiny foyer, I convinced her to part with Rick's last name, Garrison, and to give me an address, even though she thought it was no longer a current one.

"I don't think she'd go to him. Honestly."

"Where would she go, if she were in trouble?"

Mrs. James' face closed. "We don't believe in abortion."

I hadn't even been thinking of that kind of trouble. "Is she close to any of her sisters?"

"There's such an age difference between Ronni and Jayme." She bit her lip and her fingers tightened on the door handle. "And Jackie, well, she's still in school. . . ."

I insisted on their phone numbers, too.

"Helen!" Jack had quite a voice when he let it fly. It boomed over the TV blare and made the woman glance guiltily over her shoulder.

"Have Ronni call me," she whispered, "soon as you find her. I'm worried to death. We watch TV all the time. You'd think he'd know what it's like out there."

TV ain't life, lady, I felt like saying. Turn off the

fucking machine, breathe the real air. Instead I thanked her. Then I sat in my car and phoned each of the sisters, one after the other. Neither Jackie nor Jayme had seen Veronica, neither knew Peter. I saved Elsie—Mom and Daddy's darling—for last.

"Certainly not," she said firmly when I asked whether Veejay was staying with her. Her voice, low and gentle, annoyed me, since I'd imagined it nasal and hard.

"Do you have Peter's phone number?"

"Who?"

"Do you know a friend of Veronica's named Peter?"

"No comment."

"Listen, lady, I'm not from the *National Enquirer*. I'm trying to help your sister. I didn't tell your parents, but Veronica took off in a car she doesn't own."

"She stole a car? Oh, my lord."

"No one wants to press charges. Not if I find her soon."

"Maybe Ronni doesn't want to be found, you ever think of that? Oh, just leave me alone. Leave my folks alone, too. You people never quit, do you?" She hung up with a righteous bang, leaving me wondering what "people" she was talking about.

Had Dana Endicott phoned? Or was someone else asking questions about Veronica?

CHAPTER 11

"Hey, I'm sorry, kid. Ya must have had a hell of a long day." Eddie stuck out his hand and we shook. No embrace.

He'd chosen a North End pizzeria as a rendezvous, a thick-crust Sicilian joint. In another month or two, we might have eaten outdoors at a small table under a Cinzano umbrella, sipped espresso, watched street life pass down Hanover Street. I'd driven straight from Tewksbury, parking semi-legally, too close to a hydrant. It was rainy, dark, windy, and like the other patrons, we chose to eat indoors.

"I called the General," he went on. "The official line is no change. His condition's listed as—"

"Grave, but it's worse than that, Eddie. I talked to a guy. They're keeping him on life support long enough to round up people who can use his organs. He's not coming out."

"Who told ya that?"

"Guy I know. Guy I trust."

"Damn. Here, why don't ya sit down?"

Indoors, the cracked plaster needed paint; the carpet, replacement. There were seven tables—first come, first served, seat yourself. Customers came for the puttanesca sauce, not the kitschy Chianti-bottle décor or the sketchy ambiance. Fire blazed in a brick oven in the far wall. At least it was warm.

"So, is this going to be a black mark against Horgan Construction?" I took off my coat and draped it on the back of my chair.

"Ya wanna order?" Eddie's clothes were rumpled, and he looked older than he'd appeared at our previous meeting, old enough that I wondered how beneficial mozzarella and pepperoni would be on his weakened heart. We decided to split a big pie. Two smalls, you wind up with nothing but crust.

He tapped nervous fingers on the table. "It's bad, any accident on the project is bad, causes trouble, but I don't think we have to worry. Nothing to do with the stuff I asked ya to look at."

"Still," I said.

"Still what?"

"There are things I'd like to know. For instance, I haven't talked to anybody who saw the guy fall."

"Insurance dicks will cover that."

"You want me to stick to stolen equipment?"

The waiter interrupted and took our order. Eddie asked for Bacardi and soda. I stuck to Pepsi. I was still working.

As soon as the waiter left, Eddie motioned me closer, lowered his voice. "Listen, another call came in yesterday on the hotline. About the Horgans."

"What?"

"Carlotta, I don't like being used. Politically. Ya know that, right? Even when I was a cop, I didn't let the suits shove me around."

He was giving himself the benefit of the doubt, but I nodded in agreement.

"If I thought this was just political, I'd quit. Thing is, I'm not sure what it is."

"Eddie, you know me from when I was a cop, too. If there's nothing there, there's nothing there."

He blew out a breath, smiled. His fingers touched the collar of his shirt like they wanted to loosen it. "Okay, Carlotta. Sometimes I gotta hear it. I'm sorry."

"Hey, you hired me, you can fire me. I'll keep my eye out for smoke and mirrors. I've got no grudge against the Horgans."

He nodded, sipped water.

"What's with the new hotline call?" I asked.

"Selling dirt."

"Selling *dirt*?"

"Guy says somebody's selling dirt offa Horgan's site. Illegally."

"There's money in dirt?"

"When you're talking thirteen million cubic yards of it, there is. Ya know how much dirt that is?"

He was itching to enlighten me so I shook my head.

"Could fill Foxboro Stadium thirteen times."

The New England Patriots play football in Foxboro Stadium.

"Who pays for dirt?" I asked.

"Depends where it goes, depends who hauls it. There's deals with the state, capping landfills, making a new park over on Spectacle Island, ya know. Some private guys are in there too, filling in a quarry to make a fancy country club, sending it out to landscapers in the 'burbs.''

Spectacle Island, in Boston Harbor, used to be not only an eyesore, but a stinkhole. Use an area as a garbage dump long enough, that happens. Increased in size, sculpted and landscaped with Dig dirt, it was being touted as a future day-trippers' delight, only a ferryboat ride away.

I said, "Dirt off one site, though, the price tag couldn't be much."

"Exactly."

"The complaint give specifics?" I asked. "Names?"

The waiter brought the pizza, a misshapen circle smelling of garlic and tomato, too hot to touch. I inhaled and salivated. They'd scored it into six generous slices, left the knife on the side. I cut Eddie a wedge and dumped it on his plate, but he didn't seem to notice.

"C'mon, before it gets cold," I said.

My half had artichokes and anchovies in addition to pepperoni. It was squishy, hot, and delicious, twice as good as its Quincy Market cousin, and I vowed to bring Paolina here. Maybe she could bring a friend and we'd avoid the loaded silences.

Eddie tasted a small bite, wiped his mouth on his napkin. "Listen, Carlotta, there's nothing says this dirt business or the thing about stuff walking off-site has anything to do with a lousy accident. I been on this, ever since I heard. I got my sources at the General, too, and the docs think the man fell."

"Yeah, you show me a doc who can tell the difference between fell and got shoved, Eddie."

"You think it's like that?"

I envisioned the scaffold staircase, remembered the queasy sensation in my stomach the first time I'd descended to the pit. "I don't know. You want me to check with the paramedics, see if he said anything?"

"In the ambulance?"

"Horgan rode with him."

"I'll take care of it," Eddie said.

"I'm going to ask Spike to run a criminal check on Fournier, okay?"

"A CORI? Sure."

I wondered if I should expand the criminal records search, include Harv O'Day and Leland Walsh. O'Day could over-order supplies and equipment even more easily than the Horgans. And Walsh—what exactly made me suspicious of Walsh? Good looks? The way he'd watched me take the steps to the trailer? His disappearing act following Fournier's fall?

"Anything else you want me to cover, Eddie? Will the site close if Fournier dies?"

"Hah. The big boys will send flowers and regrets, but this is a money deal. You stick to equipment theft—plus check out the hauling contracts."

"Horgan had a disagreement with a trucker day before yesterday."

"Yeah?"

"Norrelli."

Eddie took a long pull on his drink, leaned closer. "Interesting. Maybe you oughta *use your contacts*, you know what I mean?"

He concentrated on his pizza, avoiding my eyes.

"I don't like it," I said.

"What?"

"Eddie, you know sometimes on a case, your gut tells you look here, look there. Mine's not giving me directions yet, but there's something. The site's way too tense—"

"Whaddaya mean, tense?"

"Maybe what I'm picking up is some kind of financial trouble, or maybe something personal, like a divorce. Any rumors about Liz and Gerry?"

"Shit. That would be bad. That would split the freakin' company."

I wondered exactly how much of Horgan Construction Liz Horgan owned. I didn't feel like I could ask Eddie flat out. Eddie was old man Horgan's friend.

I said, "Do you have tapes of the hotline calls?"

"They're at the IG's office."

"Any chance both complaints were made by the same guy?"

"Hey, if they were, it's probably some asshole with a grudge, right? FBI lab's got sound stuff. I gotta buddy there."

"Am I good with voices, Eddie?"

"Hell, yeah. I remember."

"It's not scientific, but why not let me listen?"

I didn't think I'd be able to match the voices. I mean, if I were trying to screw somebody that way, I'd have the presence of mind to disguise my voice, or have a pal drop a dime. But I thought I might get a fix on where the calls had been placed.

We finished the pizza, decided to skip dessert even though the cannoli were bursting with whipped cream.

It was easier to walk the half mile to the IG's office than move our cars. We passed under the Central Artery and made our way through a narrow, ill-lit Dig detour bounded by blue-and-yellow barriers. The wind whistled under the old highway and tugged at my hat.

The man who'd called the fraud line twice had made no effort to disguise his voice. I listened to the first message, then the second. The second, then the first, again. It helped that I'd heard him angry, demanding to know why Gerry Horgan refused to go to twenty-four/seven. Fournier sounded angry on tape, too.

"Shit," Eddie said. "You can't be sure."

"Right," I said. But I was.

CHAPTER 12

The next morning I hunched my shoulders and leaned into the wind again, lowering my head as I passed Sam Adams's statue in front of Faneuil Hall, using the Cradle of Liberty as shelter from gusts of grit, grateful for the windbreak, and for the fact that Eddie hadn't moved me to another site, maybe high on the new cable-stayed bridge. Just the thought of the icy wind at a hundred and fifty feet gave me chills. If you fell from a height like that, no doubt about the outcome.

I reminded myself to view the mechanical drawings, check the depth of the trench at the point of Fournier's fall. My mind replayed the tapes I'd heard the night before. *Stuff walking off the Horgan site. Somebody selling dirt.*

If you sell dirt, you don't ship it in cardboard cartons. You move it in trucks, maybe big red Norrelli trucks. Trucks mean teamsters, and the International Brotherhood of Teamsters is composed of men who live by an ironclad code: Never turn in a fellow driver.

Something falls off the back of a truck, none of your business.

Fournier wasn't a teamster. What did he know about stuff walking off the site, about selling dirt? Had he overheard a conspiracy, seen something he shouldn't have seen? And why use the hotline? Why not go to the Horgans, tell them his suspicions? Because they were involved, compromised . . . *Use your contacts.* Eddie's words echoed, but it was way too early to phone Sam Gianelli. Way too early . . . and maybe way too late.

Fournier died at 8:57 A.M. without regaining consciousness. I didn't hear it from Happy Eddie. I found out—no details, just the fact—from the look on Marian's face as she pressed her ear to the receiver. Liz Horgan knew as soon as Marian opened the inner-office door without knocking.

Liz's hands shook as she clasped them to her breast and she turned paler than she'd been when they hauled Fournier out of the trench. She closed her eyes and took deep gulping breaths. Her fair hair clung limply to her colorless cheeks as she warned Marian and me to say nothing to the press, to refer all reporters to the Dig's PR director. She instructed Marian to call the General again, get the name of the funeral home, inquire about services. Any calls from OSHA or union officials were to be put through to her immediately. We were to make additional copies of the weekly safety reports for the past month, make sure they were available. If any of the workers asked to see them, fine, we weren't hiding anything. She handed me a manila folder; would I please add the new night watchman to the payroll?

The work didn't occupy my mind. It existed on one level—my fingers tapped the keys, entering Jason O'Meara, DOB, SSN—but my thoughts strayed. The news of Fournier's death passed into O'Day's office, provoking a moment of shocked silence followed by a muttered curse.

"It's so awful!" Marian put the Kleenex supply to good use when she returned to her desk. "I mean, I know he wouldn't have wanted to stay in a coma, and brain damage and all, but it's hard to believe. I mean, he was standing right here. He was young. He was healthy. He was—"

"Do you want to take a break? I can answer the phone."

"That's sweet of you, but I ought to stay."

"Did you know him well?"

She barely needed encouragement. "Not that well. I mean, a couple of times we had coffee. I had lunch with him once. Guess he thought I'd make a good addition to the harem, but we didn't really hit it off, you know?" She sniffed loudly, used another Kleenex. "I had to get his mother on the line for Gerry yesterday. It'll be so hard on her. And on Gerry, too. On all of us, coming to work like nothing happened."

Gerry Horgan was currently walking OSHA inspectors around the site. I wondered whether he knew about the latest wrinkle in the calamity. His wife would have phoned him, I thought, or O'Day. O'Day was on his cell phone now, his voice rising angrily.

"Did Fournier have any close friends on the job?" I asked Marian.

"I'm not sure. I think he and Leland Walsh go back some. He was ambitious, Kevin, wanted to go to school, be an engineer, even an architect. Maybe Mrs. H. was just trying to help him out or something, I don't know." She opened her top desk drawer, removed a small round compact, inspected her reddened eyes and nose. "It's the timing I can't figure." Staring into the compact mirror, doing makeup repairs, she seemed to be talking to her reflection. "First thing Gerry wanted to know was who saw him fall."

I waited.

"Harry Dunegin, one of the cement masons, saw him lying down there, not moving or anything. And Harry was about the first person on-site."

"Could he have fallen the night before?"

"God, I hate to think of him lying there all night, like bleeding into his brain. But it couldn't have been like that. He punched out. I mean, I saw his time card."

One man might punch out for another. That was one reason O'Day sat so close to the time clock.

I said, "Maybe he forgot something, came back to get it."

"After the gates were locked?"

"He could have crawled under the fence. There are a couple of spots—"

"Maybe that's why he wasn't wearing his hard hat."

I'd wondered about the hard hat. "Did he punch in for the morning shift?"

"I don't know."

"I don't fucking believe this," O'Day yelled into the phone. I'd been trying to listen in on his conversation while keeping up my end with Marian, but I hadn't gotten a sense of who he was talking to, hadn't heard any names. He snapped the phone onto his belt and approached.

"Marian, any guys from R.C. show up, you find me right away. I don't want 'em in the trench unless they're with me. Got it?" He punctuated his outburst with a pointed index finger and slammed the door on his way out.

"R.C.?" I said.

"Wouldn't you know it? Today of all days? Two dead rats this morning, so we've got to deal with Rodent Control on top of everything else. Honestly, we can't stop work when somebody dies, but we can't keep going with rats. No way I'm going down there."

Leland Walsh had mentioned rats. They'd been a huge topic when the Dig was first proposed. No one knew exactly who'd started the rumor, but it had spread out of control like a forest fire. Rats, people said, would be everywhere once the Dig began. Thousands of previously harmless wharf rats, driven from harbor hideaways, would raid the North End, the Back Bay, downtown. They'd swarm out of the bowels of the city, swim up pipes and toilets, scurry as far as the suburbs. The truth never measured up.

I said, "I thought the rats were an old wives' tale."

"We haven't had any problems till lately, and all Gerry needs after yesterday's slowdown is rats. Until the site's certified rat-free, we can't move. The trucks are waiting, the crews are standing around."

I wondered aloud if some of Fournier's pals might have stashed rats on-site, to force the powers that be to stop, take note of his injury.

"Ugh," Marian said. "Who'd touch a rat?"

I pondered symbolic rats. Rats who talked when they should have stayed silent, rats who telephoned hotlines. For once, I regretted the trailer's bathroom. With an excuse to get outside, I'd make for a secluded nook, phone the morgue, find out when the autopsy was scheduled. I tapped my feet on the floorboards in frustration. I wanted to know what the OSHA inspectors were seeing and doing. I wanted to be out on the site, viewing the scaffolding, walking the path Kevin Fournier had walked.

"God," Marian said, "this coffee tastes like muck."

"How about I make a Starbucks run?"

"Great. I'll take some down to Gerry."

"Say hi to the rats."

"Shit."

"I'll take it down. I don't mind."

Her speculative gaze wondered if I might be after her job.

"You take yours black, right?" I looted petty cash and took off before she could change her mind.

My morgue guy was out. Eddie didn't know when they'd scheduled the cut. Starbucks was crowded. Marian brought coffee in to Liz Horgan, reminded me to grab a hard hat.

Nothing less threatening than a Styrofoam tray in the hands of a secretary. I passed the kit-of-parts barrier, chain-link fencing stuck into a concrete Jersey barrier, topped with blue-and-yellow signboard. Someone had scrawled KEEP OUT in red paint on a storage bin. I got a lot of "Hey, is that for me?" on the way across the decking. Arrows pointed toward the pedestrian sidewalk across the street. Signs warned cars to yield to pedestrians. I peered down into the trench as I crossed what would someday be park land above six lanes of unseen high-speed traffic, listening to my footsteps echo on the heavy planking. The view was strange. It wasn't like looking down from an airplane, nothing like that. The few human figures at the bottom of the pit were shortened and diminished by the steep angle, their individual features impossible to recognize. They were simply tops of hard hats, sloped shoulders, orange vests with legs. The trucks at the bottom weren't toys; they were more like half-size models, covered in mud. I paid particular attention to the scaffold staircases. From this angle, each looked almost like a cage. Four two-by-six-foot aluminum landings joined by steeply slanting steps, ten per flight.

Three men were huddled at the first landing of the east scaffold steps, one of them Gerry Horgan. The staircase plunged as steeply as a ladder. With both hands holding the tray, if someone behind me shoved— I cast a quick glance over my shoulder. A flashbulb dazzled my eyes, left a yellow glow.

"Nobody comes down here," one of the two strangers barked. "Go back up."

"I thought you might like some coffee." The containers steamed enticingly. The men exchanged glances; if one broke the other would.

"Coffee, Mr. Horgan?" I asked.

"Sure. Thanks. You guys finished yet?"

"Couple more shots."

"You said that twenty minutes ago." Horgan raised his eyebrows. "I know, I know. It's your job. Okay, but it's my job to get this job done! I got cement trucks need to move today. They don't move today, some other job gets them tomorrow. Understand?"

While Horgan took a breath and tried to hang onto his temper, I glanced down to see whether they'd marked the place where Fournier had landed. An orange stake was thrust into the ground slightly to the right of the bottom step. I tried to trace a trajectory. If he'd fallen over the railing, landed on the edge of a metal tread, that might account for the head wound. How would he fall *over* the railing? Had they marked the spot accurately? I doubted anyone had taken photos in the rush before moving the man.

The safety inspectors reconsidered, accepted coffee, and I retreated, retracing my steps. From the very top of the staircase the view was obscured, dark, the pit covered by decking and walkways that cast deep shadows. I walked another twenty feet, seeking a better view. To my left, a group of hard hats leaned against the chain-link fence. One smoked furtively, one drank from a thermos, one from a Styrofoam cup. As far as I knew, no one had publically announced Fournier's death, but from the gloom and the grim set of many jaws, I figured everyone knew. I wondered how much of the morning the workers had been idle, how much of the day they'd stay idle.

"Hey Leland, you the one fuckin' butchered those rats?"

The name caught my ear. One of the group was the black man who'd tried to question me. I slowed my steps, wished myself invisible.

"Not me. No way." It was Walsh's voice. I knelt,

set the tray down, untied the thick shoelace of my workboot, readjusted the bulky tongue.

"Thought maybe you used that hammer you say you're missin'," the first voice continued. "Got rat blood all over it, so you fuckin' buried it in the hole."

"Anybody uses Walsh's hammer to crush rats gonna find himself in trouble," another man observed.

"Anybody do that?" Walsh didn't need to raise his voice to sound threatening. I picked up the tray, moved behind a pile of metal girders. How long had his hammer been missing? Doctors might not distinguish a hammer blow from a fall. I wondered if medical examiners would.

"Any of you kill those rats?" Walsh increased his volume. "Hey, listen up. I asked a question!"

I peeked between the girders. The workers seemed to be listening, but no one stepped forward or gave anyone else away. A man with wire-rimmed glasses twitched his lips.

Walsh said, "Yeah, well, I know it couldn't possibly be any of you guys, but if you do it again, could you dump 'em on another site?"

"Guys next door probably dumped 'em here," wire-rimmed glasses muttered.

"Or better," Walsh went on, "next time bury the suckers. Whatever, so we can keep working. This is getting to be one sorry site."

"Come on, Lee, give us a break. You're the one slowing things down, hunting for those fuckin' tools."

Were Walsh's tools among the stuff that had walked off-site, the stuff Fournier had mentioned on the hotline? I considered my secluded spot behind the girders, and the way Walsh had suddenly appeared while I was talking with Liz Horgan. Plenty of hiding places onsite. Had Fournier made his calls via cell phone from somewhere nearby? From the phone in the trailer? Had someone overheard him? I'd need to go over those recordings again, find out if there was a record of the time each call had come in. You dial Boston 911 and your number pops up on a computer screen before you say a word.

Had Fournier told someone about his hotline calls? Why would he?

A dead man couldn't give the inspector general's office further details about stuff going missing, or about selling dirt. Fournier could have been silenced because someone discovered that he knew more than he should, that he would talk, that he had talked. His fall had temporarily closed the site, slowing progress. Was that the goal? To slow the site, to shut it down?

The Dig had been fought by preservationists, environmentalists, neighborhood activists. Most had been bought off, one way or another. The Fire Department, wary of having to respond to emergencies in the new tunnels, had been soothed by the purchase of a new fireboat for the harbor. Neighborhood organizations had been quieted with participatory councils, environmentalists placated with facts, figures, revisions.

Most critics made do with irate letters to the press, calls to the talk-show nasties. The most-offended filed lawsuits. If anyone—unplacated by Dig officials, unsatisfied by the law—*had* resorted to sabotage, why select this site? What would a slowdown or temporary

work stoppage on one site prove? How would it help?
Who would it help?

I needed to study maps, contracts. What other work
was predicated on the completion of this section of tunnel? Was an on-time-performance bonus at risk? According to Eddie, Horgan Construction was bidding on
other contracts. If work slowed or stopped at this site,
Horgan would be less likely to win other bids. Rival
contractors would pounce.

"Took your sweet time," Marian observed when I
got back to the trailer.

CHAPTER 13

If I hadn't had Veejay to find, I might have haunted the morgue after work or hounded Fournier's relatives. But I had Veejay—and Eddie, who assured me he had a handle on things as I hurried toward Government Center, cell phone to ear. The autopsy, booked for late afternoon, would most likely get held over till morning. The family hadn't been keen, but the doctors had persisted, pressed by insurance investigators.

"They have the tox results yet?"

"Partial. No alcohol in his blood. They'll get the rest ASAP. They can prove he was tanked or tranked, the insurance guys'll eat it up."

"Find any ex-cons on the payroll?" Earlier I'd shipped a list of Horgan employees to Spike at Eddie's office.

"Nobody rings the chimes." I could almost see him shrug. He knew what I knew: Ex-cons change their names, borrow social security numbers.

"Ya find out anything about dirt?" he asked.

"I'm making a list of trucking companies, anybody

who's driven in and out. Call me as soon as you hear on the autopsy, okay?"

"Carlotta, maybe you're jumping in a little too deep here."

"You think so? Some guys fall from heights like that and get nothing but bruises. This one's dead."

"Yeah. Well, don't hold your breath is all. I seen a lot of cuts where what they come up with is what ya call inconclusive."

A car horn blared. "What? Sorry, Eddie, didn't catch that."

"First off, we got no proof this guy was the guy made the hotline calls. Second, we got no proof the guy dying is anything but an accident."

"You can get proof that he made the calls, Eddie."

"He ain't talkin'. He's dead."

"Everybody's got a message machine, right? Get the tape off his. Take it, and the hotline tapes, over to your FBI pal."

Silence.

"You put me on-site, Eddie. You want to pull me off?"

More silence. In front of Faneuil Hall, signs advertised the great April Nineteenth Patriot's Day tribute, calling it a rededication of the Cradle of Liberty. I wondered which ex-presidents were booked to speak—Carter, probably, Clinton, the senior Bush. I wondered who was responsible for security, who got stuck with deciding which one delivered the first address. The protocol would be sticky. I thought Senators Kennedy and Kerry were scheduled, with Senator Gleason, the conservative from Idaho, balancing the ticket.

Eddie finally spoke. "Just remember you're working for me on this one. Don't embarrass me."

I assumed he meant no unauthorized activity, no B&E's at the trailer or the Horgans' home, no troublemaking. I told him not to worry, and for the moment I meant it. I had other fish to fry.

Dana Endicott was late.

She'd picked the spot, a high-traffic Harvard Square café. Any location far from the Dig was fine with me; I wouldn't risk running into a hard hat from my secret life. I dumped my backpack on a round table in a corner and went to stand on line.

I got two cups of the daily special, doctored one to suit myself, and set the other down on the table just as she came in the door. She wore a mid-calf navy cashmere coat paired with high, sleek boots, another thousand-buck outfit. She cast her eyes over the tables, spotted me quickly, and approached.

"Have you found her?" She jerked her chair back with such vigor it clanged against the table and spilled the coffee. "I got a message from her mother. She says she's okay!"

"If you want cream or sugar, it's do-it-yourself."

"Black's fine."

I explained that Veejay hadn't spoken to her mother at all, that Mom had merely relayed a message from Peter.

"She didn't talk to her? She just—accepted the guy's word? What kind of mother—" her voice trailed off.

"Exactly. What kind of mother is she? What do you

know about the family?" I kept my voice low. The couple at the next table were practically entwined and I doubted they were monitoring anything beyond mutual attraction, but it's a habit.

"Hardly anything. Veejay didn't seem to mind going home, but she never got excited about it either."

"Was she close to her sisters?"

"She only mentioned one. She and her sister bought a dog together, when they were young, but she wound up taking care of it."

"Jayme, Jackie, or Elsie?"

"Are there three?" She shook her head. "I don't know."

The place was noisy with chattering patrons and the whirr of an espresso machine. Mass Ave traffic sped by the window.

I said, "Did Veronica ever mention this Peter to you?"

"Maybe he works at the dog place, or the bar."

I'd called them both. "No."

"Damn," she murmured. "I'm scared to read the papers. Seems like every day there's a plea from some missing kid's father, or they find an unidentified body in a pond in some town I never heard of."

"Did Veejay mention anyone named Rick?" I watched her face. There was barely a flicker in her eyes.

"Maybe. I think so. But Rick and Peter don't sound remotely alike—"

"Do you know Rick's last name?"

"It could be in one of these." She held up two small books, one spiral-bound, one with a floral-fabric cover.

"Address books. They were in the junk drawer in the kitchen. I brought them for you, and her phone bills."

"You didn't have to. I could have picked them up."

"Well, that's the thing. Tonight's not going to work. I have a meeting this evening."

"I thought we were going to your house."

"This meeting just came up. I'm sorry, but since I brought the phone bills and the address books, it's not like you'll be spinning your wheels. Peter's probably in there."

"I need to see her room. I've talked to her parents, her sisters, her coworkers. I've talked to you. But I'm not getting a fix on her, on who she is, or where she'd go."

"There's no way I can fit it in tonight. I have time to grab coffee and run, that's it. Let me pay you for the coffee. Or why don't you just add it to my bill?"

"Why not lend me your keys? I'll check out her room and leave the keys wherever you want. If you tell me where you'll be, I'll return them to you. Won't take me more than a couple hours."

"I'm sorry. That won't work."

I sipped coffee without tasting it. "Why?"

"Look, I'm sorry. It's impossible. There's the alarm. I'm not going to tell you the code, and then have to reset the whole thing. And besides, there're the dogs. You can't go in without me."

"And this meeting can't be rescheduled, and you can't be late."

"Right."

"What if Veejay suddenly came home? Could *she* get in? Now? Tonight?"

"Of course."

"She knows the alarm code."

"Yes."

"When will I be able to see her room?"

"Well, I'd hoped with the address book and the phone bills—"

I shook my head.

"How is your sister doing? She is so beautiful, those big brown eyes." She dropped her gaze and stared at the table's gleaming surface, her hand clutching the coffee cup. "You're not going to quit, are you? I'm sorry about the timing, about the house. There must be something I can do to—"

"I've been giving some thought to filing on your car."

"As a stolen vehicle?"

"The cops find the car, we're ahead. It's a lead, and you can always say you forgot you loaned it to her."

"I don't like it."

I didn't like it much myself.

CHAPTER 14

Veejay's tight, ornate handwriting was halfway between script and print. After Dana left, I drank another cup of coffee and slowly thumbed pages, squinting and wondering which of the two address books was the most current. Both seemed like relics from another age, pre-Rolodex, pre–Palm Pilot, entries scribbled and crossed out. I found a Penelope, a Pamela, but no Peter.

The ex was in the floral-covered book: Rick, with the same phone number Mrs. James had reluctantly offered crossed out, and a new one squeezed beside it. Maybe not such a dated artifact after all.

I tried him on my cell, but he wasn't home. I consulted my wristwatch. If he held a traditional nine-to-five job, he could be in transition from job to home, on the road.

I walked home, armed myself with additional caffeine in the form of a twenty-ounce Pepsi, and began again with the As, dialing each and every number, playing area-code roulette with those that didn't specify, trying 617 first, then 508, then 781, 603. I spoke to a considerable number of people who recognized Veronica's name, but I didn't get a single hit. No one sounded troubled or guilty or startled at my inquiries. No one knew Veejay's buddy, Peter.

I turned to the phone bills. In the past two months, Veronica had made only seven long distance calls, all to her parents' Tewksbury number.

I called Claire at the Registry and learned that no tickets had been issued on the black Jeep. If it hadn't been for the dogs, I might have considered visiting my client's house while she was away, entering without key or permission. Alarms don't faze me, but four large dogs gave me pause.

Temporarily stymied, I paced the living room, tugging at a strand of hair, regretting the loss of my red curls. The dye had altered the texture; my hair felt as phony as a wig. Eddie didn't want me to proceed on the Dig case, didn't want me to push it. Just play secretary, behave, wait. Dana Endicott wouldn't let me in her house.

It reminded me of when I was a cop. Cops seldom have the luxury of handling one case at a time. There's always something on the back burner, something boiling over up front, a cake in the oven, chops broiling on the grill. Plus most have families.

How do cops manage the frustration of dead ends? They get divorced. They drink. I considered taking my cell phone and moving my base of operations to a bar, someplace with dark mahogany, secondhand smoke.

I revved my computer and hit an online cross-directory service instead. The address for the man

Veronica's dad termed her ex was in Waltham. I decided to try him again.

The voice that answered belonged to a woman.

"Hey, Veronica?" I said cheerfully.

"I'm sorry, you must have the wrong—"

"Don't hang up. Is Rick in?"

"Just a minute." She held the receiver away from her mouth while she shouted. I couldn't hear what she said, but she didn't sound pleased.

I waited. Someone smacked the receiver down on a table, hard, or dropped it.

"Who's calling?" a low voice demanded abruptly.

"Caroline. Caroline Grady, from Charles River Dog Care, in Boston." I'm often Caroline Grady, although Caroline has different jobs. I keep a slew of business cards in her name. Caroline, if I do say so myself, has a great voice, low and sexy, a little breathy. A phone-sex voice. Guys talk to her.

"Thanks," he said slowly, a little regretfully, "but no thanks."

"Oh, but Rick—Mr. Garrison, isn't it?—I was given your phone number as an emergency contact."

"Is this some kind of joke?"

"Not at all. Far from it. It's very serious. I have a dog in my care belonging to Veronica James. You do know Miss James?"

"Well, yes, but—"

"Oh, good, I'm so relieved to hear you say that."

"Why?"

"I expected her to pick up her dog on Sunday—"

"Look, this doesn't concern me. You're talking to the wrong guy."

"Rick Garrison, right? She gave me your number. I was sure you could help me get in touch with her."

"Don't you have her number?"

"Sometimes one of our clients writes down the wrong number by mistake—"

"I don't have her phone number. Look, hang on a minute."

He held the phone to his chest to muffle it. The woman who'd answered the phone was saying something in an angry tone.

"Honey," I heard, "it's nothing. Business, that's all." Then, "Hello?"

I said, "Would you be willing to come and get the dog?"

"No way. Now I—"

"Excuse me, but is Miss James the type who would abandon a dog, leave it and walk away, knowing that we'll have to take it to the pound, most likely. I mean, we're not a charity."

"You're telling me Veronica forgot to pick up the dog?"

"Correct. And no one seems to have any idea where we can reach her."

"Her parents live in Tewksbury. It's Jack James. He's in the book."

"I already tried him. You're my second contact, my alternate contact. Her parents said they didn't know where she was. And they wouldn't come for the dog."

"Look, I'm sorry—"

"Her parents thought she might be with a friend named Peter something. Would you have any idea—"

"My relationship with Ronni ended more than a year

ago." He spoke as though he were issuing a public announcement. Or maybe a private one, for the woman who'd answered the phone.

"Relationship. Oh, I'm so sorry. I didn't mean to bring back bad memories, Mr. Garrison."

"No problem."

"I probably shouldn't ask, but is Miss James someone we shouldn't take on as a client again? Is she unreliable?"

"Not with dogs."

"Well thank you. You wouldn't know any names of friends she might be staying with."

"Sorry."

"Maybe a new boyfriend?"

"I doubt it."

"I mean if I don't find her I'm gonna be stuck with Dana—"

"You're kidding, right?" He laughed, long and loud, ending in a hiccup. "Is Dana the dog?"

"Yes."

"A real bitch, right?" He was off again, laughing.

"I don't understand."

"Hey, you don't have to. You gave me the first laugh I've had today. Don't apologize. The bitch."

He hung up and I quickly dialed the bitch in question. Just in case she'd lied to me about the meeting as well. One ring, two rings, three. A recorded voice answered. I had reached 617-555-9687. If I wished to leave a message—

Dammit. If I couldn't proceed on one case, I ought to be able to move on another. Strike out on one, try again. I decided to go to a bar. And not alone either.

Eddie wanted me to look into possible mob connections. My fingers punched Sam Gianelli's number. It was an impulse, like naming a mythical dog after a client. It was pure impulse, and I'd known I was going to do it all along.

CHAPTER 15

Raquela's looked the same but I didn't. I'd changed my fade-into-the-background snoop garb for more feminine attire, although I should add that my idea of feminine runs more toward tight black jeans and a turquoise sweater with a low scoop neck than anything trimmed with flowers or lace. I'd traded sneakers for slides, used lipstick to make up for the missing color in my hair, dabbed perfume in the hollow of my throat.

You go see the old flame, you want him to regret the passing of the spark.

Carl was behind the bar, chatting with a crewcut male. Heidi waited tables. I didn't spot my brassy-haired whore, but a couple of her sisters were laughing and drinking with a group of suits wearing convention-eer's name tags.

The joint was Friday-night noisy, abuzz with animated post-work-week conversation. Potential customers formed a ragged line by the door, but Sam already had a table. You get a good table in this town if your last name is Gianelli.

He's the son of Anthony "Big Tony" Gianelli, mob underboss. He's also the first man I slept with, an event that seems long ago and just like yesterday. I was driving a cab nights, making a stab at my first year of college. The passion and the heat rose like steam in the back room at Green and White Cab, and we kept the office door locked all hours of the night. He was my boss, and I was dumb enough to think it didn't matter.

The spark can lie dormant for months, but never seems to completely cool. A soft breath can send it flaring. Who knows what it is, that thing that makes one man deliciously sexy, another seem like a cartoon cutout?

Sometimes I think it's his voice. There was a time I used to dial his answering machine when I knew he wasn't home, shiver at the husky rumble as he promised to return my call. Must be the voice, I thought, moving toward the table, iron drawn by a magnet. There are things I like about the way he looks: tiny wrinkles around his eyes, the way his shoulders meet his neck. He's solid, tall, good-looking enough, if you're partial to stubborn jaws and dark hair. But he's no male model, no movie-star clone. He was wearing a dark suit, charcoal gray with a faint stripe, a deep maroon shirt.

We've been married, but never to each other. We're both divorced. In spite of all I've learned from the vast experience of a nineteen-month marriage and way too many men, Sam exerts a pull I can't explain or deny.

"Margarita? Beer? Or I could order a bottle of champagne." His lazy smile brought more wrinkles to the corners of his eyes than I remembered.

Saying yes to champagne would be as good as saying the night would end in a tangle of sheets and limbs. My stomach tightened and I sat quickly, hoping no color had flared in my cheeks. If we started with champagne there would be no way to ask the questions Eddie would expect me to ask.

"What kind of champagne?" I asked.

"When I got your call, I wondered if you'd started drinking without me."

"You think I'd need to get drunk to get up the nerve to call you?"

"Not at all. I hope not. What's with the hair? I'm not complaining; it's fine. It's just not—"

"Yeah, it's not me. I'm not supposed to be me."

"So who are you?" He lit a cigarette, offered me the pack. I shook my head.

"Just a secretary."

"You need work? I can always use a secretary, especially if you take dictation."

"Nobody takes dictation anymore, Sam."

We'd settled easily into the old routine, speaking with our eyes, saying what we had to say between the lines.

Heidi appeared at the table, a lot more quickly than she'd come to take my order when I'd been alone. I wondered how much of that had to do with the Gianelli pull. "You wanna order?"

"I'll have a margarita," I said.

Sam lifted an eyebrow. "A martini for me. Bombay Sapphire."

"How're you doing?" Heidi's smile sparkled in a

way it hadn't when I'd been traveling solo. "You talk to Veejay?"

"No. You?" Her smile went to Sam, hoping for an introduction.

I decided not to oblige.

She said, "Carl found somebody else for her job. You want salt on that margarita?"

I nodded.

"What's that about?" Sam asked me as she left.

"I'm looking for a waitress. A woman who disappeared."

The clink of glasses and the tinkle of laughter ebbed and flowed around a Sinatra tune. The lighting seemed dimmer than last time, the plants greener. The ceiling fans spun rising smoke into mist. I glanced up and my eyes met other eyes in the mirror over the bar. The man looked down abruptly, muttered to his companion.

They wore suits too expensive for cops, but they had the look of cops. The heavier one should have told his tailor to allow more room for the shoulder holster. The slimmer one wore a pinkie ring.

Sam said, "Is it this missing woman you want to talk about? Or did you just . . ."

"Miss you?"

"That's what I want to hear."

"It's not the missing woman."

"Sure you don't want champagne?"

"It's a different case."

"Oh . . ." He took a long drag on his cigarette and I wished I had one to hold, to wave for punctuation.

"Eddie Conklin says hi. I changed my mind, can I bum a cigarette?"

"I wouldn't want to corrupt you, Carlotta."

"Too late." The motions of lighting up will never be foreign to me. Like riding a bike. I can always flick a match or guide a gold cigarette lighter to my lips.

"I heard you were working for Eddie."

Boston's a small town disguised as a big city. You hear about people you know, people you don't know. I inhaled, felt the smoke stir in my lungs. I was pleased that Sam listened to what people said about me.

"It surprised me," he went on.

"Why?"

"I thought you were so damned independent. Working for Eddie."

"It's partly the insurance."

"How's your leg?"

"Fine. Yours?"

His was shattered when a bomb went off in the Green and White offices. For a long time I considered it my fault. I regretted mentioning it, wondered if he'd waited for me at a table instead of the bar because he didn't want me to notice his limp.

"Fine." The silence might have been awkward if not for the cigarettes. "How's the kid?" I fished in my backpack, found my wallet, and passed him a photo.

Paolina's most recent class picture is almost too revealing. It's not the low-cut blouse, or the too-red lipstick, or the over-styled hair. She looks proud of her femininity, but I see fear behind the arrogance. To me, she looks scared of how grown-up she's getting, how grown-up she is.

"She's gorgeous. A babe."

"She's smart." My voice was sharper than I intended. "She's also pretty messed up."

Paolina used to play this game where I'd marry Sam, we'd adopt her, and we'd all ride off into a glowing sunset. That kind of shit is pernicious, especially for girls. They market it in fairy tales, in movies geared for the six-to-ten-year-old set. Happily ever after. It's the sort of thing that puts me off marriage. Permanently, I think.

"You seeing anybody?" Sam asked.

I was ready for the query, parried it. "Mostly I'm working, looking for the missing waitress, doing this stuff for Eddie."

"On the Dig."

"Some questions came up and—"

"You figured it was dirty so you came to me."

"I figured you'd give me the word. It's not that Eddie's people are gonna step in and shut it down or mess it up. It's that we want to know what we're dealing with."

"It's always good to know what you're dealing with," he said.

Heidi brought the drinks, my margarita the size of a birdbath. We clinked glasses. I rolled salt crystals around on my tongue and watched the two men in the mirror watch me.

"You're dealing with me, Sam. Nothing's gonna come back on you."

He shook his head. "You're asking me is the Dig dirty? Come on. How mobbed up can it be, with politicians up the wazzoo? You wanna know about the Dig, I'd say it's a different kind of dirty. Cover-your-ass dirty. Who-gets-the-contract-and-why dirty. There's a trail of dirt goes all the way to Washington and all the way back to the Reagan administration and before. It's dirt with governors and congressmen and lobbyists involved." It was a long speech for him, and I was surprised by the passion in it.

"Let's drink to old Tip O'Neill," he suggested. "And to all the congressmen who supported the Dig in order to thank Tip for all the pork over all the years."

"What I'm talking about, specifically, is Horgan Construction. Gerry and Liz Horgan."

"Horgan? How'd you pick them?"

"I didn't. Eddie did."

"Eddie's not as smart as he used to be if he thinks the Horgans are paisans. Horgan, he'd be into the Irish."

"Is he?"

"Don't ask me. I'm a paisan."

"Norrelli Trucking."

"Probably paisans, too," he said flatly.

"Sam, what do you hear about kickbacks on dirt hauling?"

His eyes narrowed. "That's the big deal Eddie's working?"

"He's wondering if the teamsters are working a scam."

"And you figure they'd give me the nod. Dirt hauling?"

"Selling dirt." I deliberately used the same phrase Fournier had used on tape.

"Dirt as in what?"

I raised an eyebrow. The way Eddie'd presented it

I'd only considered dirt, plain old dirt, Boston clay, the stuff that comes out of the ground.

Sam said, "You got your dirt as in shit. Brown heroin. I know guys call that dirt."

Street lingo changes fast. Brown heroin used to be called Mexican shit.

"I've heard nitro and fertilizer called dirt," he added. "Makes a big bang."

"You're full of possibilities, Sam."

He smiled. "Glad to hear it."

My mind was ticking. Selling dirt . . . I hadn't really considered other meanings. Could be dirt as in information. As in blackmailable info.

"Anything you can tell me, Sam? So I don't veer off in the wrong direction. Anything about, say, Norrelli?"

"Nothing having to do with our business, Carlotta. I'm not your field guide to the mob anymore."

"If dead rats turned up on a site, would that mean anything to you?"

"Like I said, I respectfully refuse to answer."

I'd heard the rumors. They didn't need further confirmation, not with the two restless-eyed goombahs seated at the bar, nursing tall colorless drinks that were probably soda water.

"I don't know if you've heard. My dad hasn't been well."

I swallowed tequila. He was in the organization now. No longer a Mafia son, but one of them. The two suits at the bar weren't there for decoration. They were watching the heir, guarding the boss. Making sure nobody threatened the boss.

I felt the change like a hard knot in my gut. And I

knew I'd been right about avoiding champagne, in spite of the longing.

I'm a cop's kid. I always will be. There are places I don't go.

CHAPTER 16

Morning dawned as cold and gray as a margarita hangover. I sat up in bed in forgot-to-set-the-alarm-clock panic, then lay back down and stretched. It was Saturday and while other sites worked weekends, the Horgan site was generally quiet. Sometimes, Marian had told me, specialty crews were brought in at odd hours, and if there was a crunch, all schedules went by the board, but today the site would be especially silent. With burial arrangements still incomplete, Fournier would be waked this afternoon.

If his death were considered an unlikely accident, chances were I'd recognize a few guests at the funeral home. Cops attend wakes; cops attend funerals, though I've never heard of a perp, overcome by grief, confessing graveside. That's not why they go.

I'd seen the light in Fournier's watery blue eyes, heard the urgency in his voice, but by the time homicide gets brought in, it's too late for the cops to meet the victim, shake hands, inquire about passions, loves, hatreds. Eulogies humanize the victim. Friends and family—who comes to the funeral, who doesn't, how big a turnout—tell the cops about the victim, but some cops don't drop by to learn about the victim at all. They come to recharge their batteries, rededicate themselves to the job, to justice or vengeance or both.

When a person disappears, like Veronica James, there's no wake, no funeral. A few get immediate publicity, a news-flash hue and cry, a search, printed flyers, yellow ribbons. Most are gone for weeks, months, before anyone raises the alarm, and then there's no general panic, just paperwork. In some countries, people routinely disappear. Off to prison, to the gulag, to the provinces. In Chile, so many people disappeared for so many years that they became a *cause célèbre: Los Desaparicidos*. Gone without a trace, some of them tossed alive from army transport planes over the South Pacific.

Paolina knows that if she disappears I'll find her. But here's a thought that keeps me up nights: If I disappear, who'll look for me? I used to assume it would be Sam.

We'd talked late into the night and while the subject had shifted, we'd done most of the dance to the tune of working for someone else. He'd spoken obliquely; I still didn't know whether he considered himself to be working for his father or working for his father's thing, for the mob. I wasn't sure it made a difference.

I was working for Eddie and wondering how far I could trust him. To his credit, he'd told me up front that he was biased, that he wished the Horgans well. But was he acting on their behalf to blunt my efforts? If Spike's search revealed that someone on-site had a criminal record, would Eddie tell me or withhold the

information? He had manpower, a web of associates to
trace paper trails, but could I trust him to deliver the
goods?

I wondered whether he'd managed to grab the tape
off Fournier's answering machine, taken it, along with
the other tapes to the FBI lab. Would he tell me that
Fournier didn't have an answering machine, used one
of those movie-star-taped greetings? Would I believe
him if he said he found the tape mysteriously erased?

I got up and stood in front of the closet, considering
what to wear to the wake. I didn't want to overdo it—
I'd hardly known the man—but I didn't want to seem
disrespectful, either. I selected a navy skirt and jacket,
a white blouse that didn't need ironing, and hung my
great-aunt's locket around my neck.

I left a note on my refrigerator/message board, asking Roz to heat up the computer and determine the
financial status of the Horgans and their company, with
an emphasis on what would happen to the company in
the event of a marital split. With her weird hair and
tattoos, I think twice before sending her into the field,
but there's no doubt she has an effect on men, so I also
assigned her the task of finding the EMTs who'd rescued Fournier. Eddie had said he'd find out whether
Fournier had spoken to them. Roz *would* find out. I
could compare and contrast.

Roz is the computer wiz, but I'm not that bad myself. Before leaving the house I ran a little search of
my own. I'd already done some checking on Dana Renee Endicott, but my primary goal, I'll admit, had been
to determine her solvency. Now I delved for background, employment, a bigger picture. As the only

daughter of Franklin and Emily Farr Endicott, her pedigree was as elite as any show dog's. Educated at private schools and academies, she had passed the bar in '92 and currently sat on the board of Smith College, three major corporations, and four charities. She tended to stay out of the newspapers, while her parents were relentlessly photographed at every society gathering in New York. Franklin and Emily sat on twice as many boards as their daughter. Emily was an officer of the Daughters of the American Revolution.

When Eddie called to tell me the autopsy had been delayed, I told him I'd spoken to my contact, but heard no relevant tales. I wondered if he knew Sam had taken over for his dad, if every damn cop and private op in the city knew.

Fournier's not an Irish name, but the funeral home was O'Hara's, a three-storey white clapboard in Southie big enough to be mistaken for a church. It must have housed a huge family in bygone days; now urns flanked the wooden door and the foyer was hushed with heavy carpet.

Come by and pay your respects, sign the book, spend a moment in the long candlelit room with the dark closed coffin. But the real deal was two blocks south, around the corner, and down a few steps to Mikey Finneran's Pub, closed to all but family and friends of the deceased.

Mikey's was jammed by the time I entered, although the crowd was less dense on the far side of the bar. Like most nighttime places—movie theaters, dance clubs—it looked eerie in the afternoon, off-kilter, faintly wrong. Sunlight shone through the streaked windows and warred with the overhead lighting. I spotted Marian, short black suit and pink blouse, twenty paces away, stopped to grab a beer at the bar before working my way over to her.

Some of the mourners had come straight from work, in jeans and flannel shirts. The family had let it be known that workboots were fine, no offense taken. Workboots went with the worn red-leather bar stools, the weathered wood paneling. I glanced around for a likely girlfriend, ex-girlfriend, a woman in whom Fournier might have confided. I picked out several older women at a back booth, aunts or family friends, severely clad in black, wondered what they thought of the boisterous crowd, the smoke and music, the chatter and laughter. Three women in tight sweaters seemed to have places of honor at the bar, but I didn't see the sadness of a young widow in any of their faces, and went on scanning the crowd. The serious mourners might be absent, too worn by their hospital-bed vigil to manage such a gathering.

Leland Walsh, reflected in a mirror, chatted quietly with Harv O'Day. I couldn't spot Liz Horgan, but her husband moved purposefully from group to group, resting a hand on a man's shoulder here, an arm, a back there, nodding his head in sympathy before moving on. I heard general complaints about the site, specific ones about the weather.

"Fuckin' concrete cracked like peanut brittle."

"Hands so cold, couldn't fasten rebar worth shit. So whatchya gonna do?"

A fiftyish bantamweight ordered a shot of tequila, said he wouldn't be surprised if the next thing his crew unearthed was the fuckin' mummy's tomb.

A younger man laughed, said the weirdest thing they'd dug up so far was that Colonial woman's privy. Loaded with cherry pits, too, and whaddaya think of that?

"Stomachache, for sure. I heard Jody Fargo found half a boat. Lumber from a boat, anyways."

I set my beer down and lit my first cigarette of the day. A boat wouldn't be so odd. Much of downtown is built on landfill, the place-name the only remnant of former landmarks like Fort Hill—the fort dismantled, the hill dumped in the bay to enlarge the town. Archeologists still worried that Colonial artifacts might be unearthed and unwittingly destroyed by Dig workers. Like most citizens of the Commonwealth, I'd been unaware that Massachusetts *had* such a thing as a state archeologist until teams began panning for gold along the Dig route. I knew the Horgan site was near the Mill Pond and Paddy's Alley, the most thoroughly excavated and examined archeological sites thus far.

"Way things are going around here, we're probably sittin' on an ancient Indian burial ground."

"Indians are over on Spectacle Island. Here we just got that Colonial shit."

"This site ain't got the mummy's curse, it's got the Horgan curse."

"Hey, shut it. I worked other Horgan sites and they never had no curse."

A man in a denim workshirt mounted a bar stool and banged his glass with a spoon till the crowd quieted.

He offered a series of toasts to Kevin Fournier, and there was much clinking of lofted glassware.

Marian, at my shoulder, said, "Hey, it's nice you came." Her sheer blouse was the same shade as her glossy lipstick.

"You look terrific," I said.

"You don't think the blouse is too much?"

The body was too much, but I wasn't about to say so. "Hey, you know if Fournier ever got a chance to talk to Mrs. Horgan?"

She shrugged. Blouse and body rippled.

I said, "He seemed upset that morning, you know, about not being able to talk to her."

"Yeah, well, he asked me for her home number, but I told him he was out of line."

"Is his family here?" I asked.

She tiptoed and craned her neck. "I don't think so. Not yet. I mean, they chose the spot—Gerry's buying the booze—so they ought to come. It's not a big family—mother, father, couple of aunts, on his mother's side, I think, and a brother overseas, in the army. I'm not sure if he's on the way or what. Some of these guys must be army buddies."

Army and construction. No wonder the boys outnumbered the girls. Marian moved on and so did I. Nodding to familiar faces and unfamiliar ones, I caught a glimpse of myself in the mirror over the bar. Not much chance of anyone recognizing the woman with the mouse-brown hair and glasses. Maybe my profile, caught just right.

I kept moving purposefully, eavesdropping. Most of the one-liners I overheard had nothing to do with Four-

nier or his death or the Dig. I heard about a great deal
on a used Toyota four-by-four, a girl who'd do damn
near anything for twenty-five bucks. I heard about a
guy got hit by a truck, but he was gonna be fine,
shoulda looked where he was going, that haul road behind the South Boston Postal Annex was a death trap
and no mistake.

I didn't see any obvious cops, and I didn't make any
of the construction workers for undercovers. I was re-
newing my search for a grieving girlfriend when Horgan's baritone caught my ear, part of a trio, with Harv
O'Day, the site super, and a muscular man I'd seen
near the trailer. Horgan's voice was aggressively loud.
I edged closer, but it seemed I'd missed the meat of a
heated argument.

"Hey, maybe it got misfiled. You ever think of that?
Happens all the time." The muscular man was trying
to oil the waters, make peace.

O'Day muttered, "Could have, Dennis, I suppose,"
in a conciliatory tone.

"Sure," the man called Dennis said. "Your girl's
thinkin' about her hair, her nails, her boyfriend. That's
what happened. You two make up now. Hey, come on,
Gerry. He didn't mean nothing by it, for chrissakes."

Horgan, aware of the attention of the crowd, seemed
embarrassed. "OSHA and everything, it's fuckin' making me crazy, Harv. Guess I was outta line. Sorry."

Instead of clasping his outstretched hand, O'Day
glared and walked away. I thought the boss was going
to go after him, spin him around, turn the disagreement
into a brawl, but Dennis quickly moved in and ordered
another round of drinks. I thought I could probably

paste a name to him. Dennis Marcantonio was a masonry sub-contractor whose smaller trailer abutted ours.

O'Day's charge led him close. "Hope you don't think *I* misfiled anything," I said.

"Crowded here, huh?" The wiry man's cheeks were flushed, but his voice was level.

"Problems?" I wondered what grievance he harbored against Horgan, or vice versa, whether alcohol had primed the dispute.

O'Day thumped his glass down on the bar. "You're a temp, right?" I wondered if he meant I should butt out. I nodded, a look of earnest sympathy on my face. O'Day should know whether Fournier had punched the time-clock the morning he'd been found.

"What agency sent you?" he asked.

"Franklyn Mellors."

"Yeah, well, Horgan says you do good work, but don't count on edging out Miss Marian."

"There's enough work for both of us, maybe a third, if the company lands another contract."

"There's always work, and look at everybody, drinking it up, taking it easy. Plenty of these guys barely spoke to Fournier. You hardly even met him. No discipline, that's what it is. Carelessness and no damned discipline."

"You saying Fournier was careless?"

He lowered his voice. "Man's dead. I ain't gonna speak badly of him."

"I heard he wasn't wearing a hard hat."

"Yeah, well, what does that tell you about a man? *Carelessness and no damned discipline.*"

With that, he made for the exit, edging his way through the crowd. *Damn.* I could have stopped him and tried to learn more about the time card, but I doubted whether anyone had punched in or out for Fournier with O'Day staring at the clock. And O'Day wouldn't admit he'd been away from his desk, not to a mere temp. I wondered why he'd asked about my status. If he checked on me at Franklyn Mellors, I'd come up roses; Eddie had a deal with them. I wished I'd overheard his argument with Horgan from the beginning, knew what had been misfiled.

Leland Walsh appeared on my left and asked if I could use another beer.

I nodded. "O'Day and Horgan were really going at it. You know what it was about?"

"Sounded like it was about you. You the girl who can't file?"

"Want to hear me recite the alphabet? Frontwards? Backwards?"

"Some other time." A black leather jacket buttoned over a black tee made him the best-dressed man in the room. "Carla, right?"

"I heard you were at the hospital. Do you know if the doctors found anything—any reason for the fall?"

"Reason?"

"I don't know. Like if he had a stroke. You know, the way drivers do sometimes. Crash through a red light, ram into a tree."

"Drivers in their eighties."

"Maybe there was something wrong with his shoes. Or his balance."

"Or his luck. You always need a reason when somebody dies?"

"I prefer a reason."

He smiled. "Like when somebody gets lung cancer, you want to know did he smoke?"

I tapped out my butt in an overfilled ashtray. "Got a light?"

"Maybe." He fished in his pocket and his face changed. "Damn. Hang on, I'll find you some matches—"

I got a flash of gold as he closed something in his fist. "There's a pack on the bar. What's that?"

"He gave me this, Kev did, a few days ago. Some kinda good luck charm and I wish to hell he'd kept it."

"He must have wanted you to have it."

"Well, it wasn't like he was *giving* it to me, more like he wanted me to hold onto it for a while."

I held out my hand. "Can I see?"

He opened his, displaying but not offering a flat gold oval with a tiny round hole at one end. It could have hung on a chain as a pendant. It reminded me of an army dog tag. There was a design, in color, maybe enamel, on one side. He flipped it over before I could make out much beyond a deep red star.

"Only thing I can do with it now is give it to his mother—or toss it in his grave."

He stuck it back in his pocket and before I could ask to examine it more closely, Marian was there, fluttering at my shoulder.

"Lee, I just wanted to tell you how sorry I am. Carla, honey, gotta run. See you Monday."

"You're leaving?" Gerry Horgan was still at the bar, and I'd have thought nothing but his departure could have lured Marian away. She was in her element, aglow, working the room.

She pursed her lips. "I thought Lady Liz would make an appearance, but no, I'm gonna have to truck all the way out to the house. It's in my job description, general gofer, message delivery, on- and off-site. She raced out last night without signing this contract thing that's gotta be signed, sealed, delivered this afternoon or it's down the toilet. All the fucking way out to Brookline, or sign it myself, I guess."

Part of me wanted to see the gold disk in Walsh's pocket, and part of me wanted to wait for Fournier's family, but a glance at an important document and a chance to see Liz Horgan's home at the same time . . .

"I could do it," I volunteered. "Bet it's in my job description, too. Where should I bring it once it's signed?"

"Would you?" A slow smile spread over Marian's lips as she glanced at the room full of men. "You are just too good to me. First the vet, now this. Could you bring it to me here?"

"Not a problem," I said.

"Oh, but—"

"But?"

"I was hoping to see Tess. And Krissi."

Tess was the dog, Krissi the kid. "Up to you."

"I have this little book I bought Krissi, a dog book. Would you mind—"

"If it weighs less than fifty pounds, I'll take it."

"And if I wrote her a note?"

"Sure."

"But you'd need to give it to *her*—not her mother, you know what I mean?"

"Absolutely." I gave her a selfless smile and almost missed the speculative glance Walsh aimed in my direction.

CHAPTER 17

Marian might have grabbed a cab or ridden the Green Line. I chose a more roundabout route, taking the Red Line to Cambridge and stopping off at home first.

Gerry or Marian might have phoned Liz, told her to expect immediate delivery, so I quickly steamed the flap, removed the single staple from the top lefthand corner, copied the seven sheets, replaced the staple, and neatly resealed the envelope. I gave the document only a cursory scan before sticking it into a blank envelope and placing it underneath the Yellow Pages in the bottom drawer. I noted that Elizabeth Horgan's name was listed first among principals of Horgan Construction.

There's no quick and easy path from Cambridge to Brookline. By the time I'd twisted through back streets into Allston, it was raining again, a light spitting sleet that did nothing to improve traction. If Liz asked what had taken so long, the weather gods had given me an excuse.

Brookline is a money town, but it's not Weston or

Dover—isolated, white, and removed from the fray—
too close to Boston for that. North Brookline is almost
big city, apartment buildings and two-families, a scattering of college dorms. The real money hangs south
of Route 9 near The Country Club with a capital T, a
golf course that recently conceded the need to integrate.
I checked the address Marian had scribbled. Definitely
south.

In my guise as a cabbie, I'd driven computer gazil-
lionaires home from the airport, left them in the shadow
of their gated mansions, but I don't think I appreciated
how much money there was in construction till I saw
the Horgan place. Land in the Boston area is scarce
and pricey, and this house crowned two acres. Not
much if you're talking Kansas farmland, but two acres
of Brookline equals property taxes, plus.

The house stood on a rise, two storeys of elegantly
weathered brick in front, probably three in back, ram-
bling and spread out, with enough windows to make
some heating-oil company ecstatic. Two tall chimneys
smoked above the shingled roof. The long driveway
divided into a circle and took a dive under a porte-
cochere. As I eased under its sheltering arm, I felt like
Cinderella arriving at the ball.

Halogen lamps popped and lit, almost blinding me.
My neck prickled and I wondered where the closed-
circuit TV camera was hidden. The front door opened
before I had a chance to push the bell, and Liz Horgan
stared at me blankly. Her disheveled hair was shoved
off her face, held back with a headband. When I got
close enough I could smell the liquor on her breath.

She smelled as though she'd been holding her own private wake for Kevin Fournier.

"What do you want?" There was no welcome in her voice.

"Marian needed your signature, and—"

"I told her to send the damn thing by messenger. I told her I was—"

"I was coming out this way," I lied, wondering if Marian had slipped one over on me, seen an opportunity to get me in trouble with the big cheese. "What a beautiful house. Is there a pool or a garden out back?"

It should have been a lead-in to "Won't you come in?" but Liz wasn't having any. She went on as though I hadn't spoken. "Oh, what's it matter? I'm sorry. In this weather, too. I don't know. I'm sorry. I thought you were—"

She spoke softly, almost as though she were talking to herself, and I thought she might answer if gently prompted. "You thought I was . . . ?"

She closed her eyes and pressed her fingers to her temples. "Never mind."

"I'm not sure if both you and your husband need to sign this, or just you," I went on. "Maybe Mr. Horgan ought to take a look at it, just in case. I don't want Marian to bite my head off."

"Gerry's not home. Give it to me." She ripped the envelope open, started to read. I could have taped the thing shut for all the care she paid to the fastenings. She had to be freezing in corduroy slacks and a sweatshirt, with terry house slippers on her feet. The porte-cochere kept the rain at bay, but the wind was high and even in my zipped parka, I was far from warm.

"Would it be okay if I, um, use a bathroom?" I asked.

She hesitated. "It's—the house is such a mess."

I gazed at her pleadingly, until with visible reluctance, she opened the door.

An Oriental rug lay crookedly across the marble-tiled foyer, one corner flipped up to trip an unwary guest. A broom rested against a wall near a scattering of cigarette ashes. The flowers in the vase drooped. I peered through an archway into a vast living room where elaborately carved chairs were shoved haphazardly against walls. A huge, white sofa piled with laundry sat next to an ebony Steinway.

"It's on the left," Mrs. Horgan said sharply. "Two doors down. The light's on."

A place this size had to come with a housekeeper or two, so the mess intrigued me. It was all of a piece with Liz Horgan forgetting to sign important documents, running late for meetings. I almost tripped over a dog-dish half-full of water.

The bathroom had marble tile, too, and delicately flowered wallpaper. The basin was scalloped like a shell, the fixtures bronze. There were two rustic landscapes on the walls, no medicine cabinet to rummage. It was the kind of fancy powder room used only by guests, but the effect was spoiled by a black leather travel case perched on the back of the toilet, a silver-backed brush, and a can of spray deodorant.

The travel case contained an outdated prescription vial, an antibiotic prescribed for Gerald Horgan. The hair in the silver-backed brush was short salt-and-pepper. Someone had used the basin to shave in.

Not laundry. The mound on the white sofa could be wadded sheets and blankets if Gerry Horgan were sleeping on the couch, shaving in the powder room. I flushed the toilet, ran the sink, and wondered how much on-site tension could be accounted for by marital discord.

Had marital discord shoved Fournier off the scaffold staircase? There was a puffiness to Liz Horgan's eyes and face and I wondered if she'd been crying as well as drinking, sitting alone in her gigantic house.

There was no buzz of TV or radio. No music, no evidence of Marian's favorite child, the photogenic Kristal, the girl to whom I'd been instructed to secretly pass Marian's message. The big empty house made me sad. It meshed into Paolina's failed fairy tale of me and Sam, another broken promise. A house like this ought to enclose a happy family, I thought, a welcoming dog, a daughter cheerfully practicing piano while dad poked at the fire in the fireplace.

I pasted a smile on my face. "This place, has it ever been photographed for a magazine?"

"No."

"Do you play the piano? Or your daughter?"

"The papers are signed." She indicated the door, but I ignored the cue.

"I stopped by Kevin's wake; it was really nice. I know the family must have appreciated it." I was aware that I was piling it on, talking too much, but I couldn't seem to make an impression, get any reaction out of the woman beyond alcoholic befuddlement. "Oh, and I almost forgot, I brought something for Kristal."

"What? Give it to me!"

"Hey!" Her hand had clamped around my wrist like a vise. She regarded it as though it belonged to a different person, disengaged her grip slowly.

I rummaged in my backpack. "Look, it's no big deal. Marian asked me to give her a book. I'm just doing her a favor."

"I'm sorry. I misunderstood. That's very kind of Marian. I'll give it to her."

"If she's home, I'd love to give it to her in person. Marian talks about her a lot. I have a little sister around the same age, at Cambridge Rindge and Latin. Does Kristal go to Brookline High? Or one of the private—"

I was trying to prolong the encounter, to see whether the phone would ring, or the doorbell, to find out why she wanted me gone so badly. I wasn't prepared for the anger that flooded her face.

"What are you doing here? What do you want?"

"Marian needed your signature—"

"I've already signed the damn thing."

"I needed to use the bathroom. Sorry."

"Did you see everything you wanted to see? Krissi isn't home. Gerry isn't home. Give me whatever the hell Marian sent, and tell her to keep her goddamn gifts to herself from now on, or give them to Gerry at the office."

Her fingers had refastened themselves around my wrist, but I don't think she knew she was exerting pressure. I let my umbrella and backpack clatter to the floor and gave her a little pressure in return, a taste of the cop's come-along hold. She dropped my hand like it was on fire.

Her eyes narrowed. "Which agency did we get you from?"

Same question O'Day had asked. I answered, and with her hand to her mouth, she muttered words I wasn't sure I caught, maybe "they told me," or "they warned me." She'd had way too much to drink.

"I'll see you Monday," I said.

"You goddamn snoop." Her hands fell to her sides as though she'd lost control of them. "You're fired. Don't bother coming in anymore. You are fucking fired."

Slowly I picked up my things. "Mrs. Horgan," I said, "I work for you. If there's anything I can do to help—"

"You can get the hell out." She didn't slam the door on my heels, but she came close.

I drove back to Southie wondering who had warned her to keep an eye out for snoops. Thinking maybe Happy Eddie Conklin might have slipped her the word. Wondering if he'd shared the bulletin with her husband.

I dropped the envelope off at the near-empty pub to Marian's grateful hug. She'd had a bit to drink as well and clung to a tattooed ironworker named Dave. Between giggles, she told me she'd given Leland Walsh my phone number. She hoped I didn't mind.

Here's the beauty of working two jobs: Get fired and you've got something to fall back on. I drove to Dana Endicott's Beacon Street address, thinking my navy suit would blend in well in such an elegant neighborhood. It was Saturday; she might have gotten back from New York, probably wouldn't be at a board meeting. I was planning to ring the bell, accept no excuses, search

Veronica's room. Find out why Rick Garrison had laughed and called Dana a bitch.

An ambulance and a cop car were parked out front, cherry lights flashing.

CHAPTER 18

The Area A squad car was vacant. The ambulance, from the same company that had responded at the Dig, idled. I swung into a tow zone and surveyed street numbers. The emergency vehicles were parked directly in front of Dana Endicott's four-storey brownstone, and the door to the brownstone was ajar.

I punched on my emergency flashers and exited the car in one motion.

There was movement in the doorway, a squeak of rolling wheels, and I had the sensation that I was back in the shadow of the overhead highway, watching orange-clad figures lift a prone and motionless Kevin Fournier. The illusion lasted a long heartbeat before I realized that the woman on the gurney was conscious, waving her hands in protest.

"Please, I'm fine." Polite as always, Dana Endicott.

A stocky woman in a shapeless sweater followed the procession down the narrow walk, arms folded over saggy breasts, a stream of Spanish pouring from her lips.

"What's going on?" I demanded.

"Take off, lady," the thin-lipped EMT responded automatically.

"I'm a friend. Is she all right?"

"Will be if you quit blocking the way. Move it."

I stepped aside.

"Miss Carlyle?" My client reached out and grasped my hand, her grip reassuringly strong.

"Yes."

"Please, stay, wait for me. Esperanza, stay with her. Help her. Show her—"

"*Señorita*, please. I come with you."

"Stay with . . . my friend."

They lifted her into the back of the ambulance, a pressure bandage over her left eye. There was a trickle of blood from the short dark hair, more than a trickle, over her ear, down her neck. Blood soaked the collar of her pale beige cardigan.

Esperanza watched them drive off, biting her thumb, shaking her head, murmuring *"Ay Jesus, Dios mio,"* over and over until I said, *"¿Hay policias en la casa?"* Are there policemen in the house?

"Ay! Los chupos!" She ran back inside and I followed.

To enter the vast room in which we stood, we'd passed between the glass walls of enormous twin fish tanks. If I hadn't been tailing the quick-moving Esperanza so closely, I'd have stopped to gasp at the bubble and hiss of compressed air, the darting colorful fish. On the far wall, a painting over the fireplace blazed with shades of yellow and red, colors that rivaled the exotic fish. The high ceiling had pale wooden beams hung with crystal chandeliers. Half an acre of Oriental rug framed champagne-colored sofas and upholstered chairs, enough to seat thirty, maybe more. There were other paintings on the walls, and I hoped I'd have time to study them more closely.

The short cop spoke slowly, as though he were talking to a child. Esperanza's calculating eyes took in his assumption, and her English, which had been good, began to deteriorate as she decided to play it dumb. I might not have recognized the ploy if I hadn't seen it demonstrated so often by Marta, Paolina's mother, a resourceful woman who loses her English in a flash if a conversation doesn't go the way she wants it to go.

"She is no moving. There is blood."

"Show us where you found her."

"I call nine-one-one. I tell you what I know, all I know. *No más.*"

There was a smear of blood on the polished wooden floor at the foot of a back stairway. I watched the cops quickly inspect the steps, searching for some defect, a wrinkle in the green runner. The tall cop scribbled notes in his incident book and seemed content. Esperanza tried to hold back a shudder when he asked her name.

She gave it reluctantly. "You go, now, *por favor.*"

"Should we call someone? Her husband, a brother?"

"No. You go now."

"They'll take her to Mass General. You need the number?"

"I'll find it," I said. I knew it by heart.

"Good thing you found her." The short cop smiled at Esperanza.

The smile really scared her. *"Virgen Santisima."* She crossed herself as she locked the door behind him, leaning against the wood as if she needed the support. I couldn't decide if she was in her thirties or forties. Her dark eyes looked old.

"¿Estas bien?" I said.

"Me siento desmayar." I feel dizzy.

"Te preparo te." Let me make you some tea.

My Spanish isn't going to win any prizes, but it helped to separate me from the cops, made me into one of us, not one of them. The fear in her eyes faded, and we climbed the stairs to the kitchen, one flight up, passing through a dining room worthy of *Architectural Digest*, not showy, but beautifully designed with warm woods and deep colors. The kitchen had pale yellow walls and counters that were either granite or something pretending to be granite. The refrigerator was camouflaged as a cabinet, copper pots hung from an iron rail, and the two sinks gleamed.

Over Esperanza's protests, I made tea, and tried to convey the idea that the best way to help Miss Dana would be to give me free rein in the house. Suspicion flooded her eyes again; she suspected me of being a real estate agent, and Miss Dana had said nothing about selling her beautiful house. Worry pressed her lips into a thin line, but she conceded there would be no harm if I examined the place while she watched.

The very lowest level, she explained, was the old servant's quarters. Not that Miss Dana had servants, very modern, she was, and Esperanza came in only four days a week to help. She kept some clothes there, in one of the small bedrooms. There was also the wine cellar. No one lived down there. She would, of course, live in if it were asked, dress in black like a maid, work every day if Miss Dana wanted, but this way was good, too. She worked for other people, too. She lived with her sister, her sister's family.

The street level had the spectacular aquarium room, a smaller sitting room, a music room with two Steinway grands. The place was the goods; it made Liz Horgan's Brookline mansion look hopelessly nouveau. I climbed to the next level, an increasingly nervous Esperanza my shadow. The silver centerpiece on the dining room table had probably been fashioned by Paul Revere. Each book in the panelled library looked like it had been dusted that morning.

"You look here, okay? I must work." The smile on Esperanza's lips didn't make it to her eyes.

I waited one minute, two, followed her quiet footsteps to the next level.

Light flooded the landing. The ceiling was high, the roof opened by skylights, the room jammed with plants, asparagus fern, palms, spider plants, more than I could name. The furniture was rattan, the upholstery flowered. The air smelled of potpourri. Two large Teddy bears, seated at a round table set with a sprigged china tea service, added to the impression of a grown-up dollhouse, a secret garden. One wore a straw bonnet, the other a fitted cloche. A passageway led to a master bedroom with vine-painted walls and pale green carpeting. To one side, a separate sitting area had the look of an enclosed patio, with huge windows and rattan lounge chairs.

The housekeeper knelt beside a flowered chair,

arranging cushions on the rug. I shoved them aside, and examined the darkness on the pale green wool.

"Por favor. No llames a la policia." Esperanza swallowed quickly. Her tongue went to the corner of her mouth.

I told her, in careful Spanish, that lies to the police were one thing, but lies to a friend of Miss Dana's were another. I couldn't help Miss Dana unless I knew the whole truth of the matter. Blood didn't lie, and the blood on the carpet told a different tale than the one she'd given the cops.

She bit her lip.

"Cops don't need to know everything," I added, more gently. "A person doesn't lie for no reason."

"Es verdad. I find her here."

No sharp corners on the rattan furniture. The carpet was deep and soft.

"I find her here, like she is sleeping. *Habia mucha sangre.* There is blood. I call *policia*, but then she wakes, and she is so angry that I call. She says I must help her downstairs, quick."

If Dana Endicott had been struck with a weapon, it had disappeared. There was nothing sharp or heavy nearby, no ashtray, no vase, no fireplace tongs.

"She says I tell them she fall downstairs. But I no lie. I say only I find her, and she is there. Is no lie."

There are liars and then there are liars.

"I had to call *policia*," she insisted. "Miss Dana's eyes are not right."

Each of the nightstands was strewn with personal items. Four cardboard cartons were stacked to the right of the huge four-poster bed.

I see cases as giant jigsaw puzzles. Each fact is a tiny uniquely shaped piece, each one matters. Dana had stalled, prevented me from seeing Veronica's room. Veronica's "ex" had reacted harshly to Dana's name. I'd assembled some pieces, but now it looked as though I'd fitted them together incorrectly.

They shifted: Dana didn't want cops up here, didn't want me examining Veronica's room. Because Veronica's room was her own. The neat cardboard cartons hadn't been brought by intruders intent on theft. Realizing she couldn't put me off forever, Dana must have decided to move Veronica's stuff, down the hall, or to another floor. Why bother with such a deception, now, when family newspapers shriek of gay sex clubs and deviant Scout troops?

If a wife disappears, the husband is always a suspect. Their relationship made it more likely that Dana was involved in Veronica's disappearance. But she had come to me, initiated the investigation. I considered the wealth of the surroundings, the value of the house, the paintings, the silver. Wondered if someone were trying to get to Dana through Veronica, blackmail her.

"Señorita," Esperanza said pleadingly, *"no llames a la policia."* Don't call the police.

"If you don't want me to call, you have to answer my questions truthfully."

"Sí. Ay, Santa Madre, Virgen Santisima."

"Who was here besides Miss Dana when you came?"

"No one. Truly. No one."

"Not Miss Veronica?"

"You know Miss Veronica?" she said eagerly.

"Yes." *More than one liar in this room.*

"She is not here."

"What was on the floor?"

"*Nada,* only trash, papers from the drawer."

No one knows a house like the one who cleans it. I instructed her, by her faith in the *Virgen Santisima,* to look around, tell me if anything was missing, anything, no matter how small an item.

She turned in a tight circle, her eyes traveling over each console and armoire, searching each surface while I tried to imagine what had gone awry in this cool oasis. Had Dana, busily packing the boxes, heard footsteps on the stairs, glanced up? Had she known the intruder, greeted her warmly?

"*Las fotografias.*" Esperanza's troubled voice broke into my thoughts.

"What pictures?"

"I don't know who is in them, but pictures Miss Veronica keeps on her table. *Yano están las fotografias.* They are gone." She gestured with her hands, maybe five-by-seven, maybe smaller. She had dusted them only yesterday, she thought. In silver frames that needed polish.

I said, "Tell me, today, when you came in, was the door locked?"

"*Sí.*"

"The alarm set?"

"No."

"And the dogs? *Are they gone?*"

She clapped a hand to her mouth. "*Dios mio,* I forget. *Los perros.* I put them in the back closet, Miss Dana tells me to do this, so *policia* no hurt them." She was off, clattering down the stairs, calling the animals by name as though they were children.

I followed, but didn't make it to the basement. The dogs stopped me, wagging their tails, barking, sniffing, curious about the interloper. Esperanza pointed out Veronica's Tandy, fifty pounds of intelligent-looking beast, face like a shepherd, body like a husky. The two golden retrievers barked and pushed their snouts against my legs. The Lab, older, lay gracefully on the rug.

Four dogs running free in the house. I used my cell phone to call Mass General. Patient Information was sorry but they could tell me nothing about Dana Endicott. No such person had been admitted.

I hung up and tried another number, the number of the man who'd given me the scoop on Kevin Fournier's condition. He put me on hold, then told me a Dana "Smith" had been admitted through Emergency with a concussion. She'd been taken directly to the VIP floor and would spend the night.

Could I get in to see her?

He thought it likely I'd be admitted; she'd given my name as next of kin.

CHAPTER 19

Gloomy, rainy, Sunday morning.

I made the effort to sleep late, to soothe myself with thoughts of a day minus typing and filing, but I rolled and tossed, punched the pillow, and finally sat up in disgust. Liz Horgan had fired me, Dana Endicott was in the hospital; a rotten track record all around.

I'd assumed last night that giving my name as next of kin meant Dana Endicott wanted to talk. I'd assumed wrong. She didn't want to talk; she wanted to hide, from any of her associates at any of her uptight boards, most of all from her parents, who knew nothing about her real life, who would never know anything about her real life if she had any say about it. Her mother, especially, would be dismayed. The DAR lady had no clue about her daughter's lesbianism. Dad might some-day run for office as a conservative from a conservative district. She'd given my name because the powers-that-be required her to fill in the next-of-kin blank, Veronica was gone, and I posed no threat being merely an em-ployee.

What had I learned from my long Saturday night at Mass General? That they get most of the gunshot wounds in the city, but I already knew that. I'd been taken there myself, bleeding on a gurney. My leg throbbed in the cold hallway, the overheated waiting room. I learned that the VIP area is well-guarded. I'd done some fancy talking to gain access.

I actually saw my client for less than ten minutes, during which time she professed that nothing was different, nothing had changed, except that now I *must* see that it was more urgent than ever that I find Veronica. Now I'd fully appreciate that this was no careless departure. Veronica loved her; adored her; she loved Veronica. It was, she insisted, *a committed relationship*. Veronica would never leave her without a word. Certainly she would never leave for a week or a month or any time with a *man*. She'd dumped Rick Garrison for Dana. She had no *use* for men, wouldn't waste five minutes on anyone named Peter.

And what had happened at the house? Who had hit her? We'd wasted little time on falling-downstairs fantasies. Men, she said. Burglars. Faces bulgy, like in films. Men in stocking masks. I played along. How many men? Did she recognize them, by any chance?

She thought two. Two that she'd seen, anyway, but it was over so quickly that she couldn't describe, much less hope to identify them. She'd caught only the barest glimpse, terrified they would kill her, rape her. The doctors said that, except for the wound in her scalp, she was unharmed. It was a casual break-in—*they happen*—and if nothing valuable was missing, well, that was simply because Esperanza's arrival had scared them off.

I listened quietly till her voice lagged.

"What about the dogs?" I asked.

Well, yes, of course, Veejay would never leave the dogs. She had already told me that. Really, she was getting tired.

"No. I meant, what about the dogs in the house today?"

"What do you mean?"

"Did they bark? Go after the men who attacked you? Did they sit there and drool?"

"The dogs." She'd closed her eyes, kept them closed so long I thought she might have fallen asleep.

When I asked her again, she pressed the button attached by a cord to her mechanical bed, told the responding nurse how terribly exhausted she was, and had me politely ejected.

I got up and dressed, hauling out a black suit from the back of the closet. Kevin Fournier's graveside rites were scheduled to begin at eleven. I came early by prearrangement, to meet with Happy Eddie, found his big beige Oldsmobile parked near the side gate of Saint Joseph's, on the VFW Parkway, motor idling. As I pulled alongside, he rolled down the window, shouted for me to come inside; he had coffee.

I found a parking place further down the street, moved from my car to his.

"Ya take it regular, right?" He handed me a Styrofoam cup. I suspected he had doughnuts stashed in the car as well, an observation that owed less to intuition than to the sprinkling of powdered sugar on the lapel of his navy suit.

"Crappy day. Geez, the rain. Gonna start up any minute again. Ya got news for me?" He produced a Dunkin' Donuts box, offered a choice of glazed or jelly.

I described the scene with Liz Horgan between bites of glazed doughnut, watching Eddie closely to see if I could tell how much of the story he already knew. He handled his face like a pro, plus he had a coffee cup and a doughnut to hide behind. I wasn't sure.

"She went ballistic," I concluded. "Fired me. I don't think there's a way to get back in her good graces."

"Well, she *was* drinkin'," he said hesitantly.

"She wasn't falling-down drunk. She'll remember."

"Damn."

"You might have to put somebody else in, Eddie."

"You said her husband's sleepin' on the couch?"

"Yeah."

"I been there," he said ruefully. "Whaddaya think, it's just family shit, ya can give 'em a clean slate?"

I brushed sugar off my fingers. "I think I haven't seen the autopsy report. They're burying the man today, Eddie. They must have done the post. You got it?"

"Haven't read it yet."

"I want it."

He sipped coffee. "Well, if you're off the site . . ."

"I can get my own copy if I have to."

The funeral home procession entered the gate and pulled to one side of the curving road. Seven cars followed the hearse, less than I'd expected from the size of the gathering at the pub. Maybe the family had requested a quiet graveside send-off. Maybe the weather had discouraged crowds. Maybe the Dig honchos had wanted the funeral hurried up, kept silent. Eddie gave me a nod and we got out of the car, keeping behind a screen of fir and hemlock. I might be off this site, but it would do me no good to be seen with Eddie, identified as one of the inspector general's troops. The calendar said the first day of spring had come and gone, but there wasn't a hint of it in the yellow-brown grass of Saint Joseph's. The wind whipped the branches of the evergreens and it started to rain in earnest. I'd left my umbrella in the Toyota.

"Eddie?"

"Yeah."

"I'll go in and clean out my desk tomorrow. She has to let me do that, right? I've been making a list of trucking companies. I can grab that, review it. And—"

"What?"

"Is there some kind of tape recording, a phone number drivers can call, that gives them a Dig update, a traffic update?"

"I don't think so. Commuters can check the Web site, and the newspapers run a daily column. Why?"

I was thinking about the phone call I'd intercepted on Liz Horgan's cell phone, my second day in the trailer. I didn't reply.

The rain settled into a steady beat. The first car following the flower-covered hearse was a rental limo. A somberly dressed fiftyish couple emerged. The man helped the woman from the car and they held hands, stunned and pale. A young man in military uniform patted the woman's left shoulder. He'd made it home in time to bury his brother.

Eddie said, "I'll put ya on another site. I forget, ya scared a heights?"

"I want to stick with the Horgan thing."

"She fired ya, kid."

"There's stuff I can do without being on-site."

"Yer not trying to stiff me, are ya? Tell the truth, Carlotta. That damn Fabian hire ya for security at Faneuil Hall? I hear he's hiring every freelance in town, payin' more than I can."

"Nothing like that, Eddie."

"Shit. It's the friggin' timing's got 'em worried. April nineteenth. Patriot's Day. The Wacko Waco bunch has been quiet lately, ya know? The foreigners are out there, blowing up embassies and shit, but the homegrown nuts come out to play on Oklahoma Bombing Day. I mean, if I'm a crazy, what would I like better than to watch a bunch of ex-presidents fly through the air? Plus ya got half the regular cops dressed up like Minutemen, all to hell and gone in Lexington."

The cemetery workers had erected a green tent and covered the brown grass with rolls of green astro-turf, leading to the gravesite. It kept mud off shoes, but looked oddly out of place, as though the mourners were thinking of playing a round of mini-golf after the coffin disappeared into the ground. The rain came down more heavily and people slid gratefully under the tent, closing, then reopening their umbrellas as they realized how inadequate the shelter was. The parents sank into the first row of folding chairs. The brother remained standing, with military stiffness.

"Can I do some follow-up, Eddie?"

"And no questions asked?" He sighed. "Let me think it over."

Liz and Gerry Horgan were there, with Harv O'Day and Dennis Marcantonio and three or four men who had the look of construction workers, men I might have recognized in jeans and hard hats. Liz wavered on her heels, took a seat at the end of the row. She looked like she was ready to pass out.

"What do you figure happened with Liz yesterday, Eddie?"

"Whaddaya mean?"

"I was a good temp, Eddie. I went out of my way to help, and then wham."

"Drunks," he said, shrugging his shoulders.

"Is she a drunk?" He'd admitted to a relationship with the old man, but was he a family friend? Exactly how much did he know about Liz and Gerry?

"Hey, Carlotta, ya know what I mean. Somebody's been drinkin', they do stuff. Who understands it? Look, I'm not blamin' ya for what happened. Your pride wounded?"

"A little. I mean, I wasn't that obvious, Eddie."

"Hey, there's gossip makin' the rounds. Ya know, people say the FBI's got people on the Dig, the attorney general's got people. Ever since the financials went berserk, there's rumors, investigations, subpoenas, grand juries, you name it. Maybe somebody gave her the tip."

"Maybe she's worried her husband's having her watched," I said quietly. "Followed."

"A divorce thing? I could ask around."

"I'll do it, Eddie. And I'm definitely gonna see the autopsy, right?"

"I'll messenger it. And if there's nothing there, maybe you can write me up a report about how it's probably a personal thing between husband and wife."

"Since when is stuff walking off-site a personal thing between husband and wife?"

He was silent. I hadn't read the contract bid yet, but I wondered whether Horgan Construction was going in as a woman-owned enterprise, whether that designation gave them a leg up in the contract wars. Maybe Liz and Gerry were trying to hold it together till they landed another contract.

"I'm gonna go," Eddie said. "Damn cold rain. Call me when you got the report ready."

"Send the post-mortem to my house."

CHAPTER 20

I've done my share of funerals: my mom's, singing and wailing and chanting; my pop's, a sea of blue uniforms; my Aunt Bea's, quiet and dignified. Even with time, they don't blur together; each is a frozen chunk of time. I've viewed my share as a cop, too, from mob jobs where you note the license plates, to hit-and-runs where you wear the full dress uniform to let the family know you take the crime seriously. I've seen graveside fainters, graveside screamers, slapped cheeks, wrestling matches, and once a real brawl that knocked a frocked priest off his feet.

I decided to join the crowd, but stay near the rear, off to one side, the better to watch without being watched.

Eddie had said nothing about searching for a tape of Fournier's voice to send to the FBI lab along with the inspector general's hotline tapes. Either he was playing it close to his vest or doing nothing at all, hoping I'd let it go, hoping the Horgans could bury the accusations along with the man, go on as if nothing had happened.

It was getting colder, the rain changing to slush. I plunged my hands deep in my pockets and felt the faint crackle of paper. I'd given Liz the book Marian had sent to her darling Krissi, but not the note that went with it, the note I'd been instructed to deliver in person. I ran my fingertips over the sealed flap. Marian wasn't among the sparse crowd under the tent. When I went to clean out my desk I'd give it back to her, apologize. After I steamed it open and read it. The priest's voice rose and an answering sob came from Fournier's mother in the front row.

Leland Walsh stood alone under an umbrella, half-sheltered by the tent. I joined him, using his umbrella, and my lack of one, as an excuse.

"Glad to see you," he murmured.

The priest spoke of the resurrection sure to come to whosoever believeth in Him, and Fournier's family wept along with the sky. I counted the crowd and tried to place a name on the burly figure next to Harv O'Day. He had buzz-cut light gray hair, posture more erect than the soldier brother's. I didn't think I'd seen him on-site. There must be bigwigs present. Dig officials and union bosses. PR flacks. I identified a reporter from the *Herald*, another from the *Globe*.

I'd gone through news files online last night, searching for previous Dig accidents, looking for patterns. Two carpenters had had their legs smashed at the bottom of an excavation pit under Atlantic Avenue near Beach Street. Two workers had died: one in '98, when a backhoe trapped a man against a concrete barrier; one in '99, just last year, from a fifteen-foot fall. A forty-two-year-old woman working the roof of a highway tunnel near South Station had fallen thirty feet, survived.

An insignificant number considering the project's size. That's what the papers would say, but I didn't think any of the reporters would try to tell it to Kevin Fournier's mother.

Fournier couldn't have fallen more than twelve feet.

As the coffin was lowered into the pit, Leland Walsh swallowed audibly. The man standing near O'Day took a seat next to Liz Horgan, muttered something in her ear. She lowered her head to her hands. I hadn't thought her face could turn any whiter, but it paled.

"Who's that?" I asked softly. Leland Walsh had been watching, too. I was very aware of his eyes, his movements, his strong bare hand clasping the umbrella handle.

"New night watchman. I don't know why he's here."

"Friend of the Horgans?"

He shrugged. "Maybe. Maybe he knew Kev from another job."

The priest stopped speaking. Mrs. Fournier stood shakily and tossed a white rose into the grave. The military brother sent a spadeful of dirt after it, returned the spade to the pile of upturned earth with a crunch.

"Was there an *old* night watchman?" I murmured.

"What?"

"If he's the new night watchman, how did they handle the watch before?"

"Three, four sites share a man. Old guy, does a few rounds, probably sleeps most of the time. Nobody worries much because of the detail cops."

It's Massachusetts law: Any construction site that

intersects auto traffic must pay an off-duty policeman to caution drivers and direct the cars. With so many cops so close at hand on the surface streets, the contractors would feel safe.

A sudden gust of wind caught the umbrella, tilted it. I reached to steady the handle at the same time Walsh did. Our hands touched. I felt the fine hairs on the back of his dark wrist, and an almost electric tingle.

"I won't be coming back to work," I whispered.

"Why? What happened?"

I shrugged as if to say it was too long a tale. Which it was. I didn't want to meet his eyes.

He lowered the umbrella to cut us off from the crowd. "You busy tonight? Someplace we can get together, have a drink?"

"You know a bar named Raquela's?" I asked.

"How about seven? We can have dinner. It's that place on the pier, near the site?"

I nodded.

"Yeah, close by. That'll work out real well. You want to borrow my umbrella, give it back tonight?"

I shook my head and he moved away, falling into conversation with a man in an expensive topcoat. I stayed till the end, watching the mourners file by the site, some shoveling a farewell spade of earth. I took note of who got into which car with whom, tried to sort the suits from the workers, the family from the friends. The new night watchman, Jason O'Meara, whose name I'd entered on the payroll, left without speaking to the Fournier family or Gerry Horgan. I kept an eye on Leland Walsh, but he didn't get close enough to the grave to toss any mementos after his friend.

I didn't pay my respects to the family. I didn't know them. Instead I threw a handful of dirt on the coffin after everyone else had gone, remembering the man who'd wanted to speak to Liz Horgan so badly, remembering his angry voice on the tape. I'd pay my respects by going over the post-mortem with a fine-toothed comb. Whether Eddie sent it or not.

CHAPTER 21

By 11:52 I was back in my car, drenched to the bone. I gunned the engine, punched the heater on full blast, felt an answering trickle of lukewarm air. I could go home, change clothes, watch the minutes and hours pass till Eddie sent the autopsy report, or failed to send the autopsy report. I flipped on the windshield wipers, glanced over my left shoulder, and pulled into traffic. Cops know it, PIs know it. When you investigate, you can change the course of a case, roil the waters. Observation alters the process observed.

I'd gone to the Horgan site to check out anonymous phone calls. A worker on the Horgan site had died. The two weren't necessarily connected. Even if Fournier's death hadn't been an accident, it might have happened whether I'd poked my nose in or not. He might have simply slipped, lost his balance, fallen.

I'd taken on Veronica James's disappearance, visited Raquela's and Charles River Dog Care, the two places she worked. Then her mother got a phone call from a stranger, assuring her that Veronica was okay, asking her to pass the good word along to the woman who'd hired me. Coincidence? I slid a Chris Smither CD into the deck, flicked a switch to increase the speed of the windshield wipers, and tried not to let the shivers affect my driving. The Toyota's heater was hopeless. Rain slicked the roads, salt smeared the windshield, and traffic crawled, giving me plenty of time to inspect the three black Jeep Cherokees that crisscrossed my path like cats. None had the right license plate.

I'd spent nearly a week as Carla Evans, two weeks as Kate, the laborer, three weeks as Kitty, the truck driver. The relief I felt now, behind the wheel, as Carlotta, me, myself, a semi-independent PI, was palpable, gritty as the salt on the windshield. No more curb on my tongue, no guard in my mind. I was more than ready to give up my assumed name, but I wasn't ready to give up the Horgan case. Eddie was too damn eager to close it, for one thing. I felt a keen sympathy for Liz Horgan, for another, even though she'd fired me. She was trying to do it all, raise a kid, handle a non-traditional job. Plus, I admitted, I was interested in Leland Walsh. When I met him for dinner tonight, I'd need to make a decision: Carla or Carlotta? Would Walsh, attracted to Carla, the secretary, be put off by Carlotta, the PI?

Names change. Route 128 is now Route 95, although locals still call it 128. Veronica James, Ronni to her dad, was Veejay to Dana Endicott. Was Veronica as adept as her lover at keeping her personal life secret? This business, this art, of deception, of keeping daily secrets, hiding a side of your personality, intrigued me. Was the flowery bedroom on the top floor of the

Endicott mansion the one place where Veronica could relax and be at ease with who she was? Did hiding get easier with practice? Did the guard on your tongue slip into gear automatically?

I pictured the Horgan site, the long trench covered with decking, the buzz of secret activity beneath, wall building, dirt removal, welding. I drove ribbon-straight Route 3, but I couldn't have described the scenery. Behind the metronome-like wipers, I saw Veronica's photograph. What lay beneath the surface of her dark and placid eyes?

Veronica's oldest sister was Elsie Lerner now, her home a Chelmsford ranch with pretensions, no larger than its lookalike neighbors, but with the garage enlarged to house three cars. Garden ornaments lurked in the shrubbery, small gnomes and even a gaudy pink flamingo shivering on thin legs. Before ringing the bell, I checked the garage for the black Cherokee.

She answered the doorbell with a faintly inquisitive air, bordering on suspicion. Her eyes approved of the long coat I wore over my funeral suit. Maybe I wasn't from Greenpeace after all; she wouldn't have to decide whether to fob me off with a check or tell me to scram. She looked like her sister in basic ways, eye color, hair color, skin tone.

I handed her my card and watched her jaw clench. She was going to have killer wrinkles if she kept that up, but for now, her face was pleasant enough if you didn't note the incipient lines of dissatisfaction. She wore charcoal slacks, a maroon sweater that stretched across her chest.

"I don't have to talk to you," she said sharply.

"Won't cost you a nickel." My foot got ready to move. For a minute I thought she'd slam the door, but she shifted her eyes left and right and her mouth tightened further. "You'd better come in. I don't want the neighbors to—"

Like parent, like child. The Jameses seemed more concerned with what the cops would think if they reported their daughter missing than with any harm that might come to her.

Elsie's living room was formal and stilted, the white sofa covered with see-through plastic. I chose a chair, shuddering at the thought of plastic against my legs. She didn't ask to take my coat, didn't offer coffee.

"My husband will be home any minute, and I don't want you saying anything in front of my kids."

Grandma must have made copies of her photos, doled them out. The sisters' high school graduation photos had the same brass frames. The children, beribboned and bow-tied, looked unhappy. Elsie had placed her younger self dead-center on the wall over the laminated sofa.

"Who's paying you?" I didn't have to get the ball rolling. Elsie preferred the role of inquisitor.

"Dana Endicott."

She made a sniffing noise.

"You know her?"

"I know *about* her, Veronica must have come to her senses and moved out. The way they live, it's—" She searched for a word, her nose wrinkling with distaste, and finally came up with "unnatural."

"Your sister left most of her clothes, her shoes. Makeup, jewelry. Her dog."

"You went there?" She looked like she wanted to demand a detailed description. She also looked like she wanted to question me about my sexual preference, inquire whether I was "natural."

"Has your sister been in trouble before—juvenile runaway, drugs?"

"Why would you think so? What makes you ask something like that?"

"Your parents won't file a missing persons report. I thought they might have a reason."

"We're private people."

"Your mother told me she got a reassuring phone call."

"If she says she did, she did."

"From Peter."

"I told you, I don't know any Peter."

"What if the call were from Pamela instead of Peter. Would your mother change the name, to protect her daughter's reputation?" *Better a missing daughter than a lesbian daughter*?

"I think you should leave before my husband—" She pressed her lips together and stared at the photos on the wall. "Haven't we suffered enough?"

I followed her gaze, lifted my eyes to the brass frames, and found myself experiencing the same sensation of shifting puzzle pieces I'd felt in Dana's bedroom. Four daughters, four grandchildren on the Jameses' wall. *Elsie, Jayme, Veronica, Jackie*. I double-checked the graduation shots on Elsie's wall. None of them seemed to be the same sister, photographed twice, in different poses.

"How many sisters do you have?" I asked.

Elsie's eyes were on the carpet now, counting the tweedy threads. "One of my sisters is dead. She . . . died. You have to go. My husband will be back, and I haven't finished putting the groceries away—"

Three things had happened since I'd taken on the James case: Mom had gotten a phone call; someone had attacked Dana Endicott. Someone had removed photos from Veronica's bedside table. If I'd been a thief in that mansion, I'd take paintings, silver.

"When did your sister die?"

"I'm sorry, you'll have to leave *now* . . . The groceries. The milk will spoil."

"Which is her photograph?"

She hesitated before pointing. The fifth sister's hair, long and parted in the middle, gave her the air of an old cameo. She had unusually narrow eyes, a high-bridged nose, and for an instant she seemed familiar, as though I might have seen her in a shop or a restaurant.

"What was her name?"

Elsie stood. "If you're not out of this house in thirty seconds, I'm calling the police."

I felt the urge to shove her aside, search the place, steal the goddam picture off the wall. When the flash of anger receded, I got to my feet and Elsie practically ran down the hall to hold the door. I made my way to the car, turned on the engine, flipped on the heat.

The Jameses hadn't rearranged their photo wall simply to accommodate more grandchildren. The central constellation had changed with a daughter's death. They hadn't mentioned it, but so what? Maybe they never did. How would you bring such a loss into casual conversation? Would Mrs. Fournier, when asked, say she had a son in the army? Or would she say, always, I have two sons, but one of them died. I debated ringing Elsie's bell again, asking to borrow the dead girl's photo. I considered driving to Tewksbury High School. Yearbooks have graduation photos, but the high school would be closed on Sunday.

Sunday. Gloomy, rainy Sunday.

Police stations don't shut down on weekends. I drove to Tewksbury Center.

Officer Ralph Danforth wasn't impressed by my credentials, and didn't see how it was any of my business. Good family, the Jameses. Lived here a long time. Girl died in a traffic accident. He had a bland smile as effective as a mask and I couldn't rile him or get past him, so I drove back to Boston wondering what the true story was. If she'd died in a traffic accident, why wouldn't he give me the day, date, and time? If she'd died in a traffic accident, why had her parents taken her photo off the wall?

I drove past my Cambridge home, followed Storrow Drive inbound to Clarendon, circled the Public Garden, cruising Dana's neighborhood, looking for the black Jeep. I didn't think I'd find it, and I didn't, but I found a parking place, that elusive rarity, and took advantage. I banged doors, asking Dana's neighbors whether they'd noticed a black Jeep parked, maybe double-parked, on the street the evening before.

Ask any cop: Sometimes the job feels like door-to-door sales. I knew a cop banged a door once in search of a witness to a hit-and-run. Man wearing a T-shirt and cutoffs answered the bell, stuck his hands in the air, and turned over a quarter million dollars worth of cocaine.

If you look, you could find, my grandmother used to say in Yiddish.

Tenants were out, owners knew nothing. People in the high-rent district kept themselves to themselves. An elderly woman regarded me with suspicion, as though I were a robber casing the joint for my crew. After a frigid hour and a half I realized I was wearing out shoe leather, freezing my hands, simply to blunt a feeling of failure. No way to deny it; I'd been fired off the Horgan site.

CHAPTER 22

Back home, I shivered and stamped my feet, trying to restore feeling to my toes as I steamed open Marian's note. I made cocoa from boiling water and a packet of mix, sat at the kitchen table to read.

> *"Honey, you mad or what? Maybe you think I pushed you too hard about learning to type. Whatever, I'm not mad at you! Call or come see me.*
>
> > *Miss ya, M."*

The first postscript read: *"How are all the stiffs at Goldsby?"* The second: *"How's Tess? She's soooo cute."* I was glad I'd made cocoa; at least I'd gotten something from the steam. Why on earth had Marian been secretive about a few scrawled sentences? Why would such an innocuous note need to be delivered directly into the girl's hand?

I curled my fingers around the mug, let the warmth seep into my palms. I'd brought the contract bid into the kitchen, the one I'd Xeroxed and stashed under the Yellow Pages. I took out the seven photocopied pages, worked my way through sentences chock-full of contract-specific RFPs, DSCs, and permanent IPCS signage. Performance bonds. PERT schedules.

"Is that chocolate?"

Roz, my tenant, appeared in the doorway, lured by the smell. Other people show up with their hair wrapped in a towel, you assume shampoo. Roz, you assume hair dye. I wondered what shade she was attempting. Sometimes she experiments with her own dye blends, with unusual and unexpected results. She opened the fridge, regarded the contents solemnly before yanking a jar of peanut butter from the cupboard.

"There's more cocoa, if you want it. What do you think of this?" I handed her the note.

"It's in code," she guessed.

"I doubt it. Did I get anything by messenger?"

She shook her head. "No calls, no packages."

Shit. I'd have to call my man at the morgue, use up more favors, the valuable coin of my trade.

I said, "You talk to those EMTs?"

"They're very cool."

"Fournier."

"Man who fell. Didn't say a word."

"What else?"

She'd been busy with the Dun & Bradstreet. I glanced through her report, stopping to run a finger over the officers of Horgan Construction. Gerald Horgan was listed as CFO, Elizabeth as CEO. Leonard Horgan, Gerry's dad, headed the board of directors. The company was closely held, and the smallest venture to assemble a large number of Dig contracts. That meant they had bid low; the process was competitive.

When I say small, I don't mean a mom-and-pop operation. The other players were huge multinationals like Bechtel/Parsons/Brinkerhoff, national firms with New England roots, like Perini. Modern Continental, a direct competitor, was the largest contractor in New England.

I read on. Horgan specialized in state-of-the-art equipment designed for confined work spaces. They had become slurry wall specialists by virtue of their Dig work, now had road and tunnel contracts across the New England states, a bridge project in New York.

So what were both their chief officers doing on one site?

"Anything that's not in here?" I asked Roz.

"They recently hired new counsel. Bates, Eppes, Morgan."

"Where'd you get that?"

"Lexis-Nexis."

Bates, Eppes, Morgan is the firm most hired by local businesses thinking of putting together a prospectus and going to the market. "Interesting. Good job."

The cocoa was almost cold; I'd lost my taste for it. I glanced at my watch, did some calculations, pushed the cup away. "Roz, you gonna be here awhile?"

She tapped her towel turban, nodded.

"Ring my cell if anything's messengered from Foundation Security."

"Okay."

"And how's this for vague? I want to know about a girl, last name James, don't know her first name, died, say in the past five-ten years. In the nineties. Went to high school in Tewksbury, graduated."

She made keyboarding motions with her peanut-butter-smeared fingertips. "Okay, but—"

"But what?"

Her eyes narrowed speculatively. "You gonna let your hair grow out your regular color or what? I could maybe—"

"No, thanks."

Upstairs, I removed the jacket of my funeral suit and tossed the creased white blouse in the hamper. I didn't want to wear the same thing I'd worn to meet Sam at Raquela's. It seemed like bad luck. I chose a deep green sweater that looked better when my hair was red. At least I could take my hair out of its topknot, let it swing free.

I left early. I had time for a stop on the way.

CHAPTER 23

Instead of entering the Charles River Dog Care lot, I parked by the river near the Cambridge Victory Gardens and walked back, crossing Soldiers Field Road at the Everett Street lights, hugging my arms against the cold. The rain had stopped, but the clouds were heavy and threatening.

I'd asked questions in two different places and then Helen James, Veronica's mother, had gotten a phone call. In an hour, I was due to meet Leland Walsh at the first place. I reviewed the people I'd met at the second, pictured them in my mind, the slightly pompous owner of Charles River Dog Care, Rogers Walters, helpful up to a point. Harold, Veronica's coworker, quiet in his gray scrubs, driver of the dog bus. When I'd given him my card, offered him a quick fifty for Walters's client list, I'd felt sure he'd call. Walters had admitted to paying lousy wages, yet Harold hadn't tried to get in touch.

I skirted massive puddles on the sidewalk. The gray light was starting to fade from the sky. The wind picked up and rustled the bare branches of a small beech.

No matter what had happened since the night she'd disappeared, Veronica—according to my client—had packed for the weekend and left under her own steam. If she'd intended to spend time with a new lover, she might have tried to keep Dana in the dark so as not to louse up her rent-free arrangement. If she'd spent the weekend with a new lover, where had she met—my mind started to say *him*, but I wrenched it in another direction. Not *him*, quite possibly *her*. There was another woman who worked at Charles River Dog Care, a part-timer, Erica Mullen. I wanted to speak to Erica, see Erica, learn about Erica. I wanted their client list, too, wanted it more than I'd wanted it yesterday. There was something about those dogs at Dana Endicott's, barking at me, but supposedly silent during a home invasion.

What was the deal? Had Veejay told the new lover about Dana's fabulous home? Had the lover lifted Veejay's keys, decided to take a look for herself? Were Dana's stocking-masked men real or fabricated? The concussion was real. There was *some* truth to my client's words. But not all the truth. No, not all.

I passed Boylston Auto, and my mind took off on another tack. Could Veronica have seen something that led to her disappearance? The area had two auto body shops, and body shops go with crime like dogs go with bones. Both shops seemed deserted, with locked bays and darkened windows. None of the car-theft rings I'd investigated as a cop had ties to either place. They weren't known as chop shops.

Directly across the street from Charles River Dog

Care stood a cut-rate gas station, with an insurance company to one side and a square brick office building on the other. I studied the sign in front of the office suites. Two accountants, another insurance broker, a chiropractor. A glass-fronted bank held down the corner lot and the only other nearby shop was a Store 24. The cocoa seemed a distant memory, and the idea of wrapping my cold hands around a large takeout coffee appealed almost as strongly as the idea of a look around Charles River Dog Care. I promised myself coffee later, strolled casually down the driveway. The parking lot was empty, even the painted school bus gone. The back door was shielded from Trade-All Auto Body by a low wall. A squat brick shed blocked the view on the other side.

I'd checked the lot for Veronica's Jeep the last time I'd visited, but ignored the shed, assuming it belonged to the body shop next door. Now I reconsidered. At first glance, it looked abandoned, overgrown with dead ivy, but when I examined the ground, I made out faint tire tracks on the gravel. Gray garage doors opened to one side, and vines had been cleared from the path. I rattled the two old-fashioned garage doors, tried to lift them, failed.

The only windows were small, high rectangles, centered over each door. I was debating how to get up for a view, whether to fetch my car and climb on top, when I noticed a pile of cinder blocks behind the garage. I hefted one, estimated how many I'd need to reach the necessary height, started moving and arranging in earnest. Three on the bottom, then two, then one. I steadied the pyramid, stood back to regard my handiwork.

From the ground it was hard to tell if the windows were smoked glass or filthy glass. I yanked a wad of Kleenex from my backpack, swiveled to make sure I was alone and unobserved before beginning the climb. Two seagulls wheeled over the river. Tires hissed on wet pavement as cars sped along Soldiers Field Road. The blocks teetered once, but the structure held, and in a moment I was perched on top, nose pressed to the glass, staring in, seeing nothing. I tried a Kleenex, rubbing vigorously. It turned black and I tried another.

The school bus was inside, with at least one other vehicle beside it, almost out of sight, but certainly tall enough and dark enough to be a black Jeep. I clambered down, moved the blocks to a new position in front of the second door, ascended with more Kleenex and this time, from the depths of my backpack, a flashlight.

It was some sort of SUV, hard to see, dark blue or black, maybe a deep green. I peered and stared and tried to shift to a vantage point where I could get a better outline of the vehicle, see a logo. The flashlight beam reflected off the window glass and only by shielding my eyes with my hand could I make out the green-and-white New Hampshire license plate, a New Hampshire plate that made it the wrong car. I bit my lip and descended, cursing a fresh tear in my pantyhose, more eager than ever to get some fact, some suggestion of a fragment of a clue, if only to compensate for the ripped hose.

I visualized the office, the file cabinet with employee Erica Mullen's address and phone number inside, along with addresses and phone numbers for an entire group of people, female and male, who'd had regular contact with the missing Veronica. Down a narrow staircase, across a cage-lined room. So close. I pressed the bell to the side of the door, counted to thirty slowly. Pressed it again, put my ear to the glass, listened for the sound of barking. Not a breath. I hadn't noticed an alarm when I visited the first time. The lock on the door was a simple one, an old friend, ripe for the picking.

The sky was almost dark. In fifteen minutes I'd need my flashlight just to find my way back to the car. I shivered and considered Store 24 coffee, the simple lock, the file cabinet, the client list.

The small window to the left of the entrance was high enough so no thief could break it and reach inside to unlatch the door. I fetched a cinder block from my pyramid, balanced it on the narrow end, and stepped on top. I glanced down, at an angle, searching for the telltale blinking red light.

The hairless, silent dog stood a foot away from the door, mouth open, tongue protruding, ears alert. I sucked in a breath and almost toppled off the cinder block. A weimaraner, I thought, well-trained, stealthy. I prefer guard dogs that bark. No wonder they had no alarm.

I hopped down, abandoning any thought of a break-in. Was it legal, keeping a silent secret hound? I imagined some run-of-the-mill injured burglar trying to sue for damages, represented by some sleazy lawyer with the nerve to stand up in court and proclaim that Walters owed it to the public to post a warning sign.

On the whole, I thought he should post a warning.

The lock was a simple one, almost an engraved invitation.

I returned my cinder block to the stack, climbed once again, sighted carefully on the NH plate, scratched its numbers and letters on a scrap of paper which I tucked carefully into my pocket. My cell rang while I was shifting the blocks again, restacking them behind the shed. It was Roz. Eddie and Foundation Security had come through with the autopsy report. I checked the time. Traffic willing, I could pick up the report and change panty hose before heading to Raquela's. I passed the Store 24 in a hurry; I'd grab coffee some other time.

CHAPTER 24

Traffic was beyond lousy and I got stuck at every light, behind some jerk who just *had* to brake at the first hint of yellow. I made it to the waterfront eighteen minutes late, opted for an overpriced garage rather than a time-eating parking-place search. I raced through frigid streets, hurrying toward Raquela's, entered, and peered into the darkened bar. Might as well have gone the cheap route. Leland Walsh was later than I was, unless he'd grown tired of waiting and departed.

Maybe he'd despised the glossy interior at first sight, decided no good could come of a relationship rooted in a dating bar. The loud and brassy music, designed to cover those awkward silences, had scared him off. The lighting was too low, the plants too healthy. I grabbed a cigarette, found matches at the bar, and lit up.

Probably he'd been delayed.

Carl, the bartender, gave me a nod and asked whether I'd seen Veejay. When I said I hadn't, he sighed. He hated to admit he'd been wrong, but he hadn't figured her for the type to leave him in the lurch, and he wasn't wrong about a lot of 'em either, I shouldn't take him for a fool. Wouldn't surprise him if she turned up sick or been in some kinda accident.

"You notice a black guy in here earlier, tall guy, waiting for somebody?"

He shook his head no.

"Anybody phone with a message for a tall woman?" I caught myself in time; I'd almost said "a redhead."

"Nope."

"Good."

I ordered a Harp on tap, took a seat at the far end of the bar. The couple at the closest table was deep in conversation, the bar stool next to mine vacant. No one paid particular attention as I slid the manila envelope out of my bag, removed the enclosed autopsy report.

Neatly typed. Black words on white paper. Clinical Diagnosis, Gross Diagnosis, Clinical Summary. I was grateful for the cool, detached jargon, grateful I hadn't witnessed the cut. Oh, I've done it. The new medical examiner's digs on Albany Street are much improved, a far cry from the airless cubicles at the old mortuary. The building is clean, modern, and efficient, but I'll contentedly give it a miss till they invent an air-conditioning system that eliminates odors.

Kevin Frederick Fournier, 27, well-nourished Caucasian male, right parietal depressed skull fracture. Subdural hematoma in right parietal region. Multiple small intracerebral hematomas. Cause of death: cerebellar tonsillar herniation. The pages gave me plenty of facts: duration of hospitalization, date and time of death, date and time of autopsy, name of prosector.

Useless facts that explained nothing, gave no evidence to contradict the simplest explanation: He fell on his head and died.

When a crime isn't handled as a crime, it's harder to crack, and this one had been labeled an industrial accident from the get-go. Not only that, it had been handled in a hurry. If Fournier had been dead at the scene, at least there would have been photos of his body in situ.

You work with what you've got. The ME had checked for defensive hand wounds, for skin fragments under the fingernails. No evidence he'd put up a struggle. If he'd made a last desperate lunge at an assailant intent on shoving him off the scaffolding, he'd made no contact. His clothing had been thoroughly examined. Boots, socks, jeans, turtleneck, sweatshirt with hood. Windbreaker, gloves. Nothing out of the ordinary. I wondered if the insurance investigators had requested the hand and clothing work, or if Eddie had.

The most interesting facts dealt with time, time of injury, time of death. They seemed to confirm Marian's earlier speculation. Fournier hadn't walked on-site early, fallen, and been found within a short span. His body temperature at the time of hospitalization indicated he'd been on the ground for hours.

There were photographs enclosed in a separate envelope, up-close shots of the head wound. I thumbed through them quickly, shielding them, thinking that if I saw myself from afar I'd tsk-tsk over the woman gazing at porno pics.

"Hey, you again!" Heidi's voice came from over my

right shoulder. She must have approached on tiptoe. I smothered the photos against my breasts.

"You're in here a lot all of a sudden." Her voice was cool, and I took a closer look at her regular features, reconsidering. I'd never thought of her as other than Veejay's coworker, a casual friend.

I reinserted the stack of photos in their envelope, facedown. "I'm a private cop, looking for Veronica James, Heidi."

I read disbelief in her eyes, followed by suspicion. She didn't glance away, or try to avoid my gaze. I didn't see any reaction that I'd classify as a guilty one, but I've been fooled before.

She slid onto the vacant bar stool beside me. "Is she in some kind of trouble?"

"I wish I knew. She's missing."

"As in kidnapped? Is she rich or—"

"I didn't say anything about kidnapping."

"Right. That was dumb. It's just—I dunno. When I first saw her, I thought she kinda looked like somebody, not like a celebrity exactly, but—"

"Who?" I said softly.

She bit her lip and stared into the mirror. "I dunno. You know, you see faces all the time, like on TV. I mean, she didn't look like a movie star or anything."

"And she didn't date men."

Her eyes fastened on my beer glass, stayed there. "Hey, whatever. Doesn't matter to me. None of my business."

"You knew?"

"I wondered. She seemed kind of immune, you know? But don't get any ideas. The two of us, we talked at work, and that was it. I fuck guys. Sometimes I wish the hell I didn't, but that's the way I am."

"Is there a scene here, a gay night?"

"Here?" She glanced around. "It's guys and gals, here. Hooking up. Escort services, prostitutes, maybe. I dunno. I don't see guys with guys here. Women with women, I dunno. I wouldn't really notice, unless they're feeling each other up."

The South End is Boston's gay male community—restored row-houses, good restaurants, low crime. The dyke bars are mainly in Jamaica Plain. Brookline has a lesbian population, but one so free of crime it's largely off my map. I ran through a mental list of friends, contacts, acquaintances.

Heidi stood. "I gotta get back to work."

"Did Veejay ever mention a man named Peter?"

"Nope."

"What about her family? A sister who died?"

"Never said a word."

"Did she say anything that seemed unusual, odd?"

"Doesn't everybody? She was crazy for dogs, talked about dogs. If I think of anything else, I'll tell you. I've got customers."

I watched her walk away, black slacks, white tee. People are difficult enough to peg in their choice of clothes. Stick them in a uniform, and it's really tough. Heidi wore makeup and dangly earrings. Her fingernails were polished. She seemed distinctly feminine. And so did Dana Endicott.

I ordered another beer, waited twenty more minutes, wondering whether Leland Walsh had stood me up because he'd discovered I wasn't Carla after all. I studied the autopsy report, frustrated by my inability to read conclusions into its multisyllablic words. Contents of pockets. Key ring, fifty-two cents change, six aspirin tablets in a tin, a bag of jelly beans.

Start off for work one morning with a plastic bag of jelly beans, never see home again. The damn bag of jelly beans made me swallow a lump in my throat. And a key ring. The gold disk he'd given Leland Walsh looked like something you might hang on a key ring. I tried to recall the design, stared at my watch one more time, finished my beer. Leland Walsh had forgotten. I regretted the extra care I'd taken with clothes and makeup. Dumb. The electricity I'd felt was a one-way jolt, nothing reciprocal.

As I stood it seemed that I could hear Walsh's voice, so close his breath tickled my ear, telling me Raquela's would be a great choice, because it was so near the site. The site was closed tonight, Sunday night, so why should that make a difference? I slapped cash on the bar to cover the bill and moved quickly toward the door.

CHAPTER 25

The wind blew cold Atlantic gusts that made me long for a sweater under my coat, a scarf, a snug-fitting hat. I wished I'd left the bar earlier, drunk one less beer. Had Walsh overheard some nugget of information at Fournier's funeral, developed some idea about his death that could only be confirmed on-site? Had he planned a secret after-hours search for his missing tools?

Fournier had returned to the site alone and died.

My thoughts kept pace with my quickening steps. Atlantic Avenue was bright with street lamps, un-crowded. A few cars coasted by, a cruising taxi. Knots of pedestrians, muffled in heavy coats, rushed toward warmly lit hotel lobbies. Nights like this were a boon to cops. Too icy for crooks to be out on the street, too damp, with a cold that crept in toward the bone.

Blue-and-yellow barriers rose to block my view. I hurried past, to the chain-link fence and double gates that enclosed the site. The gates were chained tight, secured with a heavy padlock. I stood quietly in the shadows, trying to discern the night watchman's presence by the sound of footsteps or the gleam of a flashlight.

The site seemed utterly deserted.

The old highway was like a jagged wound, its iron beams dividing the city from the waterfront. In its shadow, the air seemed heavy, the darkness deep and forbidding. I knew the tourists at Faneuil Hall were minutes away, laughing and drinking in bars, so close I wondered if they could hear the pulse that beat in my wrist. I walked the perimeter, trying to convince myself that Walsh had simply forgotten our date.

I'd considered entering the site at night, challenging the trailer's alarm, searching for hidden insurance records. If I'd decided to break in, I'd have made a beeline for the area between the trailer and Dumpster, near the storage shed, the area where Leland Walsh had first approached and asked me what I thought of the Dig. I'd have worn dark close-fitting clothing, slid easily under the fence.

My coat was heavy, bulky, too long. Walsh was bulkier still, large-framed, broad-shouldered. I kept walking, my hands jammed into my pockets for warmth, wondering how Walsh had planned to enter, *if* he'd entered. A laughing couple passed along State Street. They didn't notice me.

Much of the aboveground section of the site was accessible, ungated, unbarred, with KEEP OUT notices posted to tell passersby they'd strayed from the pedestrian path. I made my way past coiled cables and stacked lumber to the section of fence camouflaged by the metal Dumpster, ran the beam of my pencil flash over the linked aluminum. The edges had been pressed together, so that it took a beat before I realized what I'd seen. Six links near the bottom had been neatly bisected. When I pushed, I opened a triangular tear big enough for a man Walsh's size.

A long time ago, I made a deal with my little sister, Paolina. I don't walk into abandoned warehouses at midnight. I don't leave my gun at home when I stalk bad guys. I don't wear filmy clothing and high heels, like some pulp-fiction heroine.

I took inventory. The site was within yelling distance of a detail cop, so that wasn't so bad. My gun was in a locked drawer in my office, but I had my own version of Mace, a particularly strong-smelling hairspray, cheaper, and just as effective. I plunged my hand into the depths of my bag, made sure it was there. If I'd had any idea the evening would call for shimmying under a fence, I'd have worn pants instead of a skirt and butt-freezing pantyhose. My boots were okay, high-cut and comfortable. My skirt was tight, but the long slit up the side meant I could run if I had to.

If Walsh had broken in to learn more about Fournier's death, I wanted in on the action. If he'd broken in to tend to business of his own, business that had to do with selling dirt—well, I wanted to know about that, too. The question was, if he'd gone in through the fence cut, why hadn't he come out in time to make our date?

I crouched low and entered headfirst into forbidden territory. The fence snagged my coat and held it fast. I reached around with my left hand, tugged, and then I was through, sheltered by the Dumpster. I stayed low, balancing on my heels, listening while traffic whooshed

overhead. I had no idea of the night watchman's scheduled rounds. Maybe he was asleep in the warm trailer,
oblivious. Maybe he'd caught Walsh and sent him
packing. Maybe Walsh hadn't met me because he was
warming a cell at Area A.

If he was, I didn't want to join him. Too many old
buddies to laugh at my plight. I thought I heard a noise
that wasn't traffic, a machine-like pulse, far away.
Nothing that sounded like footsteps. Maybe laborers on
a distant site, working the night shift.

If the Horgans' watchman caught me, I'd need a
cover story, but nothing came to mind. I decided to
move; if I didn't get caught I wouldn't need a story. I
ran lightly along the ground to the west scaffold staircase. The tunnel was lit by a single caged work lamp
and the receding glow of streetlights. As I descended I
shone my flash carefully on each tread, aware of Kevin
Fournier's fatal slip.

The tunnel was eerily quiet, the hum of overhead
traffic faint and intermittent. I played my flashlight over
the pale slurry walls, keeping the beam low. Overhead
girders cast dark shadows. It wasn't warmer down here,
but the wind cut less. I aimed the light toward the ad-
joining site to the north. A bulldozer sat next to a cement truck. In the early days they'd had to disassemble,
lower, and reassemble vehicles in the deep trenches,
but now there were temporary ramps for easy movement. The trucks seemed huge and shadowy, a herd of
waiting beasts. I walked slowly, letting the sights register, listening.

Once I thought I heard steps approaching, and a sudden vision of the silent weimaraner at Charles River

Dog Care flashed through my mind. What if the night watchman kept a dog? I started at the sound of small scuttling feet, caught the gleam of small red eyes with my flash. *Rats*.

Passing close to a heap of cement sacks near a hulking vehicle, I paused, listening again for the missing watchman. Slowly, I became aware of a sound other than my own breathing, a rhythmic echo of each inhalation, heavy and muffled, issuing from the heap.

The bound man lay on his right side, knees bent, feet drawn up behind him. His hands were tied as well, and the rope reached around his neck and down to his ankles. A thin line of darkness ran from a cut on his skull. I played my flashlight over his face. Silver duct tape covered Walsh's mouth. His eyes were open, dazed, or maybe that was a trick of the light. When he saw me, he tried to make a noise. His eyes pleaded. He squinted and I lowered the flash beam.

His head rested on the ground, almost hidden beneath the mud-guard of the giant dozer's wheels. If I hadn't heard his labored breathing, I'd have passed him by. The darkness of his clothes, the darkness of his face, melted into the night.

I whispered, "The watchman?"

He grunted.

"Did he go for the police?"

While I was speaking I was searching for my pocket knife. I keep it in my bag, not my pocket, and things fall to the bottom. In spite of the cold, sweat broke out on my forehead. The expression in Walsh's eyes said hurry. I stripped off my gloves, shoved them in my pockets, found the knife. My fingers grasped the slim hunk of metal, opened it. I attacked the rope at his feet first, slicing strand by strand. "Don't move. You'll make it tighter."

He was caught in a classic mob necktie, an arrangement that would strangle him if he struggled. I wondered why, if he didn't have a cell, the night watchman wasn't using the phone in the trailer. He'd know the alarm sequence. I cut and untied as quickly as my frigid fingers could manage in the dim light. I could have used another pair of hands. Walsh's seemed useless, cold and bloodless. He fumbled at the strip of tape on his mouth.

"Stay quiet," I warned. "Did he recognize you? Does he know who you are?"

"Let's go. I cut the fence by the Dumpster."

A length of iron pipe lay near Walsh's feet. "He use this?"

"I dunno."

There was a dark streak at one end that could have been blood. I slipped my gloves back on, picked up the pipe, hefted it.

"C'mon. I think he went for liquor." Walsh raised a hand to his head and groaned. "Make it look good, like a fucking accident when some driver pancakes my head in the morning."

"The watchman?"

"I don't know that it *was* the watchman. I don't know who clobbered me. I just know I don't want to be here when he gets back." His hand, where it clutched my wrist, was icy.

We took the west scaffold stairs, moving slowly in spite of the need for speed, because Walsh was having trouble balancing. Breathing heavily, he lurched from step to step. I slipped a hand under his elbow, worried about concussion. The fence cut was as I'd left it. I shoved it open, helped him through.

A car came along Atlantic Avenue, a big black ship, sailing without lights. I ducked and yanked Walsh into the shadow of the Dumpster. The Jeep Cherokee passed slowly, then stopped near the trailer.

The license plate light had been disconnected, but a street lamp did the trick. The plate wasn't Dana's. I only caught a glimpse, but I thought New Hampshire, like the one I'd seen earlier in the day. Green on white. "Live free or die," the controversial motto. I waited, we waited, hunkered down behind the metal Dumpster. Two men got out of the Jeep. One must have had a key to the gate. I heard it creak as it opened.

"Can we get the fuck out of here?" Walsh managed in a whisper.

I wanted to stay, creep closer, see more than outlines, shapes, and shadows. Walsh swayed and tugged at my sleeve. His teeth chattered and his skin looked gray in the dim light.

We both heard it, a sharp cry of surprise, anger. There might have been five, six angry words, but the one that registered was "gone." Abandoning caution for speed, we ran.

Some date.

CHAPTER 26

I eased the chunk of iron pipe under the driver's seat, relieved that the long stumbling journey to the garage was over. "The General? New England Medical? Preference?"

"Neither." Walsh sank into the passenger seat; his breath came hard and fast. "No way."

With his arm tight across my shoulders, mine around his waist to steady his gait, I hadn't felt the biting cold the way I had earlier in the evening.

"Look at me," I said sternly. "What's your name? Where are you?"

He gave me a grin. "I'm fine, coach. Put me back in the game."

"Show me your eyes."

He lowered one eyelid in an exaggerated wink, reopened it. His pupils were the same size, the whites so white they seemed almost blue. Now, he was goofing, fooling around, his grin infectious, but fifteen minutes ago he'd looked and acted as though a trip to the ER was inevitable. His sudden recovery made me question his earlier behavior. Had he simply felt a strong desire to get off-site, a reasonable one considering his reception, or had he wanted to hurry me away before I saw something I shouldn't?

"If you don't want a hospital, what about a cop?"

"No." No hesitation. "You live near here?"

"Cambridge."

"Got any Band-Aids?"

When I leaned forward to crack the dash compartment, he stopped me by taking my hand. "At your place?"

"I can drive you home," I said slowly.

He didn't release my gloved right hand; he held it in his left, moved his right to cover it. "It's early yet. We could talk. You live alone?"

"Depends what you mean by alone."

"Single," he said.

"Formerly married. I have a house. A tenant."

"Man?"

"Woman."

"Fine. Is that all the heat this car can do?"

I nodded. He gave an elaborate shiver, then let go of my hand so I could back up the car and ransom it from the garage attendant. Walsh stayed silent, head bowed, while I negotiated the ramps onto 93, the turns onto Memorial Drive. Along the river, cars drove fast and exhaust hung in the air like mist. The triangular Citgo sign in Kenmore Square pulsed red on the Boston side of the Charles.

I pulled into my narrow drive, used my key on the front door. Walsh followed me in, turning from side to side in the foyer, peering up the stairs as though expecting someone. The house looked deceptively occupied, the lights I leave on to trick the burglars glowing cheerfully.

Walsh eyed the living room suspiciously. "This what they call a safe house?"

It stumped me at first. "You mean the neighborhood?"

"You're no secretary."

A safe house. Could have been the absence of furniture, or maybe the man had seen too many movies. "I'm *definitely* not CIA."

"I thought FBI. I heard they're all over the Dig."

"Come into the kitchen," I said mildly.

"Spider to the fly." The grin was back.

"Stay here, if you'd rather, but there's disinfectant in the bathroom off the kitchen. I'll get you some stuff to make a bandage while you wash that cut off. Want some aspirin?"

He started to nod, thought better of moving his head so quickly.

I said, "Then we'll talk."

He disappeared into the tiny half-bath and I took the stairs to the second floor to rummage in the medicine cabinet. I chose gauze and tape, marvelling at the amount of stuff I'd collected to treat and bind wounds. Must be in the wrong business.

I put the assorted goodies on the kitchen table, fired up the kettle. The toilet flushed and Walsh emerged, his face damp enough that I wondered whether Roz had neglected to replace the towels, his skin so dark it glistened. I watched as he made an expert job of the bandage, staring into the small mirror over the bathroom sink.

"Very tidy," I said.

"Army medic."

"Is that where you met Kevin? In the army?"

"I know him from way back, before high school. What? You don't believe me?"

Even in the mirror, he picked up on the slightest facial changes, practically read my thoughts. I'd need to be more careful. "At the funeral, you kept your distance. His family—"

"His family never liked me. Wrong color."

"You want some coffee?"

"Black." He smiled and busied himself rewinding strips of gauze and replacing them in the carton. "Unless there's brandy."

"With your head, I'm not sure."

"It's my head. Brandy will do fine."

I put a filter and grounds into the pour-through gizmo. Walsh seemed content to wait in silence. He'd recovered enough to look rakish, with the bandage across his forehead and a single gold stud gleaming in his ear. I wondered how I'd missed the earring earlier. He must have removed it before breaking and entering, reinserted it after applying the bandage.

Bonnie Raitt sings a plaintive Joni Mitchell song that starts with a syncopated guitar riff. *"I met you on a midway at a fair last year, and you stood out like a ruby in a black man's ear."* I instructed myself to quit hearing the seductive melody. Songs are for romantic interludes, not the aftermath of attempted murders. *If that was what I'd seen.*

"This is a nice room. Nice house. Yours?"

My kitchen is big and square and so old there's a butler's pantry off to one side. If I were to put it on the market, the realtor would list it as unspoiled, which means I've never had the money or the inclination to renovate. The only dishwasher I have is Roz.

"What happened tonight?" I set a cup of coffee on the scrubbed-oak kitchen table, added a generous slug of brandy.

"Who are you?" Walsh said.

"Someone who wants to help."

"Bullshit."

"Someone who saved your ass, then. And who exactly are you?" I countered.

"All I've got with me is my driver's license. Shoulda left that home, too, considering my plans for the evening."

I held out an expectant hand while he sat and undid the laces of his left workboot, reconsidered, tried the right. The card, tucked inside his sock, gave a Jamaica Plain address, listed his height as 6'4", his weight at 205. I'd have guessed less. After a brief internal debate, I handed him one of my business cards: name, address, phone, private investigations.

"Carlotta," he said. "I like it."

"I'd appreciate it if you'd keep it to yourself."

"Who do you work for?"

"Myself, usually, but you could say I work for the Dig."

"Attorney general?"

"Inspector general. They're playing on the same team."

"All that stuff is so much bullshit. Where'd the money go? That's what they want to know, they say, but they don't want the real answers."

"I do."

"It's a fucking expensive project. Christ, anybody's ever built something, rebuilt something, put a damn pool in the yard, knows you don't find what you expect to find. The problem was always the estimates. Politicians wanted the green light so they made up good numbers. They counted on things being right and they went wrong every step of the way. It's human nature, what happened. Anybody says they know what's down there before cutting into the ground is nothing but a mind reader, a freak, a circus performer oughta go on the fucking road."

Best thing to do when somebody starts a rant is to keep quiet. I got the feeling he was talking in order not to talk, going on and on about the Dig to avoid something else, maybe to avoid answering the questions I wanted to ask.

"Man, they found a mess down there. Red-tape mess, environmental mess, utilities mess. They found old shit that the archeologists wanted saved, and ground too soft to tunnel through, and ground too hard to tunnel through, and rock where there wasn't supposed to be rock. You got utilities where they ain't supposed to be and old tunnels and sewers and—You know where else the money went?"

I shook my head, sipped coffee.

"Keeping the city open. Building temporary ramps and roads so commuters can still get to the office. Plus they paid everybody off. Called it 'mitigation' but it's just payoffs by another name. And now, when there's only so many contracts left, they're gonna check those firms out three ways to Sunday and make everybody look bad."

"I wasn't brought in to make Horgan look bad."

"Now they're blowing money on investigators. I heard there's an ex-cop on the take, making things smell good where they stink and stink where they ought to smell good."

Jesus. I filed that one.

Walsh had run out of steam. He closed his eyes momentarily.

"You want to visit the ER after all?"

"No."

"How about the cops?"

"No."

I raised an eyebrow.

"I'd rather not."

"An ice pack?" I took one out of the freezer.

"You get smacked around a lot, job like yours?"

I wondered what he'd say if he saw the bullet wound in my thigh, and then I wondered what he'd say *when* he saw the bullet wound in my thigh. "No," I said softly, thinking about the big difference a small word could make.

He held the ice pack to his head. The cut was high on his forehead, not much damage considering the heft of the pipe under my car seat.

I inhaled, blew out the breath slowly. "So tell me about the evening's plans."

"Carlotta, are you checking out Kevin's death?"

I liked the way my name sounded on his lips, so I

tried his on mine. "Leland, think about it. I was there before he fell."

"That's not an answer."

"More of an answer than I got."

His repertoire of grins ranged from rueful to charming to full-bore sexy. I put this one in between boyish and disarming. "Hey, I was only gonna break into a storage shed."

"For fun?"

"Things disappear and reappear, for chrissakes! I put my tools away, I expect to damn well find 'em where I put 'em." He reached over, added more brandy to his cup, offered me the bottle. "There's this storage hut, pretty much like the others, except nobody has the keys. That's where I think my tools must be. Hell, I don't know what's in there, but nobody can find the keys and that makes me dead curious. So tonight I went in to bust it open and find out what the hell's in it and why everybody gets bent out of shape whenever I ask."

"Everybody?"

"Horgan. O'Day."

"And what happened?"

"I remember cutting the fence. I was pretty full of myself. Gonna do a little spying, brag about it to a pretty woman."

I raised one eyebrow. "Do you remember going down the scaffold stairs?"

He shrugged.

"Did you see who hit you?"

Another shrug.

"What do you know about selling dirt?"

"What's that supposed to mean?"

"Your friend Kevin called the IG's hotline, said things were walking off the site."

He sat up straighter. "Tools and shit. I told him that."

"He called again. Second time he said someone on the Horgan site was selling dirt."

Walsh shook his head slowly. "I don't know jack about that."

With effort I kept the exasperation off my face. When I'd found him, almost under the truck wheels, it seemed as though I'd stumbled onto another accident about to happen. If Kevin Fournier hadn't slipped, if he'd been killed because of something he knew, it followed that a second accident might have been arranged because Walsh knew the same thing. Dammit, if he didn't know anything, why risk killing him?

Walsh said, "Fuck, if they'd checked, those pathologists at Albany Street, they'd know he hadn't fallen down any stairs."

"They did check." Someone could have *thought* Walsh knew, *assumed* he knew. "I've got the report."

"Can I see?"

"He was your friend. There are photos that might be hard to forget."

He hesitated.

"I used to be a cop. I've gone over it and there's nothing there. A skull fracture's a skull fracture. Pathologists can't tell what caused it, a fall or a blow. And they can't tell if he fell or was pushed, either."

"Shit." Frustration brought his hand down hard on the table, and the sound echoed in the small room. "I'll save myself the grief then, but goddammit, I wish I could do something."

"Maybe you'll remember more about tonight later. Sometimes it's like that with a hit on the head."

"Sure you don't get hit a lot?"

"Not often."

The slow grin again. "Hit *on?*"

I drank coffee.

He got to his feet, returned the ice pack to the freezer. When he came back, he stood behind my chair and rested his hands on my shoulders. "They shifted most of the dirt the end of last year, start of this one, December, January. Day after day, trucks pulling up to the bucket, dump trucks, whole line of 'em."

If it happened months ago, why had Fournier chosen to drop his dime now?

"You sure he said dirt?" Walsh's fingers pressed against my shoulder blades and I had difficulty suppressing a moan. Sam Gianelli had asked the same question, and I realized I'd been thinking about Sam for awhile, watching Walsh move, comparing him to Sam, his stature, his build. I wondered if I'd ever see a man completely as himself, not in comparison to Gianelli. The thought made me sad, and then—I don't know—defiant. I wanted Walsh to help me forget Gianelli.

"Other room we passed through," he murmured. "Is there a couch, something soft to sit on?"

"Used to be. Now it's just pillows on the floor."

"Sounds fine." He didn't ask for an explanation and I liked that.

We moved to the living room, set about building a fire in the fireplace. He had a system: He liked to place the logs vertically, didn't approve of newspaper for kindling, but decided to roll a few sheets tightly rather than rummage for shim shingles in the cellar. He claimed that making and lighting the fire exhausted him to the point that he had to lie down on the rug. When I offered a pillow for his head, he said he'd prefer to rest it in my lap.

"Or do you want to talk politics first?" I'd thought his other grins were sexy, but this one was devastating.

"I'd rather talk music."

"That's what you like to know about a guy? Before?"

"It's one thing I like to know. Before what?"

He ignored the question. "Me, I'm kind of a musical throwback. Temptations, Marvin Gaye, all that Motown shit. Dancing and listening, both. I like to dance. Slow stuff, you know?"

Delta blues is my passion. My ex-husband, a bass player, shared it. Sam likes more modern stuff, mainly big band, some alt rock, but we could always agree on Bessie Smith. I thought I could deal with Motown. Hell, I could probably deal with a man who adored overweight Wagner-singing sopranos; it's musical indifference that leaves me cold.

"You're so pretty, you know that? Hey, you don't like it when I say that?"

I hadn't pulled away, nothing as strong as a flinch, but he read me well. It's true; I don't like pretty. Pretty seems to me a weak word, and I guess, above all, I want to be strong. I'm not a girl who wants to be a boy; it's nothing like that. I love the melting, aching feeling I get when I'm with a man, but there's only so

much I'll give up for that feeling, so in the end, I know
I've got to be strong.

"Hey, come back. You want to talk about your ex?"

"No."

"How about religion?"

I laughed. "You get far with lines like these?"

"Always. You bet."

"Half Jewish, half Catholic, if you need to know.
You?"

"Jewish and Catholic both?"

"Yeah, I'm gonna feel real guilty afterward."

"After what?"

I raised an innocent eyebrow.

He said, "Me, I'm a pagan. You ever go with a
brother before?"

"Hasn't happened, but I don't go by black or white."

"What do you go by?"

Chemistry. That was the simple answer. And unfail-
ingly, I got it wrong. My cop friend, Mooney, once
said he'd arrest any man I got the urge for, with total
confidence that the bastard would have something
arrest-worthy in his past.

"I don't know," I said.

"We could try it on a little."

He reached up and touched my cheek, circled my
neck with one hand, drew me down to meet his mouth,
and I felt the old familiar tingle in my stomach. He
smelled of coffee and brandy and disinfectant. It was
warm by the fire, the rug thick and soft. We both wore
layers and layers of clothes against the outdoor cold,
which made undressing nothing like the scenes in movies, more of a frantic race against the clock than a

languorous cinematic seduction. Face it, panty hose and long underwear and camisoles are funny. So are condoms. We laughed a lot and then we didn't.

"Do you happen to have a bed?" he asked after a long time.

"Upstairs."

He sighed and tugged a strand of my hair. "I thought maybe you just had pillows in all the rooms. Wouldn't be a bad thing. Your hair smells great."

"It's usually red. I dyed it brown for the Dig job."

"Can you dye it back?"

We started collecting our scattered clothes, and something, maybe the jingle of change when he lifted his pants off the floor, reminded me. I asked if he'd show me the key chain token Kevin had given him, the good luck charm.

He reached into his righthand pants pocket, reached deeper. Then he groped the lefthand pocket. "It's gone."

"What do you mean, gone? You sure you didn't take the thing out and leave it home?"

"I don't think so. No. It must have dropped out of my pocket, or . . ."

"Do you remember the design?"

"A circle. With sort of wavy lines."

"Could you draw it?"

His mouth tightened. I found a piece of paper and a pencil on my desk, and slowly, with much erasing, he drew an awkward replica while the dim glow of the dying fire gleamed against his dark skin.

"It's not my best skill," he said when he was through.

"No," I agreed.

We went upstairs, made love again, less urgently this time, slowly, rhythmically, satisfyingly. It took me a long time to fall asleep afterward. Black Jeeps haunted my dreams.

CHAPTER 27

"What on earth did you do?" Marian gawked at me from behind her desk.

For three seconds I thought she'd seen love-bites on my neck or read my mind, knew I'd spent the night entwined with carpentry foreman Leland Walsh. Why wouldn't it show, the way I felt: loose, easy, and well-used?

It occurred to me that she was probably asking why I'd been fired.

"I'll fill you in later, call you with the gory details," I promised hurriedly. "I don't want to run into Liz Horgan."

"You can say that again. She's in a mood."

"She's here?"

"Down the trench with some union safety officer."

"Two things, Marian, okay? That's all." While I spoke, my fingers were busily yanking items out of my desk drawers. "I came across this weird stuff with the trucking invoices. Most of them were for work done in December and January—"

"Who asked you to check the invoices? I thought you were doing the look-ahead schedule—"

"Liz asked me to do it," I lied. "She said there was another trucking company, just recently, and I can't find any invoices on that firm."

Marian pouted her lips. "There was a trucker in, maybe a week ago, for a couple loads. I saw him pull up."

"Which outfit? Norrelli?"

"I can't remember the name, but they had a red diamond in the logo, if that helps."

"You're fabulous, Marian."

"I'm so sorry you're leaving. Jeez, they'll have to bring *somebody* in. I'm drowning here. Hey, did you give my note to Krissi? Did she say anything, send a reply?"

Shit, I'd left the note in the car, which was parked in a nearby tow zone. "I never saw her. I'm sorry. I gave Liz the book."

"Oh, never mind. It's nothing. Throw it out. I'm just worried about that kid."

Worried about the kid's dad, more likely. More specifically, worried about ingratiating herself with the kid to earn points with the dad. Still, I wasn't sure. Her interest might be genuine. Over-suspicion can be as big a job hazard as lack of suspicion in my business.

"Worried about the dog, too," Marian said with a sigh.

"But I told you—"

"Yeah, but have I seen the dog? Did *you* see the dog?"

"No."

She gave me a look.

"One other thing, Marian, did some keys go missing from here?"

"Keys?"

"To a storage shed."

"I don't know anything about that." She seemed puzzled. "Mrs. H. didn't accuse you of stealing, did she?"

"Nothing like that."

I got out as quickly as I could, with promises to stay in touch that rang false on both sides. I walked down the concrete steps, steadying myself on the rough wooden handrail. The thud of hammers and the rattle of rebar blended with the hum of overhead traffic; the earth smelled rich and damp. When I had a chance, after I found Veronica James, I'd ask Eddie for a job where I could get dirty, work with my hands, make a small piece of a lasting tunnel.

I would have said good-bye to Harv O'Day and the handful of workers I knew to speak to, but I was wary of spotting Walsh. He'd planned to turn up on time, make as if nothing had happened. He'd promised to watch for reactions, tell me if anyone asked him pointed questions about his whereabouts last night, if anything brought back memories.

Of course there might be no work on-site today, if those red eyes I'd seen last night meant rats were still hanging around. *Rats.* Were other sites closing because of rats? Another oddity for my report, along with the weird phone call reciting Dig-related traffic closings, the husband sleeping on the couch . . . I thought about Liz Horgan's haggard face and limp blonde hair, her empty house. If something were wrong with the daughter . . . If something were wrong with the daughter, it might account for her parents' moodiness, but not the disruptions and tensions on the site.

I like to wrap up cases. I like to solve them, type neat final reports, get paid, and feel that I've earned every penny. Instead I'd have to set about salvaging remnants, slapping together a patchwork summary to pass along to the next operative, assuming Eddie Conklin didn't override my judgment, ignore the hotline calls, declare Fournier's death an accident, and give the Horgans a green light.

Dammit. I shouldn't have gotten fired. I listened to the radio on the way home—rock, cranked as loud as I could stand it—but it didn't drown the reproachful chorus in my head.

You don't need high-tech gizmos for fingerprints. You can pull decent prints with basic tools and I had them, the black powder, the fine brush, plus the length of pipe used on Walsh's head. Twenty minutes later in my office, I bent to work wearing disposable gloves. I didn't think I'd find anything. Crooks use gloves, too; that's an axiom of the business. But I'm a glutton for tying loose ends.

I splashed powder the length of the pipe, and damned if someone hadn't been foolish enough to grasp it with ungloved fingers. A slow smile spread over my face. Crooks are dumb; another axiom of the business. I could plainly see, not a thumb, but three well-defined fingertips. I had Scotch tape and three-by-five cards handy.

A storage shed that couldn't be opened. Which one? Why didn't Marian know anything about it? What could be kept in one of those small huts that would be worth killing to protect? I let my mind wander while my hands worked. Counterfeit hundreds. Pirated video discs. Kiddy porn. Drugs. I hadn't come up with anything pointing at cocaine or ecstasy or heroin, unless selling dirt meant selling heroin. I lifted the prints to the cards, labeled them, placed the pipe in a plastic bag, stuck it under my desk. Eddie could run the prints for me.

I could almost hear Walsh's deep voice, talking about an ex-cop who gave bad sites clean slates, made trouble for sites that had no trouble. Eddie certainly had been eager for me to make a quick entry and exit on the Horgan site.

Exactly what should I include in my final report? Would Eddie run the prints if I told the tale of Walsh and his nighttime adventure? Did I even want to mention the locked storage shed?

Maybe I'd get better results if I asked Eddie to run the prints as a favor, told him I wanted to check out a potential tenant, a boyfriend of Paolina's. *Damn. Who do you trust? Who can you trust?* My current tenant's footsteps raced precipitously downstairs while I was pondering the question.

"Want work?" I yelled.

Roz usually moves fast, so the speed of her descent didn't alarm me. Slower, heavier footsteps followed, which didn't faze me either. Roz sleeps late, and seldom sleeps alone, or with the same guy twice, for that matter. She wore a fuchsia T-shirt with the motto "Yankees Suck," and her hair had come out navy blue.

I asked her to photograph the print card and make

three copies in her cellar darkroom. I'd keep one, send one to Eddie, one to a cop pal, probably Mooney. If Moon came out with a different result than Eddie, I'd learn something. I considered asking Moon to run Leland Walsh's name and description through the system. I tugged a lock of my hair.

"Carlotta?" Roz shifted from foot to foot. Probably hadn't said farewell to the boyfriend.

"Oh, yeah, look, I need them fast."

"Good, it'll cost you more."

"This mean anything to you?" I showed her Walsh's drawing of the missing gold disc.

"Is it a tattoo?"

"I saw it on a piece of metal, same size it is now. Colored. Red, blue, green. Maybe enamelled. Could be a gang symbol, I suppose, or a tat." Pity it didn't feature Marian's red diamond truck logo, I thought.

"I can ask around."

"Could be corporate. Some logo deal." The slow voice belonged to Roz's sometime lover, sometime karate instructor, a man who goes by the single name Lemon.

"I'll run a graphics check," Roz said. "Lemon's got a great Mac setup. Tons of people want to know, like, if somebody's using the same corporate name. I'll make like I wanna use this wavy-line thing for my company logo, but I don't want to get sued by Acme Consolidated, or some other outfit already owns it, okay?"

After they left I worked on my report. "Stuff walking off the site." "Selling dirt." Why had Fournier been so fucking oblique? Was he trying to shield someone?

Holding back deliberately? *Why?* I knew jerks used the hotline to get rivals into trouble. I wondered if anyone had ever used the hotline as a threat: Do what I want or I'll turn you in. If Fournier had been motivated by the simple desire to see justice done, why hadn't he told his story in words anyone could understand?

I shoved the incomplete report into my desk drawer, shut it with a bang, and locked it. I'd finish the damn thing later. It was Monday, the beginning of a new work week. I'd been fired off the Horgan site, but look on the bright side: I had another case, a rich client in the hospital, a client who refused to speak to me.

Charles River Dog Care would be open, and I still needed Erica Mullen's address and Walters's client list. I wondered whether he'd hired a replacement for Veronica yet.

Could I convince Roz to devote a few days to pet care if I paid her enough? If so, I could drop by, bombard the staff with questions about my new puppy. *Did he need special food? Was Dr. Aronoff a good vet?*—I had a soft place for Aronoff; I'd met Dana Endicott in his office. Maybe Walters, as well as the Horgans, sent pets there. While I monopolized the staff, Roz could rifle the files, grab the client list.

It had the makings of a plan. But would Walters hire Roz, navy blue hair, tattoos, and all? Ah, well. I took a deep breath. Tewksbury High would be open on a Monday, too. The dead sister first, or Erica Mullen first? I felt like driving, so Tewksbury won.

CHAPTER 28

The high school was open, but might as well have been closed for all the details I gleaned about Veronica's dead sister. An elderly English teacher with a shiny bald head had taught other James sisters. He reminisced cheerfully about Elsie, a *truly promising student,* as we sat at a cramped table in a cafeteria that smelled like pasty mashed potatoes. Jayme was bright as well. He barely recalled Veronica, and didn't seem the type to question about her early lesbian leanings. He thought Lisa, or was it Leslie, attended some private school. Perhaps she was academically gifted, possibly a behavioral problem. He bit his lip and furrowed his brow and couldn't, for the life of him, remember the name of the school.

I got back in my car with a sigh. I could drive to Charles River Dog Care in an hour, but since I was already to hell and gone northwest of the city, I decided to drive to the James's home instead, hope Jack James's bad back had improved. If he was at work, Helen might relish a chance to talk about—

The Goldsby School.

The letters on the roadside sign jumped out, and my foot hit the brake almost before I thought. I took a sudden right turn down a winding driveway lined with elms. Right in the neighborhood, en route between the high school and the house, a private school, and if the James girl had been academically gifted ... Private schools make necessary community friends by giving scholarships to promising locals.

A long shot, yes, a hunch, but an opportunity to do a good deed and feed my insatiable curiosity at the same time. Marian's note to little Krissi Horgan was still in the car. *How are all the stiffs at Goldsby?* I transferred it to my pocket as I navigated the twisting road. Sometimes I believe that if I take care of other people's children, they'll do the same for mine. Goes around, comes around. I hadn't been doing much for Paolina lately, and she had, after all, landed me a paying client.

Who was I kidding? If I stopped at the school, gave Krissi her note, it would be because I hadn't given up on the Horgan case yet. Liz might have fired me, but I wasn't ready to write that final report.

A graveled parking lot opened at the end of the drive. The grassy quadrangle was surrounded by buildings that looked more like cozy homes than institutional structures. A grand hall, in old redbrick, blended into the landscape so well that it might have grown there like an ancestral oak. If I could, I wondered, would I play fairy godmother, touch Paolina with my wand, send her off to someplace like the Goldsby School? Did I want her to attend school where the wealthy learn to get richer and make friends with those most likely to help them climb the ladder? The Goldsby doorways didn't have metal detectors, like Cambridge Rindge and Latin's.

The forsythia bushes budded yellow at their very tips. The occasional student hurried past, flinging a backpack across one shoulder, better dressed than any contemporaries at Tewksbury High. I wondered if I'd recognize Liz and Gerry Horgan's blonde daughter if she passed. Would she be brisk, efficient, and overstrung like her mother, brusque and offhand like her father?

Daughters of undersecretaries of state, sons of business tycoons attend Goldsby. I've worked private school cases before and I knew private investigators would be given the polite heave-ho. If anyone thought I was from the press I'd be out on my ear. Asking questions about a former student was safer than asking about a current student, but no one would feel the need to oblige.

My clothes weren't bad, and New Englanders, especially old money New Englanders, show an open contempt for fashion. I could be a prospective parent interested in enrolling a child, but I wasn't sure that was the way to go. I strolled from vine-covered building to vine covered building, reading the signs to the right of each pillared door: music education, science laboratory, mathematics instruction. A small unadorned door to the rear of a larger building was labeled INSTITUTIONAL ADVANCEMENT.

I went back to my car, traded my backpack for a briefcase I keep in the trunk. I twisted my hair up and fastened it with a clip, checked the results in the rear-view mirror, used lipstick.

Then I made my way back to the small door, knocked lightly, turned the brass knob, and walked into warmth. The entryway was small and looked in through a glass door on a welcoming fire, a worn Oriental carpet and the kind of furniture your grandmother might have owned had she been a doyenne of Yankee society.

The young woman at the desk stopped tapping her keyboard and stared up at me with sharp eyes behind dark-framed glasses. She wore a pink twinset, had dyed black hair, and a pugnacious jaw. I'd been hoping for a sweet old dear.

I used one of my phony business cards, apologized for my lack of an appointment. Miss Harriman said that was okay, how could she be of assistance? When I replied that I'd come on the behest of a client who wished to make a donation in memory of a former student, I got a dazzling smile, the offer of coffee, and the news that Mrs. Bowman would be delighted to see me.

Mrs. Bowman was exactly the sweet old dear I'd had in mind. Her white hair stood out around her head in frothy waves and I could see hints of pink scalp. Her room was a trifle stuffy, but comfortably furnished in blues and golds. She greeted me gravely, shook hands firmly, and invited me to choose between a sofa and an armchair. My phony card did not identify me as a lawyer. It simply gave a name: old Caroline Grady again, and a fictitious Boston address.

My client, I informed Mrs. Bowman, wished his generosity to remain anonymous, would that be a problem? A beaming Miss Harriman brought coffee for two, adjourned, and Mrs. Bowman and I spent such a long time discussing the difficulties of anonymous philanthropy that the name of the student to be honored by the gift was almost an afterthought. When I mentioned Lisa James, I glossed over the name lightly. I said I believed she'd been a member of the class of '92, but it could have been '93. My client had not been quite sure.

Mrs. Bowman selected the '92 and '93 yearbooks from a collection on a mahogany bookcase. A faint shadow crossed her face as she ran her finger over the faces of the graduating seniors of 1992.

"You don't mean Leslie Ellin James, do you," she said in a flat voice.

"Yes. I'm so sorry. Didn't I say Leslie?"

"No, you didn't." Her voice sounded too level, as though she were trying to control it.

"Slip of the tongue."

"Miss Grady, exactly what sort of memorial does your client have in mind?" Her tone was different, almost hostile.

"Nothing ostentatious. A stone bench, maybe a garden, or a tree. I'm sure if you'd care to make a suggestion—"

"There could be *nothing* with her name on it. Nothing like that."

"I'm sorry. Is there some issue here I'm not aware of?"

"I'm afraid that I really would have to discourage your client from attempting to use this school as a vehicle for any political statement he might wish to make." Mrs. Bowman averted her gaze and straightened the cuffs of her silk shirt.

"One minute, please, Mrs. Bowman. I'm afraid my client may also be using me." I let my voice grow puzzled, then indignant. "I have no idea who this girl is other than a former friend of the gentleman who hired me. Why should the use of her name on a memorial be a political statement? My client simply wishes to make an anonymous gift—"

"Miss Grady, Leslie Ellin James did not graduate from this school."

"Her picture seems to be in your yearbook."

"She left prior to graduation. She—I suppose you could say she ran away. Then she met—an entirely unsuitable companion. She married him and when she died she was Leslie Harrow." She spoke the name emphatically, paused as though waiting for me to react.

"I don't understand."

"It's simply an event no one in this community wishes to remember. Some of us do, whether we wish to or not; we don't need any memorial plaque." Her spine stiffened and she looked me straight in the eye. "As you probably know, Leslie Harrow died the very next year, in Waco, Texas, one of those poor people—I always think of her as one of the children, although she had a child of her own by then. I think of her as one of the children, shot, or burned to death in that terrible place." She lifted her hands to her chin, fingertips to lips, almost as though she were praying.

"You're talking about the Branch Davidians." The words felt foreign on my lips.

"David Koresh, and the others. I remember so few of their names."

Koresh. I remembered that name. *Leslie James died at Waco.*

"I'll have to ask you to leave," Mrs. Bowman said. "You can see, a memorial would be out of the question."

A death at Waco was a death a family as well as a school might decide to forget. A grainy photo flashed across television screens, reprinted in news magazines, like the photos of air crash victims, but infinitely different, with *fault* and *blame* and *shame* in attendance, playing their dirty roles.

"I'm sorry," I told Mrs. Bowman.

Miss Harriman gave me a puzzled glance as though she'd expected me to stay in the inner office longer, emerge in a better mood. No doubt about it, I was shaken. I crossed most of the distance to the door before remembering the limp envelope in my pocket. Miss Harriman had gone back to her keyboarding. When I said, "Excuse me," she glanced up.

"Yes?"

"Do you know many of the students?"

"I *am* a student."

"Would you know where I could find Krissi Horgan? Kristal Horgan."

Her mouth twisted. "She hasn't been here in like a month. She's probably going to have to repeat the whole year. You'd be amazed how many kids just take off. The family goes to Gstaad skiing or something." While she had to work, her look said.

Kristal Horgan's family was very much in Boston.

I said, "She could be sick," and waited to see whether Miss Harriman would respond.

She gave a short laugh. "Most of the girls here, I'd say, they miss a month of school, they're pregnant. No doubt about it."

She seemed young to be so cynical. I wondered if she came from a family like Paolina's, if she were here on scholarship, working part-time to offset costs.

"But not Kristal," she said, going back to the keyboard. "It's all dogs with her. Boys don't even register."

CHAPTER 29

I sat in the frigid car—five minutes, ten minutes, half an hour—trying to digest what I'd learned, factor it into Veejay's disappearance. *Leslie James died at Waco.* At some point I must have turned the key, maybe only for the heater, and then I found myself zooming along Route 3, before I realized I was driving. Leslie James died in that grim inferno, a conflagration that bred other conflagrations. I must have seen her graduation photo in the paper, one of many—women and children— burned to death when the compound ignited. I remembered the gruesome television coverage. *David Koresh* was a name that echoed, and *Ruby Ridge* was another. *Oklahoma City . . . Tim McVeigh . . .*

April 19, 1993. Seven years ago . . . Leslie was close to graduating from high school in 1992, which would make her eighteen or nineteen when she died. If Veejay were twenty-one now, she'd have been, what? eleven or twelve, when she'd watched her sister die. Maybe the sister she felt closest to, the sister with whom she'd shared a dog.

What if both my client and her maid told the truth, and nothing but the truth? Masked men, entering easily through a locked door, unfazed by large dogs, stealing photographs. Veronica James had left willingly, and left her beloved dog behind. She was missing and it was my job to find her.

I had another job, finishing up the report on the Horgan site. And Krissi Horgan, who also loved dogs, *was she also missing?* She'd stopped visiting the site so abruptly that Marian feared she'd done something to anger the girl. She hadn't been at school in nearly a month, didn't seem to be at home. Loved dogs. Couldn't be pregnant, only loved dogs, boys didn't register . . .

Mooney, my cop friend, razzes me about "intuition." I can't help it. I pick up hints, changes in intonation, shifts in tone. They register, often subconsciously, submerge, then resurface. I see them as thin silk lines, each seemingly independent, that come together, interweave, form a web. Or jigsaw puzzle pieces, shifting, changing. I tugged my hair, drove faster than I should, considered black Jeeps in the shed behind Charles River Dog Care, under the dim street lamps near the Horgan site.

I disapprove of all those assholes making cell calls while speeding along major highways, driving over yellow lines, never mind white ones, endangering themselves and others. Me, I've driven a cab; I'm a pro; I can handle it. I punched Claire's number at the Registry, asked her to try another plate for me. New Hampshire JN 6794, the one I'd seen through the dirty window of the shed. I used Information to get Dr.

Aronoff, the vet's, number, even though it was somewhere in my notebook. I didn't want to pull off the road, not on 128. People *drive* on the damn shoulder of 128. I tapped it in, warned the receptionist not to put me on hold. I needed to know whether Dr. Aronoff had an arrangement with Charles River Dog Care, if he handled their emergencies. He did.

I pulled into a rest stop, yanked my hair, stared at the cell phone. I hit redial, and when Aronoff's receptionist answered, I raised my voice to Liz Horgan's pitch, identified myself, and told her I wanted to reschedule Tess's checkup.

"I'm sorry about last time," I said.

"Yes, well, this time, if you can't make it, be sure to call. No-shows are extremely inconvenient. Dr. Aronoff is such a busy man."

I hung up and rooted around the dash compartment for a bottle of water, couldn't find it, tried the floor. I'd met Dana Endicott at Dr. Aronoff's, while on an errand for Marian. I found the bottle, tilted my head back, and drank. The Horgans could be Charles River clients. Maybe Veejay picked their dog up every day, took it to the vet, taught obedience classes in which Krissi Horgan participated.

And? So? I didn't know yet, but I remembered that cop, banging routine doors, looking for his ho-hum hit-and-run witness. If you bang the door looking for a witness, and a big-time dealer comes out with his hands up, you've got to be ready with the handcuffs. *Damn.* The Fresh Pond Rotary would be a mess, construction everywhere, but I decided to take Route 2 anyway, risk a traffic jam.

I called Roz, told her to run Leslie James Harrow through the Internet with a focus on Waco.

"Waco? As in massacre? Okay. And the copies are almost dry."

"Stay on the clock. Run a print card over to 425 State Street, Foundation Security, tenth floor, give it to Eddie Conklin, tell him it's from me, ask him to run it as an urgent favor. Use your charm."

"Wiggle my boobs?"

"Whatever. Is Lemon there?"

"Sure."

"Let me talk to him. And before you leave the house, feed the cat."

I could hear her holler, hear his approaching footsteps. "Yeah?"

"Hey, Lemon, you want some work?"

"Always hungry."

"Still got the dog?"

He gave a snort. "Hannibal? What do you want with him? He's no bloodhound."

"Has he been to obedience school?"

"Are you kidding?"

"Perfect."

At the Fresh Pond Rotary, I almost made a three-sixty and drove back to Goldsby, thinking someone, *someone* there would tell me more, more about Veronica's sister, more about Krissi. But when I recalled the silent weimaraner and the black Jeep and April 19, 1993, I kept driving, edging through traffic, to meet Lemon in the parking lot of the Store 24.

CHAPTER 30

Traffic was one problem, Lemon another. I'd given detailed intructions; he'd told me to expect him in fifteen minutes. He runs a dojo in Somerville, but before his conversion to clean living and karate, he did performance art on the street and took every drug on the market twice. I decided to triple his estimate, dodged an SUV at the tricky intersection of Storrow and Route 2, drove outbound along Soldiers Field Road, following the river as it meandered along the Watertown border. The dogs got plenty of fresh air and sunshine running along the Charles, according to Walters, but I saw no sign of them. I U-turned, drove past the Everett Street lights, found the pack attended by a dark-haired woman and Harold, the man who hadn't called to offer the client list, near the Lars Anderson Bridge, heading east.

A terrific sight, all that golden fur, those waving tails. I'd never seen such elaborate leashes. They looked more like horse harnesses and enabled each walker to handle multiple dogs, although if all the dogs got the notion to take off racing at once I'd give the woman, slighter than the man, not much of a chance. Harold had eight dogs, the woman who was probably Erica, six. I strained to make out details of her appearance, but both humans wore layered running clothes and sneakers, the woman a close-fitting hat. She was youngish, short, and dark. I considered their position and direction; there was little chance they'd make it back to the shop in less than an hour.

I drove to the Store 24 lot. Lemon was nowhere in sight so I went inside, bought a coffee, and tried to set the counterman gossiping about his neighbor down the street. He didn't think the business had been open long. Started seeing the bus in the fall, and here it was almost spring already. Spring in Boston lasts about two days. You sneeze, you miss it. It was crazy, he thought, using a school bus, bringing pets to some lah-di-dah play school. You have a dog, you take it for a walk, your kid plays with it. Some people, he snorted, had too much money, not enough smarts.

I took my coffee outside, sat in the car, flipped radio stations. An airplane had gone missing off the South China Sea. A man had been struck and killed by an MBTA commuter train. The town was gearing up for the marathon and the great Patriot's Day debate at Faneuil Hall. *Where the hell was Lemon?* The dogs might want to run by the icy river forever, but Erica and Harold might cut the session short.

The jaunty dogs, the cheerfully painted school bus looked so normal and wholesome that I felt dirty even suspecting that the pet care place might be involved in Veejay's disappearance. And yet . . . Its doorway was hidden from public view. The shed behind the parking lot was a secret garage. A silent dog guarded the interior. An admittedly underpaid employee couldn't be bribed. Rogers Walters boasted that he ran the place like a military operation. I don't associate military precision with pet care.

When Lemon's van slipped into the parking lot, I switched to his car, and Hannibal, a large German shepherd mix, barked up a storm and tried to climb over the seat to eat my hair. Purchased as the dojo's guard dog, Hannibal never made it to that post. He proved untrainable, playful as a pup and dumb as a brick. My cat, T.C., can tie him in a knot.

"You clear on everything?" I asked.

"Sure," Lemon said. "Performance art. Up my alley."

"Obnoxious. Persistent."

"Me and Hannibal, you kidding? We don't take no for an answer."

He wanted to synchronize watches and I obliged, certain he'd strapped on a Timex for the occasion. I'd never seen him wear one before. I patted Hannibal, who went berserk, and departed, strolling up Western Avenue toward Charles River Dog Care. When I got to the door I pressed the bell, leaned on it, and waited, tapping my toe.

Walters, dressed in heavy corduroy slacks and a flannel shirt, his hair carefully plastered over his scalp, opened the door. My height, average build, no noticeable scars. When he recognized me he got a sour look on his face.

"Mind if I come in?" I moved before he could voice

his opposition, and he bit back unwelcoming words. The unwelcoming expression remained.

"Did you manage to find her?" There didn't seem to be much interest behind his inquiry.

"Did Peter call, and explain that she was away?"

"I'm sorry, no. I've heard nothing, and it's a very busy day."

"This won't take long." I plunged down the stairs, moving briskly toward his office. Not much he could do but follow, other than threaten me with a dog. Most of the cages were empty. I gave them a seaching glance, saw two small terriers, but didn't spot the weimaraner.

One wall of the office was lined with louvered closet doors. The metal desk had a shallow top drawer, three deeper side drawers. His notebook computer was on; the screen saver displayed photos of wolflike dogs or doglike wolves. The filing cabinet had four drawers, one of them slightly ajar. Not many places, but I wouldn't have much time.

"Look, I don't see how I can help. I'm expecting a phone call, and—"

"I've hit a dead end," I confessed.

"I'm sure she'll turn up."

"You look like a shrewd judge of people, Mr. Walters." The praise brought him up short. "I know how you feel about giving me your client list, even though I've assured you I have no interest in upsetting any of them."

"Well, I'm glad you—"

"But I'll bet you know your clients. If I could ask

you a few questions, I wouldn't have to bother with the list."

"Well, I—"

"First off, do you have a client named Peter, possibly Peters? Last name, first name?"

"No."

"You're sure? It could be the husband of a client. If you could check your list, you'd see—"

His eyes flicked toward the file cabinet. "I know my clientele."

"How long could it take?"

"I don't have time for this."

"Did Veejay show any interest in any particular client? Not necessarily named Peter. I mean, was there someone she was helping in an obedience class, a client she might have made friends with?"

C'mon, Lemon, I was thinking. *What's the point of wearing a watch if you don't use it?*

"I told you, she was good with the clients. She was professional."

"Did she ever date a client?"

"No."

"You sound pretty sure about that."

"I really don't know what she did on her own time, but no one ever mentioned anything like that to me, and if they had I'd have disapproved very strongly."

I sighed deeply. That took about two seconds. *Lemon, where are you?* Walters's irritation was almost out of hand.

The doorbell rang sharply, twice, and then the door opened with a loud creak. I'd slipped the latch as I entered. Barking, loud and furious, followed. The barker went nuts, to tell the truth, all those good doggie smells.

"Hey! Anybody home?" Lemon called. "Hannibal, put that down!"

"I guess that must be a client," I said.

"Nonsense. Excuse me."

"I have a few more questions. I'll wait."

I settled into my folding chair, made no move to leave. The barking grew louder, punctuated by Lemon trying ineffectually to call the dog to order. There was a clatter and a crash, and I thought they might have succeeded in knocking over some of the cages.

As soon as Walters was out of sight I went for the computer mouse, jiggling it to call up the open file, a seemingly harmless dog food invoice. I moved to the filing cabinet. Let's hear it for military precision, spit-and-shine polish. The files were alphabetized, in perfect order. A is for airedale, B is for beagle. Shit. If there was no single centralized client list, if records were kept by breed, I was in trouble. But who'd—C is for clients. I grasped the neatly typed sheet and pulled. A through G on the first page. I flipped the stapled sheets. H. Horgan. Brookline. At least I had that right. There was *some* connection.

Of course, it proved nothing, except that Boston is a small town, that circles overlap, that a family in Brookline might kennel their dog in Cambridge . . . My fingers raced over the files, looking for Erica Mullen's address and phone, for something that involved, mentioned Veejay or the Horgans. The noises outside the office swelled to a crescendo. I abandoned the files. I could hear barking and running footsteps, and Lemon yelling, "Well, fuck you, too, bozo. Shit, I thought this was a fucking place for dogs!"

That was the signal. He was getting ready to leave, getting thrown out, more likely. I crossed to one of the louvered doors, gave it a tug. An unremarkable closet, jackets, leashes. On the floor in a pile were three, maybe four, orange mesh construction vests, identical to those used on the Horgan site. I gawked at them for a moment, quickly shut the closet, retreated to my seat, crossed my legs. When Walters returned, I was idly examining a fingernail.

"Some people," he thundered, "shouldn't be allowed to have a dog." His clothes were rumpled, he was out of breath, and there was a red weal across the back of his left hand. He scowled. "I think you'd better go now."

I held his gaze. The damn screen saver hadn't flipped back on yet. "Have you managed to replace Veronica?"

"No."

"Would you mind giving me Erica Mullen's address? I'd like to speak to her, see if she's in touch with Veejay."

"I'm sorry. I can't give out that information." Out of the corner of my eye, I saw the wolf-dogs prance on-screen. I tried not to gulp with relief, thanked Walters politely, shaking his hand, noticing hard calluses on his palm. On the way upstairs, I wondered where he kept the weimaraner. I hadn't noticed it racing along the Charles with the others.

CHAPTER 31

Lemon's empty van was parked in front of the house. Indoors, I deduced from the yelps, my cat had treed Hannibal on the third floor. His noises were pitiful, but I ignored them and made tracks for the fridge. I'd missed lunch and a consultation with my gut told me I wasn't going to hold out till dinner. A carton of milk smelled okay. There were eggs. I could make what I call a frittata, what Sam used to term, less kindly, scrambled eggs and leftovers. I found some suspicious Chinese food in a goldfish container, tossed it in the sink. Eureka! Salami, some cold roast potatoes in a deli take-out box, an onion barely starting to sprout. I stuck a lump of butter in the frying pan.

Lemon appeared as soon as the onion started to sizzle, drawn by the aroma.

"Good work," I said.

"Guy doesn't appreciate Hannibal, what's he doing working with dogs?"

"Eggs?"

"Sure. Did I give you enough time?" He disappeared

before I had a chance to reply, maybe to rescue his dog. Construction vests in a heap at the bottom of a closet. I cracked an egg sharply on the side of a white pottery bowl. Two missing girls, Veronica James and possibly Krissi Horgan. Two dead people, Leslie Ellin James in 1993, Kevin Fournier on the Horgan site. I broke eight eggs, splashed in milk, whipped the mixture with a fork till it frothed. The various bits of information seemed as separate as the ingredients spread on the countertop, a chunk of salami here, an egg there. I glared at the phone, willed Claire Harper to call *now*. The onion sizzled and I turned the flame low, added the potatoes.

Lemon reappeared. "Hey, I looked in the shed, but there wasn't any Jeep."

"Empty?"

"Nope."

"Did you get any plates?"

"Sorry. Looked like a Porsche or a Jag or something in there. Nice car, but I couldn't read it. Sorry."

"Walters says you've got no business owning a dog."

"Hannibal owns me, so it's okay."

"Roz around?"

"Online. Checking that design."

"Ask her if she wants food."

He sauntered out. I dumped thinly sliced salami in the pan, inhaled the smell, added the egg mixture, stirring, keeping it from sticking to the pan.

"She says go ahead, she'll grab something later. Oh, and give you this." He slapped an assortment of printed pages, some stapled together, some loose, on the kitchen table. I hadn't sat there since Leland Walsh stood behind me, hands pressing my shoulder blades.

I divided the frittata onto two plates, found that Lemon had already set two places at the table. I sat in the same chair Walsh had used, imagined him smiling, holding the ice pack to his head. The eggs were so hot I burned my tongue. I read the handwritten note on top of Roz's pile while I sipped Pepsi.

"Eddie's running the prints," read the first line. "No problem. More than 6000 hits on Leslie James Harrow. Massacre victim. Either 19 or 21, depending which site you hit." On the subject of Waco, Roz, using Google as a search engine, had scored over 10,000 hits. "Some way-out stuff," she'd scrawled. "Here's a sample."

I started to read, kept on reading while the eggs congealed on my plate. There were photos, appalling shots of the devastation of April 19, 1993. Some sites featured straightforward descriptive passages, some passages of heat-seeking purple prose, declaring the Branch Davidians martyrs, used as guinea pigs for chemical warfare, as targets for experimental assault rifles. I read the manifesto of the New Revolution, the call to arms of the Kingman Militia, what passed for logic from the Patriot Sons of Valor.

Were the Branch Davidians, a reclusive Seventh Day Adventist sect, dangerous, a threat to themselves and others? Did they hoard illegal firearms and sexually molest their children? By the time I'd finished scanning the material, I realized I'd never know, so I focused on another question: Were the offshoot groups out to avenge the Branch Davidians dangerous? I could answer that one with a resounding *yes*. Proof rested in the ashes of Oklahoma City.

Leslie James Harrow, 19, was listed among the victims. And there: Zachariah Harrow, infant. Another photo that should have hung on the Jameses' wall.

At the tail end of several Web sites were what amounted to hit lists. The head of the Bureau of Alcohol, Tobacco, and Firearms was identified, pictured, his home address given. Louis Freeh, former head of the FBI. Janet Reno, of Justice. Senators who'd chaired the investigating committees that had exonerated the FBI. Judges who'd sentenced surviving sect members to jail. Several sites applauded Tim McVeigh, the Oklahoma City bomber, for his heroic role in evening the score. The Republic of Arizona Freemen thanked him for taking the blame, although they were confident he had not acted alone.

I didn't hear Roz till she spoke. "I've got a lead on the wavy circle."

"What?"

"A tat man. A guy does tattoos. Either I'm gonna run up and see him, or he'll drop by. He's in New Hampshire. Depends on his schedule. Hey, I didn't know all that shit about the FBI roasting babies at Waco, did you?"

"Roz, you can write *anything* and stick it on the Web. There's no gatekeeper."

"Like a newspaper."

"*Not like a newspaper*. A newspaper's got an editor, a publisher, a legal staff."

She gave me a look that said "big deal" and I hoped the literature hadn't converted her. Roz's politics are weird, but they've always been odd verging on anarchy rather than odd verging on extreme right-wing.

"That Eddie guy says he wants his report. Seemed kinda disappointed I hadn't brought it."

I'd locked it, unfinished, in my desk. I'd taken two or three unsatisfactory runs at it—chronologically, most important discoveries to least important discoveries, person by person. Finally I'd tried to split events into two groups: those that were definitely site-related, like missing tools, rats, a permanently locked storage shed; those that might be personal, related to the Horgans' marriage, like the aborted Fournier-Liz meeting, the Marian-Gerry flirtation, the constant tension.

I considered Krissi. Was the girl the key to the Horgans' personal problems? Did she know Veronica well? Could they have run away together, a young girl with a crush, an older lesbian? But what the hell did those construction vests piled on the floor of the closet mean? Were they used in dog training? Was I trying to manufacture a substantial connection where only the most inconsequential of connections existed, the link between dog trainer and client? I kept seeing that black Cherokee in the shed, the one with New Hampshire plates, and then later the same night, a Jeep with New Hampshire plates visiting the Horgan site, driving slowly, without headlights.

The Cherokee is an ordinary vehicle, I told myself, scraping cold eggs into the sink. Common as dirt. Maybe the fevered prose and conspiracy theories of the Waco Web sites were leading me off the deep end. I drank Pepsi, bit my lip, and let the kaleidoscope of images spin, hoping to catch a thread, a theory, something that would bind the separate ingredients like eggs and milk, transform them into a new substance. On the Horgan site: dead rats, live rats, missing tools, a storage shed with no key. At the Horgans' home: an empty dog dish, a missing daughter, tension verging on paranoia. At Dana Endicott's: a missing woman, a missing Jeep, a missing photograph.

Why steal that photograph? Let's say Veronica knew that Dana had hired me, never mind how. Or hired someone. The photo could have been stolen so an investigator wouldn't make the link between Veronica James and Leslie Harrow. Therefore the connection was important . . .

My cell made the run up the scale that passes for a ring, and I grabbed it. Claire at the DMV had a news flash: The plate I'd called in belonged to a silver Jaguar on the New Hampshire stolen vehicles list. I don't think I said a word, but I may have because Roz and Lemon looked at me strangely as I hurried out the door.

CHAPTER 32

I drove to Brookline, doing forty-five to fifty on thirty-mile-limit streets. If the cops had pulled me over, asked where the fire was, I'd have been hard put to justify my speed. What would a random cop make of Claire's bulletin about the Jeep? I'd leapt immediately to a conclusion: Dana Endicott's Jeep had been parked in the Charles River Dog Care shed, disguised by a stolen plate. Dana Endicott's Jeep had driven by the Horgan site minus headlights, stopped, disgorged passengers.

I pulled over behind the Allston fire station, let the car idle, watched exhaust fumes disperse in my rearview mirror. The windshield fogged over and I had to use the air conditioner to clear it. I punched Dana Endicott's number into my cell, bullied my way past Esperanza.

Dana professed ignorance of Veronica's political leanings, wanted to know what the hell I thought I was doing. Was I trying to get Veejay into trouble? I was simply supposed to *find* her, not investigate her politics, question her loyalties.

"I am trying to find her. Did she ever say anything, *anything* that made you think she was an extremist, either wing?"

"She wanted the government to leave her alone, that's all. Not to tell her the way to live or love. Same thing I want, and I'm no radical."

"Any political figures she hated?"

"I don't know where you're going with this—"

"Dana, please. Did she speak against say, a president, a senator?"

"Who's that guy from Idaho? Senator Gleason. She had it in for him, but I'm not sure why."

I hung up, pulled back on the road, kept heading south.

The Horgans' house looked so fairy-tale safe perched on its idyllic hill, a few interior lights gleaming, that I hesitated, feeling like some medieval bearer of bad tidings, wary of punishment even though I knew I wasn't the culprit. If I was on target, the bad thing, the irrevocable thing, had already happened.

If I were wrong, I'd apologize. I'd grovel, hat in hand. I hoped I was wrong. Surely I was wrong. Boston, once the hotbed of Patriot sympathy, the tinderbox of the Revolution, was quiet Eastern liberal establishment now. Our revolutionary days were hundreds of years ago, and modern militias, groups of so-called "freemen" were a rural, Western phenomenon. I left my car at the bottom of the drive and walked. As I passed beneath the porte-cochere, I took a deep breath, pressed the bell.

The lady of the manor answered, keeping the door chained, peering with unfriendly eyes. She looked ill and, when she realized who had disturbed her, angry.

"What the hell do you think you're doing?"

"Helping you out of a jam." She started to close the door. "Let me talk! I have nothing—"

"You can't have your job back."

"If Krissi's home, I'll leave. Without another word."

"Krissi." The name made her hands go limp. "Go away."

"You're right about me, Mrs. Horgan, but you're wrong. I'm not a secretary, but I'm not who you think I am. Let me in. I can help. It's okay. I could just be bringing papers from the site, like last time."

She closed the door, but didn't slam it. The chain rattled, the door reopened, and I stepped quickly inside. Same mess, same stepladder in the corner of the room, same broom and dustpan. They must have sent the housekeeper on vacation as soon as the horror show began, as soon as their daughter disappeared.

"Who are you?" she whispered fiercely.

"Carlotta, not Carla. My last name is Carlyle. I work for the inspector general, but I'm not working for him now. I'm working for myself now, and I hope for you. For Krissi."

"You've seen her?" She tried to keep her voice steady but failed.

"I came at this from another direction, Mrs. Horgan. We need to talk. I need to know what you know."

"What direction? What do you mean?"

"I was searching for a missing woman, and then I realized there were two, a missing woman and a missing girl. How did Kevin Fournier find out? Did you tell him?"

"I never told anyone. The goddam bastard. He knew *something* was wrong, that's all. Knew I should have had crews working twenty-four hours, overtime. He threatened me, said he'd kill our new contracts—"

"Unless?"

"Unless I slept with him, okay? I don't know—maybe I would have, to keep Krissi safe—but he fell—"

"Krissi's been taken, kidnapped?"

"Get out."

"Please, I can't help unless I know."

"How can I trust you?" Her voice was shrill. "They said—"

"You can't trust her." I hadn't heard Gerry Horgan's footsteps on the stairs because he wasn't wearing shoes. Some part of my mind registered the socks, and the khaki pants and the plaid shirt, open over a white undershirt. The gun in his right hand was aimed at my heart.

CHAPTER 33

He made his way down the stairs, left hand on the railing, a 9-mm Beretta in his right. I watched for signs that he didn't know how the hell to use it, that the gun was an unloaded toy kept in the bedside table for emergencies. His gaze didn't waver and his finger rested easily on the trigger.

"Careful with that." I made my voice cool as ice water. Sweat trickled down the small of my back.

"You carrying?" he demanded.

My S&W .40 was locked in my bedroom closet, unloaded. I shook my head as Mrs. Horgan interrupted.

"*Please*, do you know where Krissi is?"

"Shut up, Liz."

"I was pretty sure you weren't in on this deal," I said. "I thought you were just taking orders—"

"Neither of us is *in* on anything," Liz Horgan said passionately.

"Shut up! I'm not letting her mess this up." Horgan spoke exclusively to his wife. "All we have to do is lie low for another day or two, and Krissi will come home.

It will be like it never happened." Now his glance included me. "Into the living room. Move!"

He kept a wary distance as I passed. I knew I couldn't tackle him before he got a shot off, and I remembered the last time I'd met up with a gun at close quarters. The scar on my thigh began to tingle.

"Do you know who you're dealing with, Mr. Horgan? Do you know who's got your daughter?" I kept it low and businesslike.

"I don't want to know. Shut up."

"For a smart man, that's dumb. You'd never do business with people you don't know." The tingle became a throb, an ache.

"This isn't about business. This is about my only child. Sit down." He used the gun to point me to an armchair. "Now, who the hell are you? What business is it of yours?"

"Kevin Fournier phoned a tip to the inspector general. I was assigned to investigate."

Gerry turned on Liz. "I told you to cool him off."

"I tried, Gerry. Jesus, I tried."

I said, "If the people you're dealing with killed Fournier for making a phone call, what on earth makes you think they'll let your daughter go? Someone's holding a gun on her now, the same way you're holding one on me." I might have punched him in the stomach, the way he paled. If I moved quickly, snatched the automatic—

"He fell," Liz Horgan said faintly. Her words brought her husband back and I temporarily shelved the idea of a rush.

"He fell," her husband echoed. "We obey orders,

they do what they say, we get her back." It was a chant, a prayer, spoken with the flat inflection of repetition, like a nun telling beads.

"You're dealing with people who don't give a damn about your daughter's life."

"Shut up!"

"You need the facts so you can decide what to do."

"Gerry, maybe we need to know. Maybe she can help."

"You're giving me *maybes*, Liz. It's Krissi!"

"*You're holding a gun,* Gerry."

"Jesus, Liz."

"We can't be like this, Gerry. I can't be like this." She sounded ragged with hysteria, as though she might blow any minute. I was grateful she wasn't holding the pistol.

I pitched my voice low so they'd have to strain to listen. "Let's talk. Put the gun down. You aren't going to use it. Not on me."

"I'd use it to save my daughter," he said defiantly.

"Your daughter's in no danger from me."

He exchanged a glance with his wife, then crossed the huge chilly living room and placed the automatic on top of the grand piano. He moved a scant two feet away and stood there, hands clasped behind his back.

"When did they take Krissi?" The Beretta was only a short lunge away from Horgan.

"It's been three weeks and four days. Twenty-five days. The third Friday in March." Liz Horgan was back in rigid control. "She took the dog to the vet."

"She should never have gone alone," Horgan muttered.

"You baby her! She's old enough. You'd drive her around for the rest of her life—"

"If I can," Horgan said. "*If I can. I* wouldn't have let her go alone. You shouldn't have let her—"

"She had Tess!"

"She has a dog, a good dog, a real tiger." Horgan stopped arguing with his wife long enough to inform me. "She'd never—they must have hurt Tess."

I could have reassured him on that count, but I didn't. I wanted him to keep talking, to forget about the gun on the piano. "How did they get in touch?"

"We found a note shoved under the front door."

"Do you have it? May I see it?"

His eyes went to the piano, to the Beretta, to Liz. She nodded, made her way to the fireplace mantel, lifted a heavy crystal vase. The note was underneath it.

"*Your house is watched, your phone is tapped. If you go to the police or the FBI, or tell anyone, you'll never see your daughter again.*" The paper was standard-issue office bond, the text typed with the even flow of a laser printer. The single sheet had been folded twice, to fit into a standard business envelope.

"We'd hardly read it when we got a phone call," Liz said softly.

That followed, if the house was being watched.

"Did you record the call?"

"No."

"Can you describe the voice?"

Horgan said, "Electronically altered. I couldn't even say if it was a man or a woman, but I think it's the same voice every time. I wrote down everything. Liz?"

We waited in tense silence while she brought his notes.

He moved two more steps away from the piano to take them from her hand. "First, he or she said, 'Your daughter is safe.' Then I said something like, 'Let me talk to her.' Then he said, 'Listen carefully. She's staying with us for awhile.' "

"Go on."

"He told me we had to do certain things or we wouldn't see Krissi again. I thought he'd demand money. I was prepared for that, but he said I had to think of this as a long-term business deal. When he said 'long-term' I couldn't imagine—It started to sink in that he meant—I demanded to speak to Krissi—"

"She's alive," Liz said. "She's okay. She reads from the paper, the *Herald,* the 'Ins-and-Outs on the Dig' column. It's different every day, and we follow along with the text. Her voice is . . . She sounds so scared."

I'd picked up Liz's cell phone; I'd heard Krissi's voice.

"What else do you hear? Sounds, background noises." I was trying to recall what I'd heard even as I spoke. "Did you ever hear dogs barking in the background?"

"Maybe," Horgan said.

"I'm not sure," his wife said at the same time.

If I could make him take one more step. He was almost far enough from the gun for me to risk it. "Tell me about the business deal."

"It wasn't any deal. There were . . . orders. And he said he'd know if his instructions were carried out—and if they weren't—"

"What?"

"I can't say it."

I waited. He ran a hand through his hair and sucked in an uneven breath.

"They said they'd send us a piece of Krissi, an ear, a finger, and maybe that piece would be all we'd ever see."

Liz Horgan made a noise and pressed her hand over her mouth. Her husband turned to her with anguished eyes, and I was out of the chair like a shot. I beat Horgan to the automatic by half a step, not enough, had to knock it across the floor instead of simply grabbing it. It landed closest to Liz, but she was paralyzed, stuck to the floorboards. I shoved Horgan aside, snatched the weapon, pointed it at him while I checked the safety. *Fuck*, the thing was ready to fire; it could have gone off and killed me, killed anyone in the room. I set it, used the pistol to wave both of them to the sofa.

"Sit."

I was breathing hard. "Okay, exactly what orders did he give you?"

Horgan said, "Drop dead. I won't—"

Liz spoke. "He promised he wouldn't ask anything too hard, or too tricky. He might tell us to order supplies, to leave a gate unlocked. Nothing worth Krissi's life."

"Specifically," I said.

"Liz," Horgan pleaded.

"Gerry, *we have to tell someone.*"

Horgan said, "Make her promise she won't go to the

cops. I'm not going to let Krissi get hurt. She's just a baby."

There were babies at Waco, I thought, *one named Zachariah Harrow.* I've worked law enforcement in this city for years. There are Feds I wouldn't trust to follow up on a hot tip, cops I wouldn't trust with my wallet if my back were turned. There are a few cops, a very few, I would trust with my life.

I said, "Here's what I promise. The first thing is getting your daughter back alive. If that's not the Feds' top concern, I won't talk to them. I won't help them. I swear it."

Liz took her husband's hand, squeezed it.

He swallowed, closed his eyes.

"Today!" I said. *"Now!"*

His voice, when it finally came, was low and scratchy. "First, he told me to resist any pressure to go to extra shifts. When I heard that, I don't know, I thought it was some union thing."

"It's *terrible,*" Liz said. "We can't explain and we're falling behind."

"What else?"

"I can't!" Horgan protested.

"They told you to lose the keys to a storage shed, right? Which one?"

"In the trench, along the west slurry wall," Liz murmured.

"They told you to order explosives," I said.

Horgan, his lips pressed together in a taut line, nodded curtly. "Geldyne. I had to redirect shipments, make 'mistakes' on requisition forms."

"And after Fournier's death, they told you to hire a night watchman."

"Yes," Liz said. "They wanted us to hire him before."

If I called the FBI, they'd grab the night watchman, nail one of the group, squeeze him. But someone else would be watching over Krissi.

"I'm going to borrow your Beretta, Mr. Horgan."

"You won't go to the cops?"

"Not yet. Not till I run out of other ways to do this."

If I take care of other people's children, someone will take care of mine.

I tell people—no, I tell myself—that Sam Gianelli was my first lover, but that's a lie. When I was still a child, in Detroit, a wild child of fourteen, I had a baby. I gave him up for adoption. I never saw her. I never held him. I don't know whether it's a boy or a girl. I've never told anyone. Even when I shot and killed a man, and the brass made me see a shrink, it stayed my secret. But every kid out there is my kid. *All the lost kids are mine.*

I said, "If anyone asks why I was here, tell them I wanted my job back."

"Did we give it to you?" Mr. H's voice was hoarse.

"No," I said. "You're a mean sonofabitch."

CHAPTER 34

I drove by the dark and icy river. Street lamps glittered along the Esplanade and I was glad I'd taken up smoking again. If I hadn't, I wouldn't have had a pack at the ready. I'd have had to stop at a store.

When Timothy McVeigh was arrested, he wore a T-shirt with the slogan *"Sic Semper Tyrannis"* emblazoned across his chest. That's what John Wilkes Booth yelled after he shot Lincoln in the old Ford Theater. "Thus always with tyrants" is a rough approximation. The back of McVeigh's shirt was devoted to a quote from Thomas Jefferson: "The tree of liberty must be refreshed from time to time with the blood of patriots and tyrants."

I'd need to tell the cops within twelve hours, or risk disaster. I could trust Mooney, *knew* I could trust him, but on something like this, he'd bring in the Bureau immediately. I knew who'd taken Krissi: Veronica James and her Charles River Dog Care colleagues, bent on vengeance for Waco. I knew why they'd taken her: to force her parents to give them access to the Dig site.

Fournier had blundered in over his head, thinking Liz Horgan had her own reasons for stalling progress and limiting access—money reasons. He'd tried sexual blackmail, backed by veiled threats on the IG's hotline. Someone had overheard a phone call, lured him back to the site, killed him. A member of the gang that had kidnapped Kristal Horgan? Or possibly Gerry Horgan? I wasn't sure which. I ground out my cigarette butt in the dashboard ashtray. Horgan's automatic rested uncomfortably at the base of my spine.

Where would they hold the girl?

I left my car a block from Dana Endicott's brownstone in a space reserved for resident parking. A ticket was the least of my worries. I rang the doorbell, waited, willing her to be home. I knew she'd been released from the General because I'd called, but what if she'd—Someone hit the buzzer without asking who it was, an action so suspicious I almost transferred Horgan's gun to my hand.

My client answered the door in person, tying a robe around her waist. She had puffy eyes, a bandage over her right temple, an eager expression. Her face fell when she saw me.

"You ought to use the chain." It amazes me, the carelessness of city people who ought to know better.

She opened the door wider and an inquisitive nose hit my crotch. She had one dog on a leash. The others frisked around her. "What is it? Have you—"

"The neighbors don't need to hear this."

"I'm sorry. Come in."

"Will the dogs let me?"

She gave a hand signal, and they backed off.

"I'd hoped it was Veejay, but Tandy would have known," she said regretfully.

"Is that Tandy?"

"Yes. The one with the tail like a husky. She's a trained hunter. Elkhounds are almost like bloodhounds." She knelt and patted the two goldens, detaching the leash from the bigger one's collar.

"How are you feeling?"

"Okay."

I met her eyes. "Are you alone?"

"Except for the dogs. Esperanza wanted to stay, but I told her I'd be fine." She led me through the opening between the fish tanks into the room with the paintings. I wondered what the dogs made of the fish swimming behind glass. "You seem—I don't know—angry."

"I don't like to be lied to."

"I haven't lied," she said. "Can I get you a drink?"

"I know about Veronica's sister."

"I'm sorry, but—which one?"

If she knew, she was dangerous. If she didn't, she was a gullible fool. Not a muscle tensed in her face to betray her. She didn't seem alarmed or upset.

I said, "Veronica's older sister, Leslie, died in 1993 in the FBI assault at Waco, Texas. They never really figured out how many died. Some say seventy-four, some seventy-six. I've seen it up into the eighties. There were twenty-seven children. One was Veronica's nephew."

She sat down on a deep green sofa, sinking into it abruptly as though her legs would no longer support her.

"The sister had married," I went on, as my client

gaped, struggling to find words. "Her name was no longer James."

"Oh my God, poor Veejay. But she never said—"

"Poor Veejay is heavily involved in a plot to avenge her sister. And that's where you come in."

"I don't—I had no—"

"Something made Veejay very attractive to the people she's working with, and I'm guessing it was money, your money."

"I didn't pay her. I told you—she didn't pay rent, but that's all. She worked."

"You never gave her money?"

"Of course not."

"Don't try to protect her. She's been using you, living here, waiting for her moment."

"I never gave her money."

"You never gave her money for *anything*? For charity? For an old dogs' home?"

She leaned forward, elbows on knees, hands covering her face.

"Tell me."

"Oh, God. No one can know about this. If my family—"

"What charity?"

"I can't remember the name. Some fresh air camp for dogs. I mean, I give to tons of charities. Why wouldn't I give to one recommended by a friend?"

"I need the name."

"I don't remember."

"Where's your checkbook? You didn't give her cash, did you?"

I followed her upstairs, into the spotless kitchen,

helped her find the purse that sat on the floor next to a flowered chair. She handed me her checkbook with a curt, "Look for yourself," and sank onto a stool at the granite counter. I ran my index finger down the check register. The lines were close together, jammed with crabbed handwriting and the kind of sums I'll never find in my own checkbook.

"What has she done? How much trouble is she in?" Dana spoke haltingly, as though the words were being forced out of her mouth.

"She kidnapped a girl."

"You're wrong."

There were sums to Saks and Neimans, American Express, MasterCard, to well-known local charities, the Boston Adult Literacy Foundation, the Jimmy Fund.

Camp River Ridge—river as in Charles River Dog Care, ridge as in Ruby Ridge—an echo, a statement. The check was for $30,000. To her, it must have seemed like a nickel. To them? How many "patriots" had it kept afloat?

"What did she tell you about the place? Where is it?" If it existed.

She raised a shaky hand to her bandaged head. "Just a minute. Please. I'm trying to think. Okay. It was in New Hampshire. Fresh air, dogs, an inner-city escape thing. I think it had just started, or they were going to start it this summer. Yes. It was starting. Veejay thought she might want to be a counselor there. I didn't want her to go."

"Did she give you any literature?"

"I don't know. There may have been a flyer, a hand-out, but I haven't seen it in months."

"Where were you when she gave it to you?"

"I don't know. I don't remember."

"What color was it?"

"I don't know."

I kept at her. Maybe the flyer was blue, a folded sheet of flimsy paper, two pages of sparse printing. She was sure the camp was in New Hampshire, but I couldn't get a town, not even an area, southern or northern.

If any of the New England states harbored western-style militias, I'd bet on New Hampshire, with its "Live Free or Die" credo. The Jaguar whose plates currently masked Dana Endicott's Jeep had been stolen in New Hampshire. Claire Harper could find out the name of the town.

"Do you have the cancelled check?" I asked.

"You're wrong about the kidnapping. Veejay's not like that."

"How did she come to work for the dog care place? Did she answer an ad?"

"She heard about it."

"From?"

"I don't know. It doesn't make sense. Why would she tell me she was going away for the weekend? Why not just leave?"

"Why would she leave, when she's got a perfect setup here?"

"Then why didn't she say she'd be gone two weeks, a month? Why hasn't she called me?"

Why, indeed?

"A change of plans," I said.

"I don't buy it."

"Veejay's in it up to her neck. The girl went with her, trusted her."

"Give me my checkbook." She flattened it on the counter, started to write. "I'll pay you. To keep my name out of it. To save her, to help her."

"She's in too deep," I said.

She kept writing in spite of my protest, tore off the check, and handed it to me. Thirty thousand. The same amount she'd donated to Camp River Ridge.

"Keep me out of it," she said. "Try to save Veronica. I'll do anything to help."

"Give me the cancelled check."

Within fifteen minutes, she found the small slip of blue paper in a file in the study. I couldn't make out the signature of the endorser, but the name of a New Hampshire bank was stamped on the back.

I took a silver pen from a holder, a sheet of stationery from a box, scribbled a few hasty lines.

"Dana, do you recognize this mark?"

She swallowed and licked her dry lips. In her robe, with her bandaged head, and tousled hair, she hardly looked like the polished woman who'd hired me. "Yes."

"What does it mean?"

"Mean?"

"What is it?"

"I don't know."

"Where have you seen it?"

"On Veejay," she said in a small voice. "Underneath her left breast."

CHAPTER 35

The cold night air felt bracing. I'd hardly slept with Leland Walsh in my bed, but I wasn't tired. I'd passed beyond exhaustion, had no desire to rest. I wanted to keep going, keep working, but I was stuck. The Registry had closed hours ago, and while I could reach Claire at home, how could she in turn squeeze midnight information from the New Hampshire Commission of Motor Vehicles?

I didn't have the clout; I didn't have the power. But how could I sleep, knowing what I knew?

When I can't sleep, I drive. I took the Mass Ave Bridge across the river, Memorial Drive outbound, thinking, at first, that I'd try a circuitous route home. Instead I found myself exiting at the BU Bridge, cruising the back streets of Cambridgeport, chain-smoking three cigarettes in the Strawberries parking lot before changing my mind and heading downtown.

Monday night is a dead night in Boston, the theaters dark, the tourists gone, the revelers sleeping off the weekend. I spotted an empty parking space on Bowdoin

Street near the JFK Building, pulled on gloves and a hooded scarf. Gusts of icy wind tried to rip the scarf off as I crossed the bricks and cement of City Hall Plaza, descended the steps to Congress Street, moving closer to Faneuil Hall. I began counting my steps at the statue of Samuel Adams, pacing steadily eastward, toward the ocean and the site. Patrons drank and laughed in the marketplace. Diners lingered over after-dinner drinks in the restaurants. Lights twinkled off mica chips in the pavement and distant music welled from a hotel bar. I stopped walking before I got to Atlantic Avenue, took shelter behind a street lamp, and estimated the last twenty-five yards. I didn't want the night watchman to notice me.

I turned and made my way slowly back toward the hall, counting paces again to make sure I'd measured accurately the first time. The Cradle of Liberty, site of the great Patriot's Day tribute, would be jammed at six o'clock tomorrow evening, the old meeting hall on the second floor SRO. I'd heard they were planning to hook up outdoor speakers to accommodate the overflow crowd. The honored speakers, the honored guests, would be concentrated inside the hall: the ex-presidents, the Massachusetts senators, Senator Gleason of Idaho, who'd once chaired a committee that had given the FBI a clean slate on Waco.

The old hall looked serene and untroubled behind its shield of concrete barricades. They'd protect the national monument from a truck bomb, an Oklahoma City bomb. But they wouldn't protect it from explosive charges in tunnels, in old sewage or drainage tunnels widened and redirected with borrowed tools. Maybe the humming noise I'd heard the night I'd rescued Leland Walsh had come from underground machinery, from a drilling rig borrowed off another Horgan site or ordered especially for this one.

There's a post office inside the hall, gimcrack tourist shops on the first floor. It was always like that. Even in 1742 when it opened, there was space for a market as well as the meeting hall for town gatherings. Here James Otis, Sam Adams, Dr. Joseph Warren, the "Sons of Liberty," gave impassioned calls for opposition to the sugar tax, the stamp act, the tax on tea that provoked the Boston Tea Party.

"The tree of liberty must be refreshed from time to time with the blood of patriots and tyrants." Jefferson had said nothing about the blood of innocent bystanders. Jefferson hadn't lived to witness IRA bombings in London department stores, Israeli teenagers blown to bits while eating pizza in crowded restaurants.

There was no visible police presence around the historic hall, and why should there be, with the Patriot's Day event sixteen hours away? As I'd paced the distance from hall to site and back again, had I walked over a finished tunnel, or were patient tunnelers still digging beneath my feet? Did they live down there? Was everything ready? Were they waiting till D-day to bring in the explosives? I swallowed suddenly, hearing Liz Horgan describe the location of the locked storage shed in my memory. If it was flush along the west slurry wall, it could be a blind, positioned to conceal the entrance to the tunnel.

Twenty-foot-thick sections of bedrock had been blasted from the bottom of Boston Harbor to make way for the harbor tunnel. When the major explosions went off, there'd been an environmental brouhaha over the inadvertent killing of fish. The solution: a fabulously expensive "fish-startle system" to keep migrating fish away from the blasting zones. After spending a million dollars to startle fish, who'd question a few hundred bucks' worth of explosives ordered by a reputable contractor?

I shivered and backed away. I didn't think Krissi Horgan was down in the tunnel, in the darkness, but I didn't know, and that was maddening. I wanted to make a move, do *something*. I could grab the night watchman, threaten him with Horgan's automatic, force him to take me to the girl. If he refused, would I kill him? If he agreed, would he bring me to a spot where I'd be outgunned, outnumbered?

I wanted to do something, but not something foolish, not something fatal. In the morning, Claire could tell me where to look. I had time. They wouldn't blow the building till Senator Gleason was safely inside.

CHAPTER 36

They were waiting in my living room, a pair of them, like andirons flanking the fireplace, wearing dark suits and ties. Eddie Conklin was with them.

"Geez, Carlotta, you could stay in fuckin' touch." Eddie didn't look pleased. "These guys about reamed me a new asshole by now."

Roz, in black leather, emerged from the butterfly chair, yawning and stretching. I wasn't sure if her I-just-took-a-little-nap routine was genuine or a put-on. She's good.

"Hey, Carlotta, sorry. Shouldn't have opened the door." She glared at the trespassers before dipping into a sarcastic curtsy. "There are some gentlemen to see you, and they pushed their way in."

"Miss Carlyle." The elder unknown removed a slim leather folder from his breast pocket, followed it with his name, Dunfey, and the initials FBI.

"Him, too?" I nodded at the younger one.

"McNamara."

Both sets of credentials looked legit. It was possible

that Liz Horgan, unable to cope with the tension, had sprung a leak, run to the feebs. It was possible that Gerry Horgan had felt similar misgivings and opened up. It was possible that I'd been spotted jaywalking in a federal zone or openly dining with Sam Gianelli. Eddie's presence gave me a hint, but I wasn't about to speculate aloud in front of special agents Dunfey and McNamara, both still standing, both trying to peel their eyes off Roz's tight leather butt as she excused herself and rapidly disappeared upstairs.

Dunfey, skinnier as well as older, asked whether I would mind discussing a certain matter that had been brought to their attention.

McNamara, in the brown suit, showed even teeth. "A friend, a colleague of mine, goes way back with Eddie here," he said. "So far back that every once in a while he'll do Eddie a favor."

"I'm all for old friendships," I volunteered when he halted expectantly. It didn't seem like sticking my neck out.

"This bozo will even run a set of prints for Eddie, from time to time." Dunfey narrowed his eyes into slits. "It's not something he ought to do, really, considering Eddie's just a private op."

"Right," I said, "but let's not make a federal case out of it."

Dunfey's ugly smile stretched. "We can visit headquarters, if you'd rather."

His threat meant the prints that I'd lifted from the pipe were not only on file, they were of special interest.

McNamara showed me more teeth. "Believe me, we'd prefer your cooperation." He was playing good cop, Dunfey his evil twin. It wasn't a bad performance but I'd seen it before.

I knew I had to talk or call my lawyer and *dammit,* the thing was I *wanted* to talk. I needed help, specifically the kind of help the feebs can provide. I didn't have the clout, the power, and they had it in spades. They could haul the head of New Hampshire Motor Vehicles out of bed, track down the origin of the stolen Jag. They could trace Dana's cancelled check in the blink of an eye, find the bank, hell, grab the clerk who'd cashed it. But I didn't want to be shut out, and the feebs shut you out so hard you bounce. Plus I was worried they'd save the ex-presidents and the senators, and the hell with the little Horgan girl. I wanted a chance to talk to Veronica James, a chance to earn Dana Endicott's thirty grand.

Dunfey snapped, "Are you familiar with the term 'obstructing justice'?"

McNamara's voice stayed cool. "Eddie says you didn't tell him where you got the prints, and I believe him."

"So who's the guy?" I asked.

"You answer my questions, that's how it goes. Where is he?" Dunfey was getting hot.

"Is he on the ten-most-wanted? Do I win a prize?"

"Look, we've heard about you. Don't try to get cute with us."

"I've heard about you, too. About people who died because the Boston Bureau protects informers instead of citizens." Last year two agents got indicted for helping a local Irish mobster cover crimes ranging from extortion to murder.

"Those weren't citizens!" Dunfey snapped.

"Right. They had vowels on the end of their names so they deserved to get dumped in a gravel pit."

"Gianelli tell you all about it?"

They'd done some checking on me.

McNamara intervened. "Hey, it's getting late, and we're not making progress. This guy's prints kicked up and we want to know where you got 'em. You used our resources—"

"I used Eddie."

"Eddie doesn't know shit."

Conklin roused himself. "Yeah? Well, I know this: You schmucks ain't Boston Bureau."

They had to be Washington. Justice keeps files in D.C. on guys who've threatened public officials, on foreign-born terrorists as well. The feebs have a counterterrorism squad. Squad 5. I dropped Eddie a nod by way of thanks.

"Listen," I said. "Whoever matches those prints, I figure he's got to be major, to bring you guys up from D.C. And I also figure you didn't have a clue till the prints came in."

"We didn't know this particular scumbag was in this particular area, and we're glad to know," McNamara conceded.

"In other words, I did you a favor."

"You could put it like that. But we need to know everything you know about the man who made those prints."

"Favor for favor," I said.

"The hell with this! Where is he?" Dunfey was hot.

"Does Faneuil Hall mean anything special to you?"

I said. "Faneuil Hall on April nineteenth?"

The two agents exchanged uneasy glances.

"Listen, I don't want to stonewall you guys. I just want to tell my story to an agent I know."

"You can tell it to us," McNamara said.

"We're in a goddam hurry here," Dunfey insisted.

"Then the faster you get him here, the faster I talk."

"Let's take her in," Dunfey said.

"Take me in, and I clam. Not a word."

"Shit."

"You guys could be heroes." I broke the angry silence with a hint, an implicit offer.

Dunfey brought his fist down on the mantel. "I thought the guys in the Boston office were all corrupt anti-Italian bigots. We're not gonna fly anybody in from goddam North Dakota, for chrissakes."

"You won't have to. He's local, undercover. I don't think it's his real name, but he calls himself Leland Walsh."

"Fuckin' A," Eddie said slowly. "He's Bureau, and nobody fuckin' told me?"

McNamara whipped out his cell.

CHAPTER 37

"When did you know about me?"

I was ready with an answer. "From the start."

"Bullshit."

"You asked too many questions. You took too many chances. You called the morgue Albany Street. Cops do that, not civilians. When you showed me the driver's license in your sock, you made a move toward the other sock first. Your FBI creds were in that one, right?"

We shared the front seat of an old Ford four-by-four parked on the verge of a narrow gravel road. Leland Walsh—I was having trouble calling him by his real name, Leonard Wells—was behind the wheel and I rode shotgun. The deep green of the truck blended into the nearby pine woods. Mist covered the windshield and fogged the side windows, which was okay because that way no one could see inside. We were north of Derry, New Hampshire. It was an hour before dawn, and icy cold. I stifled a yawn and a shiver, drew my jacket closer. More than anything else, I'd found it hard to believe Walsh was Kevin Fournier's friend.

Walsh—Wells—was supposed to confine his activities to discovering whether minority and woman-owned businesses were truly represented on the Dig, or whether blacks and women had been brought in as figureheads to get around federal contract regulations. He wasn't supposed to go sneaking around at night, getting his head beaten in. I'd been right about who he was, and I'd been right about the fact that he hadn't submitted a report detailing his midnight escapade.

And that's why I was sitting in the truck instead of twiddling my thumbs at home or calling my lawyer from jail. I wasn't here because I'd given the feebs Kendall Heywood's fingerprints and they'd sent up every red flag in Washington from the IRS to the Secret Service. Kenny Heywood, devout soldier of the Texas Republican Army, had vowed on tape and in print to blow up the White House, torch the Capitol, machine-gun senators and representatives racing for the exits. I wasn't here because he was currently pretending to be one Jason O'Meara, night watchman, or because I'd been able to steer the FBI to Rogers Walters and his crew, or because I'd unveiled the plot to dig beneath the Dig, using a huge tunnel as a blind for a small one. I was part of this operation because I was blackmailing Walsh. My involvement was the price for my silence.

I rubbed my hands over my eyes. Walsh-Wells gunned the motor to give us a little heat. My FBI all-nighter had been divided into three stages, indignation, disbelief, and finally, planning, with disbelief taking up way too much time. Dunfey couldn't credit the fact that an organized cell had infiltrated security for the Faneuil Hall extravaganza. Ken Heywood was probably a windbag; no one would dare to blow up ex-presidents. The Bureau couldn't take a tour of the secret tunnel, and since I hadn't exactly seen it either, they preferred to imagine it couldn't exist. Walsh and McNamara brought in a Dig engineer and a Department of Utilities supervisor who backed me up. The tunnel might not be there, but it could be there; it was possible. An old sewer line, a hell of a big one, long abandoned, ran parallel to Chatham Street.

Once the feebs wrapped their minds around the necessity for action, once the bureaucracy ground into motion, the wheels spun quickly. The manpower, the money, the persuasive force of the FBI was impressive. The New Hampshire Commissioner of Motor Vehicles, eager to cooperate even in the middle of the night, identified the strip mall parking lot from which the Jaguar had been stolen. It became the first pin in the large map someone tacked to a wall. A vice president at Fleet Bank identified the small Concordia Bank branch in Derry as the place where Alicia Smith or Smithe had endorsed and cashed Dana Endicott's check. Another pin. The red diamond logo Marian had noticed on a dump truck led to Hastings Hauling, a small trucking firm, also in Derry. Pin number three.

By this time, half the special agents in New England were in New Hampshire, waking district attorneys, contacting judges, preparing warrants. Since the operation would be carried out across state lines, it was necessary to fix jurisdiction. The District Attorney's Office for Racketeering and Terrorism, the Secret Service, FEMA, had to be talked on board.

Roz came through with a lead, producing the tattoo

artist who'd done designs six months ago on three dudes who gave their address as River Ridge Farm. One was a girl of twenty or so who fitted Veronica's description to a T. The tat man was currently combing through files of known and suspected terrorists.

The tattoo, he explained, was a hybrid, part Montana State Prison—where agents immediately began checking files in the hopes of finding either Rogers Walters or Harold, his incorruptible underling—part homage to various Texas-bred militia groups. The star was straight from the stars and bars, the Confederate flag.

The FBI located the the Hastings truck driver and rooted him out of bed. Urged to do his civic duty and prompted by the name River Ridge Farm, he'd recalled delivering dirt to a small compound off a gravel road in a quiet area that would be bustling with summer camps in three months' time. He'd drawn a map, showing how many gates he'd driven through, exactly where he'd dumped the dirt.

Postal inspectors were awakened and questioned about the number of people receiving mail at the Jasper Pine Road address. The town clerk brought in a platte map. The gas company and phone company gave details about the service.

There were no landline phones, but no one knew how many cells. No one knew how many guns. Three women had been seen and a couple of kids. Two men, a mail carrier thought. A neighbor, the brother-in-law of the mailman, said it was a religious retreat house and the folks were very nice and respectful. Two families, he thought.

"Shit. If it weren't for the kidnapping." Walsh-Wells

didn't go any further because we'd been there before. If it weren't for the kidnapping it would be simple. Disarm the bombs and round up the crooks.

Tandy, borrowed from Dana Endicott, nudged my shoulder, and made soft inquiring noises. I patted her head and she wagged her tail, eager and alert. In the end, I'd gotten the two things I wanted most: participation, and an agreement that the conspirators wouldn't be grabbed until an attempt had been made to rescue both Krissi Horgan and Veronica James.

They'd keep Kristal alive until after her daily call to mom and dad, because if mom and dad talked, the entire operation was at risk. The Horgans had never received a phone call before noon. I thought we could count on Veronica as an ally in Kristal's rescue. I'd gone over my reasoning with the FBI, and by and large, they'd scoffed. She was the sister of a Waco victim, and their faces had gone still at the mention of the Texas town.

I ran through the sequence in my mind. She'd said she'd be gone for a weekend. She hadn't made the phone call explaining her disappearance. I wasn't sure what Walters had told her, how he'd conned her into helping, but I didn't think she'd grasped the enormity of the plan until it was too late. At some point, I thought, romance had turned to reality and the idea of revenge had been personified by a real girl, a bright and sympathetic girl who loved dogs.

When push came to shove, I thought Veejay would help Kristal, but I wasn't a hundred percent on it. I wasn't even a hundred percent on Kristal. Kidnapping does funny things to people. We could have two little

Patti Hearsts in there, armed with AK-47s waiting for the glorious revolution to begin. But if I was right, if I could get Kristal out alive . . . If I could grab Veronica James, give Dana Endicott the chance to hire the best attorney money could buy . . .

"You awake?" Walsh asked softly.

"Yep."

"Almost time."

I ticked off details in my mind. The black Jeep's stolen plate was known to law enforcement. Charles River Dog Care was under careful watch. No one had been arrested; surveillance was deliberately loose. Better to lose someone than to let them know the game was over.

If the game was over, they'd kill the hostage and blow the hall. It might not be as satisfactory to kill teens and tourists and lunching secretaries as former heads of state and a senator who'd helped clear the FBI of wrongdoing at Waco, but demolishing the Cradle of Liberty on the anniversary of Waco would be a coup in itself.

At Faneuil Hall, they could do nothing. They couldn't sandbag; they couldn't shut down. The National Parks Service was in an uproar. A quiet uproar, I hoped.

Walsh-Wells poured a cup of coffee from a thermos and passed it my way. I drank it black, that's how much I needed it.

"We ought to get our vests on," he said.

"Right."

"You don't have to go. We got guys can do this."

"Hey, you don't have to go, either."

"It's my job," he said.

"Mine, too. I'm getting paid."

"Jesus, let's not get into it again."

"Good idea."

He chuckled softly. "You went through my stuff, didn't you? That's how you knew what was in the other sock."

"While you slept like a baby."

He touched my hand. "Let's do it again, when this is over."

It was time; if we waited any longer the darkness would dissolve into pale gray mist, into the dawn of April 19. I unwrapped one of Veronica's old shoes, held it at arm's length for Tandy to sniff.

"Take it, girl," I whispered. "Take it, Tandy."

CHAPTER 38

The dog strained at the leash and I quickened my pace. My eyes had made what adjustment they could, but it was darker than I'd anticipated, true country dark rather than the city glow to which I'd grown accustomed. I could hear Walsh's—damn, *Wells's*—footsteps, faintly echoing my own. The dog padded silently. I could barely hear her panting breath. Underfoot, the brown leaves were limp and damp, a heavy winter mulch that sucked at the soles of my boots. The cold was thick and moist, a blanket that chilled rather than warmed. I risked a beam from my flash, shielding it, aiming it low.

The four buildings within the compound were spread out much as they'd been on the hastily sketched FBI map. There was a trailer set on concrete blocks, smaller than the construction site office, a large weathered barn where the mailman thought people slept, a narrow shed, possibly for equipment storage, and what looked like an outhouse, with a half-moon cutout on the door. Windows in shed, trailer, and barn were few and small. The

last light, a candle burning on the sill of the trailer, had
flickered and died before midnight, and no lights had
been spotted since.

The silence was heavy and deep, creeping like fog
out of the old pine forest. A murmur of wind brushed
my neck. I thought about FBI watchers in the trees as
the leash grew taut, and my spine prickled. We
emerged from the woods fifty yards from the river at
the same time a sliver of moon appeared from behind
a bank of clouds. I flicked off the flashlight and hugged
the ground, listening.

A man named Henry, Ryan Henry, a ringer for Rogers Walters, had sublet the campground eight months
ago. He ran an animal shelter, the original lessee understood, a refuge for elderly pets who might otherwise
be destroyed. Only other thing he knew, the man sent
the rent on time. Eight months is a long time to main-
tain armed vigilance and I was hoping the troops had
slacked off, trusting to the dogs that ran free within the
fences, dogs that ought to be sleeping now, thanks to
hamburger liberally dosed with sleeping pills. I tugged
gently on the leash. I didn't want Tandy eating any of
that meat.

She whimpered and urged me forward. She hesitated, sniffed the ground, pulled in the direction of the
narrow shed. I checked out the rough path as far as my
flash would illuminate. Trip wires were a staple of sur-
vivalist groups, the FBI advisor had warned. My turn
to scoff; dogs and trip wires don't mix. Advisors, experts, agents—I'd had my fill. The kidnapping experts
said it wasn't technically a kidnapping, since kidnapping is for money. They labeled it a hostage situation.

The hostage negotiating team said it wasn't a classic hostage situation either. Both groups seemed to value deniability more highly than responsibility, and a hit-and-run rescue plan had been approved only because we were running out of time and options. There wasn't time for a standoff, and no one wanted to risk coming in with guns blazing, not with potential armed resistance. No one wanted an Eastern Waco, a new rallying cry, another April nineteenth to remember. One thing the experts agreed on: If the plan was to be successful, no one communicates, no one escapes.

Tandy pulled and I moved, running lightly behind her, Wells behind me.

The shed's only door was to the northeast, blocked from view by a huge pile of dirt. A rusty bulldozer sat five yards away, just as the truck driver had described. If I were holding prisoners in an old wooden shed with warped boards, I might kill them after their usefulness had come to an end, then knock the whole damned place down with the 'dozer and cover it with cheap dirt. Two birds, one stone. Get rid of telltale dirt from a secret tunnel, build a funeral mound.

If the shed door hadn't been blocked by the dirt pile and the 'dozer, the watchers in the trees would have spotted the huge silver padlock earlier, warned us. An iron chain looped twice around the doorjamb through a slotted latch. Wells swore under his breath while Tandy whimpered and put her nose to the door. I gave her the "quiet" sign, touched her tawny fur. Wells kneeled and removed his backpack and I did the same. I pointed the flash as he unzipped a pouch, sorted through lock picks.

"Hold it steady."

"Wait. Let's check the chain." I played the light over the looped metal. At first, I saw new galvanized links, but then the chain went dark and splotchy. It was a hybrid, with a section of old rusty links.

"Bolt cutter?"

Wells supplied the tool and the upper body strength. One of the old links snapped neatly in half. Tandy pawed the ground while I slowly unwound the broken chain. The door creaked when it opened. There was a muffled snort of surpise, maybe dismay, maybe fear. I couldn't see, but I could smell, and the place smelled like an outhouse. I made sure the door was closed before I turned on the flash.

The straw under my feet was matted and dank. Two bodies—women, prisoners—were lying on the unclean straw, their arms bound behind their backs, their legs roped as well. Tandy yanked so hard I almost lost the end of the leash. Wells put a warning hand on my shoulder. He had his flash out, too, and he played it slowly over the women. I knew he had to make sure they weren't rigged, wired, connected to explosives, but it was hard not to approach them immediately, loosen the tight bonds.

I breathed through my mouth. They were filthy, one blonde, one dark haired, facedown on the straw. Dark-hair moved and tried to speak. Her voice was muffled by the bandana wrapped tightly around her face, but she managed a noise, a double syllable that could have been "Tandy."

"Okay," Wells murmured.

"Don't try to talk." I started on the thick rope at

Veejay's feet. My fingers fumbled the knots and I thought I might need the bolt cutter, but then something gave and the ropes loosened. I had to roll her to the side to get the knots at her wrists. She struggled to keep her face out of the straw. Finally my fingers released the tightly bound bandana.

"Tandy," she whispered in a rusty voice. "Who—"

"Keep quiet. Dana sent me."

"They'll kill me, kill us, kill everybody—"

"Shhh."

While I was untying Veejay, Wells was doing the same with Krissi. I could hear him murmuring soft encouragement, see tears streaking her grimy face, blood caking one corner of her mouth. Her eyes were wild and staring. She looked nothing like the glossy photo on her mother's desk and I wondered whether she could be restored like a damaged photograph, whether she would ever be the same.

"Who are you?" I heard her whisper.

"FBI. Can you move your right arm?"

The door creaked at the same time I heard the bolt slide on a rifle. Rogers Walters's voice sounded along with an explosion of light, a beam that caught me square in the eyes, made me squint. "Drop the weapons. *Now*. Let me hear them hit the floor. Drop them or I shoot the little blondie on three. One, two—"

I pressed the tiny device at my waist, the move-in signal, the Mayday. *No one communicates, no one escapes*. At the same time I dropped my S&W at my feet. A nearby thunk told me Wells had done likewise.

"Now back away. Girls, down in the straw. Do as I say, dammit!" Veronica went to her knees first. She had

to take Krissi's hand and tug to make her follow.
Krissi's face was pitiful—bewildered, tearful, and stoic
at the same time. With both prisoners wallowing
around in the straw, I couldn't hear Tandy, couldn't
see her in the shadows.

"And now you two. *Move!* Up against the wall."

I caught Wells's eye and we tried to get some distance between us, but Walters ordered us to stay close.
One of him, two of us. His rifle was a semiautomatic.

"FBI?" Walters said bitterly. "I hear you right?" He
jerked the barrel for emphasis.

"Right," Wells said.

"Then I assume you're not alone."

"We're only here for Krissi. Why not let her go?
How is she a danger to anyone?"

"How is she a danger? Hell, how was Randy Wea-
ver's wife a danger? How was David Koresh a danger?
A man of God, a scholar?"

"Did you know Mr. Koresh?" I could almost feel
Wells willing Walters to go on, keep talking, tell us
the whole story, long and detailed, *give us time*.

"No, but I know you. You're FBI and that means
you're lying. If you're FBI, the whole damned place is
surrounded. I saw one of the dogs down; that's what
brought me out. I should have woken—never mind."

"I won't lie to you," I said. "The place is surrounded." If he hadn't roused the others, they could be
taken easily. If we could keep Walters talking, keep
him from firing—

"You!" he said. "He told me—I thought you were
just a busybody PI."

"I am."

"Well, too bad. We don't take prisoners, not since Waco. We know you don't take prisoners either, not patriot prisoners, and we're all ready to die here."

"You don't have to," Wells said. "At least, send the children away. Are the kids yours?"

"Shut up, *boy*."

Wells flinched at the word. And then I saw Veronica's arm move, heard her low command, and saw the streak that was Tandy arch through the air. For half a second, Walters stood frozen; he was ready to kill us, to let his children die, but he was unprepared or unwilling to shoot a dog.

Wells threw himself at Walters, grabbing him around the knees, bringing him toppling down like a felled tree. There was a deafening blast and one corner of my mind thought, *That will wake the others, dammit*. I scrabbled inside the top of my boot, came out with Horgan's borrowed automatic. Walters had raised himself to one knee. He was aiming at Kristal, prone on the straw, hands pressed to her ears. She was screaming, screaming, and I knew I couldn't get a shot off in time, wouldn't be able to stop the execution. I couldn't see Wells, didn't know if he'd been hit or where he'd been hit.

Veronica turned, looked, launched herself, not at Walters but at Krissi, over Krissi, shielding the younger girl with her body. At the same time I heard the report, saw blood blossom on her back.

I shot Walters, kept firing till he went down. There were noises everywhere, running, lights and flares. But no one came inside the shed, no one tried the door. Krissi clutched the dog and moaned; she half-crawled, half-wriggled out from under Veejay, who lay motionless. I ripped off my coat, my shirt, made a bandage and applied pressure to the woman's back, felt my shirt grow warm and wet.

It seemed like hours before help came, but I found out later that the whole operation, from the Mayday to the round-up, took a total of eight minutes.

CHAPTER 39

Two helicopters took off from the clearing, big and black enough to furnish a thousand New World Order nightmares: First, the medical flight, airlifting Veronica and the other wounded; then the FBI chopper. I was strapped into the second bird, disoriented by the view through the Plexiglas floor, deafened by the roar of the rotor blades. Wells sat on my right. He'd been struck with the rifle butt, stunned not shot. I realized my teeth were chattering, pressed my lips together before the enamel chipped.

Kristal Horgan, on my left, rested her forehead against the smooth body of the bird. Someone had given her a clean jumpsuit that hung off her slender frame. She gazed out the window with a thousand-yard stare.

No one escapes, no one communicates. The FBI had cut phone lines, jammed wireless frequencies, silenced the local press so efficiently it was no wonder they were feared and hated. Despite Walters's defiant words, they had taken prisoners north of Derry, four of them, at least, alive. Two, Erica and Harold, I recognized from Charles River Dog Care. Two were combat-fatigue-wearing strangers, both male, with shaven heads. Rogers Walters was dead.

One of the combat-clad strangers sat across from me, handcuffed and manacled, guarded by a square-cut Fed. His slight build and callused hands had drawn immediate attention. So far he had refused to discuss the particulars of the tunnel, but I imagined pressure would be brought to bear.

I felt Walsh's—Wells's—touch. He shot me a questioning glance and I nodded to say I was tracking, I was okay.

"Where do we put down?" I yelled.

"Not Logan. Take too long to get into position."

"Why the hurry?" If *no one escapes, no one communicates* had worked, there should be time.

"Ops says there could be a fail-safe code. Something like if you don't hear from us every two hours, blow it. Wham."

"What does he say?" I indicated the handcuffed man.

"He says no. But whose side is he on?" Wells shrugged. "Another thing. Heywood wasn't at the camp, and we haven't got a line on him. Address on his employment stuff is a phony, bad phone number, too. He could be down in the tunnel, and if he doesn't hear from Walters—"

Wham.

"What about Heywood's KA's?" KA's are known associates. Prison buddies, cellmates, in particular.

"What are you looking for, Carlotta? *Who?*"

I shook my head and pressed the heels of my hands

against my eyes. Soon, I'd have to sleep. For a moment I imagined myself inside the other chopper, watching colored lights pulsing across screens hooked to the still figure of a dark-haired girl. Veronica had been alive, barely, when they'd taken off.

"When can I call my client?" I asked without opening my eyes.

"I don't know."

I'd given up my cell in exchange for a Kevlar vest. It hadn't been my choice and the cell hadn't been returned. The FBI didn't trust me, and it's true, I'd have called Dana, told her to meet Veejay at Mass General. It's not like I would have phoned *Hard Copy* to sell some scoop about a bomb under Faneuil Hall, to tell the world that depending on the time, depending on what the Feds learned from the captured "patriots," there were two alternative plans to deal with it.

The favorite: Flood the tunnel, force the bastards out while neutralizing the bombs. Much of the tunnel was thought to consist of ancient watertight sewage pipes. City engineers and Dig engineers, water and sewer employees, were confident they could quickly pump in enough water to neutralize explosives and drown anyone who refused to surrender. If I'd read the signs right, correctly interpreted the rat business from the start, I thought bleakly, it would be over by now. Where had the Horgan site rats come from if not the reopened sewer tunnel?

The fallback plan, to take the tunnel by storm, dropping agents into manholes, pouring them into the mouth of the tunnel via the locked storage shed, was favored by few. The fallback plan would cost lives. The tunnel was undoubtedly booby-trapped. One older agent, visibly shaken, had paled and left the room during a discussion that ranged from sharpened sticks to trip wires to land mines, and someone murmured that the man had been a tunnel rat in Vietnam.

"He told me," Rogers Walters had said. *"He told me*—I thought you were just a busybody PI." I opened my eyes as the helicopter swerved, shut them as my stomach lurched in reaction. *Who told him?* Who had warned him about me? The night watchman? What if neither Heywood nor Walters was the lead player? Walters ran the dog care company as a blind. Heywood came in as a night watchman late in the game. Was there a "patriot" on the Dig, someone who'd recognized the Horgan site as an extraordinary opportunity? Horgan wouldn't have kidnapped his own child, subjected her to the kind of conditions she'd survived in the camp. I considered Happy Eddie Conklin.

"Landing! Coming in." The intercom voice opened my eyes. Possibly I'd slept. Beside me, Krissi lifted her head and tried a smile that trembled, flickered, and went out like a broken bulb. I watched the ground tilt.

The helipad, atop a financial-district skyscraper, was thick with men in suits. They converged with guys in coveralls and vests, a cross between an honor guard and a posse. Walkie-talkies were standard issue and so were forty-caliber automatics. Agents urged Kristal into one elevator, hustled the handcuffed terrorist into another. He—I overheard the barked commands—would be whisked directly to a waiting van in the basement garage, shuttled to command headquarters at the JFK Building.

Time kicked into fast-forward. Wells squeezed my arm. "Stay with the girl. Her parents should be arriving in the lobby." The brisk, order-giving atmosphere seemed to have rubbed off on him.

"They could have been watching the house—" I protested.

"If they were, we grabbed them." The FBI was *we* now, I was *other*. He rejoined a group of agents. Hands slapped his back and he shook someone's outstretched hand.

"I'm coming with you," I said. "I know the tunnel entrance, the—"

"So do I. Stay with Kristal. *Stay with her.*"

I hadn't negotiated beyond New Hampshire and the woman I'd been hired to rescue, the woman who, with luck, would be in an operating room by now. Wells disappeared into the crowded elevator to the right, and I stepped into the elevator on the left, with Kristal, to avoid getting abandoned on the roof. The doors slid shut and machinery whirred.

Machinery. The FBI machine had taken charge.

The doors slid open onto Gerry and Liz Horgan, still as statues, flanked by agents, and Kristal fell into their arms. You say that, *fell into their arms*, but she really did it, taking her mother with her to the floor, where they hugged and sobbed, until Mr. Horgan joined them, kneeling, one arm around his wife, the other holding his daughter so tightly I worried about her ribs.

"Sir." The agent who spoke needed an inch more jaw to be a classic.

Horgan ignored him, pressing his face into Krissi's filthy hair.

"Sir, an ambulance is waiting to take your daughter to New England Medical Center."

"But I want to go home," the girl wailed. She'd been talking, talking, about Veronica, and her missing dog, and taking a bath, *please,* a bath.

"That woman stole her?" Liz Horgan said. "The dog woman?"

And saved her life. I wondered whether Krissi realized what Veronica had done.

"Sir, your wife will accompany your daughter to the hospital. You're with us."

"I need to stay with Krissi!" he insisted.

"Sir, we brought her back. That was our part of the deal, and now we need your cooperation." I didn't envy Horgan. I'd heard the agents talking. Every item he'd ordered, every person he'd hired, every shift he'd made in the schedule or the plans would be mined for information about the terrorists and their tunnel.

"Hey," I called to the agent who was busy peeling father from daughter. "Let me ask him something. Gerry! Mr. Horgan—"

"What? Oh—Carla—Miss—" He seemed dazed.

"A symbol," I said. "Wavy yellow lines over a blue moon, a tiny red star in the corner. Did you ever see a man or a woman with a tattoo like that, wearing that symbol on a bracelet or a necklace?" More than ever, it seemed to me, that symbol might have gotten Fournier killed. If he'd found his "good luck charm" on-site, thought it might be linked to some sort of illegal activity . . . He'd tried blackmail with Liz Horgan, maybe he tried it with someone else.

"No. No, I don't remember anything like that."

"C'mon," the agent said impatiently. "We're out of here. Let's go."

"Take care of my daughter, my wife—"

"We got 'em," the agent said. "They're okay. Let's go."

"Please." The boss tore his eyes away from his daughter and stared at me, eyes pleading.

I nodded. I'd stick.

"Thank you," he mumbled.

They bustled him off, surrounded by agents. Liz Horgan and I were left with the girl and several agents of junior rank, one an older man whose main duty seemed to be the ineffectual patting of shoulders.

Not until we were in the ambulance on our way to the hospital, with Kristal lying blank-faced on a gurney, blankets drawn to her chin, did Liz Horgan approach. I thought she might echo her husband's thanks, but she seemed distracted. She pushed her hair off her forehead and said, "Can I tell you something, privately?"

I nodded, thinking either she would or she wouldn't. She looked like the coin was still in the air, waiting to drop, heads or tails.

"I love my husband," she said.

If that was the private communiqué, it was safe with me, I thought.

"I wouldn't want him to know. I wouldn't want him to know where the FBI learned it. I wouldn't want the police to know. They talk. No one can know. You'd have to give me your word."

"Depends on what you're getting at."

She bit her lip. "You asked Gerry about—about a symbol, a—a tattoo."

I snapped to attention then. Inside, so it didn't show. "I did. Yes."

"Is it important?"

"Yes." I thought about adding life and death, but let it go. I didn't want to discourage her.

"I know someone, a man, with a tattoo like that."

"Who?"

"I wouldn't want my husband to know. The tattoo is not someplace where, um, a casual acquaintance would happen to see it."

Low on the small of his back. That's where Roz's tat man had placed them on the men.

"Who?" I repeated.

The ambulance took a sharp corner and she staggered slightly. "Harv O'Day."

Harv O'Day, the site supervisor, keeper of the time cards. Wiry and small, a born tunneler.

CHAPTER 40

The ambulance stopped on a dime, the back doors flung wide at New England Medical Center's emergency entrance, a mile and a half from the JFK Building where agents were gathering, preparing to drown the tunnel or take it by storm. I couldn't run it, not with this leg.

"My husband can't find out about this," Liz whispered sharply as I jumped to the pavement.

The agents had disappeared, vanished, melted like snowflakes on hot pavement, the car assigned to tail us either lost in traffic or diverted to some other emergency. Diverted. Had to be. How can you lose a fucking ambulance? Who knows? Sam Gianelli once told me the mob has a saying: *Organized crime thrives on disorganized justice.*

I gave up on the Feds and ran back to the entrance in time to see Krissi's gurney disappear into a sea of hospital workers. Liz followed it, and I followed her, edging through the crowd, moving quickly down a wide corridor, catching my jacket on an IV stand, ignoring the attendants who asked me just where I thought I was going, until I caught up and placed a restraining hand on Liz's shoulder.

"Do you have your cell?"

She thrust her hand in her bag, shoved the phone in my direction, and moved on. I punched the main number for Horgan Construction and Marian answered, no recording, a live and recognizable voice.

"Is Harv O'Day there?" She started to babble excuses. "Just answer the question, Marian. It's Carla. Have you seen Harv today? Is he on-site?"

"He walked out a little while ago, Carla. Everything's weird today. I don't know what the hell's going on."

A long-nosed man in green scrubs, stethoscope dangling from his stringy neck, approached and told me I couldn't use a cell phone in there, couldn't I read the signs?

"When did he leave?" I asked Marian. "Did he get a phone call?"

"Yeah, I think. Maybe half an hour ago, maybe longer. He just left. Didn't say a word. Usually he—"

"Did you see where he went?"

"What do you mean? Why do you want to know?"

"Marian, *please*."

The man in scrubs glared at me, and I glared back fiercely.

"Jeez, he went off, like, in the direction of the marketplace, but he never goes out for lunch or anything. I don't get it. Gerry hasn't come in. Liz hasn't come in. They're not answering their phones—"

"Thanks." I hung up while Marian was still talking,

reflecting that her day was only going to get worse.

The glaring man was gone. I searched the waiting room, the hallway for a city cop, found only a vacant-eyed security guard who looked too young to shave. On the average Patriot's Day, every available cop is busy, tapped for crowd control on the marathon course. With the additional burden of the Faneuil Hall debate, beat cops would be twice as scarce. Out of the corner of my eye I saw double doors part to swallow the gurney bearing Krissi Horgan. Liz stayed behind, slumped in a chair, pen in hand, scribbling furiously on a clipboard. I knelt beside her.

"I have to fill in all these damn blanks and I can't remember—"

I took the clipboard from her unresisting hands. "Liz, where would Harv go? What's his cell number? Do you know it?"

She nodded and I handed her the phone. "Get him."

"What should I say?"

"Find out where he is."

She pressed numbers, held it to her ear. "He's not picking up. Should I leave a message?"

"Dammit. No."

"Isn't he on the site? Can't Marian—"

I repeated the secretary's words.

"He probably went to the apartment," she said. "Give me the clipboard. I have to fill out the—"

"*What apartment?* Where?"

He had a tiny flat high above the marketplace, she told me, a perfect crow's nest from which he liked to peer through binoculars at the busy scene below. The windows looked toward City Hall Plaza, an excellent view.

My heart sank. With binoculars, he could watch exactly what went down at Faneuil Hall. When the routine changed, as it inevitably would no matter which plan was put into action, he would notice. With a high-powered rifle and scope, he could take out a careless agent before he could lift his walkie-talkie to his lips. She'd never seen weapons in the apartment, but he had a police scanner, kept it on most of the time, enjoyed listening in on police and fire calls, even during intimate moments.

She had a key. She wouldn't say when the affair had started. Since she still had the key, it hadn't ended. She'd always been like that, always had a secret lover on a site. She wanted my guarantee that I'd say nothing to her husband. Her key would open the downstairs door, the street door; she had no key to the apartment. Once inside, she walked up five flights, knocked in a pattern.

"Show me, rap it out."

She tapped on the clipboard: one, two, rest, three, rest, four.

"Do you show up? Do you call first?"

"I call."

"Go ahead. Now."

"What do I say?"

"Find out if he's alone. If he isn't, say you'll see him later, and hang up. If he is, tell him you're coming over. Keep it casual, however you do it. But if he says he's alone, don't take no for an answer."

"I'm not going anywhere. I'm staying here with my daughter."

"Of course you are." O'Day would never mistake me for blonde Liz. But I'd been practicing her voice. All I had to do was get him to open a single door. "Call," I urged her. "I'll take it from there."

The long-nosed man approached, face red with anger. "I warn you. If you use that thing in here again, I'm going to call security."

"Don't bother with security," I told him. "Get a real cop or you're gonna have a situation on your hands."

He wagged his finger near my face. "You're the one who's gonna have the situation."

"Shut up."

"What did you say?"

"Shut up. Fuck off. Whatever!" I pressed the phone into Liz's hand.

She punched buttons. I clenched my hands into fists and eavesdropped. He didn't want her to come. She kept her voice light and teasing, made kissing noises into the phone. When she hung up, I had her describe the flat. I made her diagram it on the back of a hospital form. A large room, a bath. Windows, she emphasized. Wonderful vistas of historic buildings. You could see the Faneuil Hall weathervane, the famous grasshopper.

"After you knock, what do you say?"

She stared at me blankly.

"Come on. You use the key, climb the stairs. Knock. Two quick, two slow. Does he ask who's there or is the signal enough?"

"He asks."

"What do you call him? Harv? Honey? Darling?"

"I don't—"

"Do you call him darling?"

"I just say something like, 'Harv, it's me. It's Liza.' "

"Liza, not Liz?"

"Liza. He likes Liza."

"Okay, I'm going to ask you one more time to take that phone outside." The long-nosed man sounded sure of himself this time, and damn if he hadn't found me a real live Boston cop, slightly overweight, out of breath, as though he'd come on the run.

"Bless you, you're a prince." I leaned over and kissed the man in scrubs on the cheek.

"What the heck's going on here?" said the cop.

I handed him the offending cell. "617-555-9572."

He stared at the phone and then at me. "But that's—"

"Lieutenant Detective Mooney. Tell him it's urgent."

CHAPTER 41

In Concord, less than fifteen miles northwest, patriots of a different stripe would be checking the hooks, eyes, and laces on period costumes. Minutemen in ragged gear would face off against British redcoats, and soon a parade would begin, a hundred marching units. Rebel troops would muster on Lexington Green and a visiting dignitary would be granted the honor of shouting Captain Parker's words: *"Stand your ground. Don't fire unless fired upon! But if they mean to have a war, let it begin here!"*

The cop dropped me two blocks from the marketplace. I considered him—overweight, slow, a desk cop moved to the street to meet the Patriot's Day demand; he'd do more harm than good in his conspicuous uniform. I reassured him that I'd scout the territory and wait for reinforcements, knowing I wouldn't. O'Day was expecting Liz.

What did he know? *What did he know?* Liz and Gerry hadn't shown up for work. That might have alarmed him, put him on alert. *He'd gotten a phone*

call, left the site. The caller could have advised him
that the plan had gone awry, ordered him to make a
quick getaway. He could be up in the flat packing a
bag, getting ready to melt into the marketplace crowd
and disappear. Or it could have been a different kind
of call, the caller saying simply, "Do it now." I considered the proximity of the crow's nest to Faneuil
Hall. O'Day could be poised over a timing device, a
trigger. Plenty of time to detonate it while Mooney
tried to touch base with the Feds and organize a response. Two small children passed by, bundled against
the cold, their father holding their mittened hands, and
it was all I could do not to yell stop, take cover.

The feebs had taken Horgan's 9-mm automatic, the
gun with which I'd killed Walters, as evidence. Maybe
they'd arrest me for using a stolen gun to shoot the
bastard, but I wasn't worried about that now. I was
grateful I'd grabbed my .40, the weapon I'd tossed
when Walters ordered me to disarm. I'd tucked it se-
cretively into my boot. I leaned forward, made as if to
adjust a sock, removed the gun, and wedged it into the
waistband clip at the small of my back.

If the FBI had already started flooding the tunnel,
they'd try to make it look like some sudden sewer problem, a natural disaster. I checked for gas company
trucks, fire trucks, anonymous paneled vans. There
seemed to be fewer people than usual in the marketplace, and I wondered if they'd begun diverting trains
from Government Center to the Haymarket. I strained
my eyes. The Hall blocked my view of the City Hall
staircase, but it wouldn't block O'Day's. If he was up
there waiting for confirmation that the Feds were on to

the plan, how long before he realized that the normally heavy foot traffic from the T-stop wasn't materializing?

The building Liz had described was old gray stone, tall and narrow, with three steps leading to a brick stoop. I'd been clutching her key so tightly it left an outline on my palm. I forced myself to relax, kept to the shadows, wary of binoculars. A kitchenware shop rented the first floor. A brass plate advertised a hair salon on two, a dentist on three. That left four and five for residential. I glanced at my watch. Interagency co-operation takes time; I was counting on that. The best chance to take O'Day without gunfire was through the Liz ruse. She'd said she'd be right over. It was time.

The key worked and the door opened easily, noise-lessly onto a dark vestibule. The stairs were steep, un-carpeted. My leg started to throb after the third floor. After the fourth, the staircase grew narrower and I moved more slowly. Liz Horgan had been okay on the phone, teasing, casual. He'd been reluctant to let her visit, but he hadn't forbidden it, hadn't sounded forced or unnatural. Maybe he wasn't sure what was going on, maybe he thought things were still moving according to plan. I listened to Liz's voice in my head, let myself breathe before knocking on the door labeled 5A, an ordinary door. Dark wood, old wood. No peephole. Two quick, two slow. My .40 felt heavy in my hand.

I pitched my voice high, made it breathy. "Harv, it's me, Liza."

If I'd been part of a team, one of us would have fronted the door, while the other kept out of sight, pressed against the wall. I lowered my weapon to my side, hid it behind my thigh, arranged my face in a smile. When he opened the door there would be a moment, a beat, while he soaked in the scene: a woman, but not the right woman. I heard the chain rattle and drop, the handle turn.

He was barefoot, wearing nothing but low-slung boxers, and a welcoming smile that froze. He had a smear of shaving cream on his jaw. He made a noise that wasn't a word, just an exclamation of surprise that was cut off when I raised the gun.

"Hands where I can see them," I said. "Take two big steps back. Now! Right now!"

"What the fuck—" His hands were empty. He took the steps.

"Turn around." Usually I don't bother with a two-fisted grip, but I was using it now, to impress the man as I backed him inside.

His shoulders slumped and some of the tension left his body. Could be faking, I thought, gathering himself to spring.

"Two more steps, quick!" I shouted. "On the floor, face down!"

"What the fuck's your problem, lady? Jesus. Carla? That's your name, right? You crazy?" He took one step, not two, brought both legs together, flexing his knees slightly.

"Goddam right, I'm crazy, so don't mess with me! Down on the floor."

He turned to face me, grinned. One short step forward, testing like a goddam toddler. I thought, damn, I'm going to have to shoot him.

"I've already killed Walters," I said. "On three, I do your right kneecap. One—"

"Shit, lady, let's fucking talk this over." He was watching my eyes, and I was watching his.

"Two."

Watching my finger tighten.

When he turned and lowered himself to the wooden floor, I could see the very top of the tattoo, tiny points that belonged to a flaming star.

CHAPTER 42

I met Happy Eddie on the second floor of Faneuil Hall just before noon the next day. The rectangular room was dark and hushed, the balconies swagged with tri-colored bunting, the small wooden stage flanked by the flag of the Commonwealth and the Stars and Stripes. The high-backed seats, more like church pews than auditorium chairs, were empty except for the one in which I sat. The noise of shoppers filtered up from below, the ching-ching of electronic cash registers.

Outside, high puffs of cloud dotted the bright sky of a clear winter's day. It hadn't rained in the past twenty-four hours, but I'd skirted puddles on the pavement, the residue of the flooding operation. Icy water had erupted in such a sudden rush that even a suicidal attempt to detonate the explosives had failed. Two men in addition to Jason O'Meara aka Kendall Heywood had emerged, gasping and soaked, from the storage shed on the Horgan site to be taken into federal custody without a shot fired.

I'd chained the door of the tiny apartment, hadn't

budged till Leonard Wells's booming voice sounded the all-clear. I never took my eyes or my gun off the man on the floor until after he'd been surrounded and cuffed. When I finally realized I could lower my weapon and my guard, I thought Wells might have to oil my joints like Dorothy did for the Tin Man. Spent, I sank into a chair near the windows. The blinds were up, the faded curtains open. A seagull veered over a panoramic view of the roofs of old and new Boston, church spires and weathervanes, clock towers and skyscrapers, the distant gleam of the ocean. High-powered binoculars rested on the sill.

A brief search of the apartment yielded three rifles, two automatics, a box of grenades. I was grateful I hadn't known about the grenades. O'Day stood at attention like a soldier, refusing even to give his name.

A federal smoke screen quickly engulfed all proceedings. Yes, the FBI had taken several fugitives into custody. The MBTA offered sincere apologies for the derailment that had forced them to temporarily shut down Government Center Station. Jaded Bostonians were hardly surprised by the closing and shocked by the apology. Unexpected groundwater near Commercial Avenue and State Street would cause yet another delay in the Dig's much-delayed schedule.

Eddie looked his age and more, climbing the stairs slowly, wearing a rumpled charcoal suit. His eyebrows lifted when he saw me, but he didn't speak till he'd seated himself, tugging at an imaginary crease in his pants.

"Hey," he said, "you okay?"

"Yeah. Tired. I thought I'd sleep for a week, but I

can't seem to." I kept having the same dream: First the fire was at my house, a copycat inferno from my last case, and then its location would shift in the magical way of dreams and the fire would be here, in this building, and I could see the blazing spire tilt from the window in O'Day's flat, see people running, hear them scream.

"Gerry's clear," Eddie said. "He didn't shove the guy off the scaffold."

"O'Day confess, or Kendall Heywood?"

"They found traces of blood in the storage shed that hid the tunnel entrance. Looks like Fournier never left the site the night he died."

"But somebody punched his time card."

"O'Day hasn't admitted it yet, isn't saying shit. But Gerry's covered. Alibi, and a good one. Not that I'd a blamed him, what I know now. Makes me wonder what's the good of the friggin' hotline, what kinda creeps use it for what kinda reasons."

"You thought there was something fishy about the call from the get-go, Eddie. Give yourself credit."

He shifted on the seat. "You thought I was on the take."

"Eddie, I—"

"Maybe I was, a little bit, not for money, ya know, but for friendship. Leo Horgan and I go back and I'd a hated to lose a friend over something like this. Hard to keep friends when you're always looking at 'em, judging 'em."

Tell me about it, I thought. If Eddie hadn't pushed me, I might have avoided seeing the change in Sam. I would have tried hard not to notice.

"You'll be ready for another assignment, say, Monday?"

I nodded. "Sure."

"Bridge?"

"Lower, Eddie. Solid ground."

Dana Endicott had entered from the other side of the hall, looking small and lost. I'd been keeping an eye out for her. I waved and Eddie's eyes followed.

"You didn't tell me you were working for somebody else," he said, "but seems like it worked out."

A dog that didn't come to the site anymore, a secretary worried she might have injured it, my little sister demanding a finder's fee for landing me a client. Their plan could so easily have worked, a building shattered, people killed and maimed. I sucked in a deep breath. The dream was a dream, the wooden bench was solid.

Dana wore a slim cranberry-colored skirt and matching jacket under her long black coat, mid-heeled pumps. She looked like a wealthy banker after a Wall Street crash, exhausted, depleted. She shook hands with Eddie, managing a weak smile until he excused himself and his footsteps faded on the stairs.

"Veronica?" I asked.

It had been touch and go all night, nine hours in the operating room, and afterward sudden bleeding that had required an immediate return to the operating theater, a second three-hour session. Walters's bullet had missed her spine by less than three-eighths of an inch.

"Alive," she said. "I sit and talk to her when they let me. I know she probably can't hear me but I keep talking, telling her Tandy's okay, Krissi's okay,

Krissi's dog is okay. And I hired a lawyer. Not the family lawyer. The man you suggested."

"Haggerty. He's good."

"I'd rather hire a woman."

"Haggerty's good."

"I can't stay. They say she'll pull through, but—I wanted to thank you, but I want to be there."

"I'll drop by later."

"Do you think she'll have to go to prison?"

I shrugged. Once it gets to a jury you never know.

"Would you testify? If it comes to that?"

I could say she'd been a prisoner when I found her. I could describe the look in her eyes when Walters raised his rifle, her refusal to watch Krissi Horgan die. I nodded.

When she stood to go, Dana shook my hand warmly.

As far as the Feds knew, Walters's dying words, belatedly understood, tipped me that O'Day was involved. After all, returning a kid to her parents, the best job a PI gets, is no good if the kid comes back to a broken home, and Gerry Horgan hadn't impressed me as the kind to forgive and forget. I hoped Liz Horgan would get her kinks out, but I wasn't about to detail them for the FBI. Nobody deserves that. And Walters wouldn't deny the tale.

I watched Dana disappear down the stairs to mingle with the shoppers and the sightseers and the working stiffs who had twenty minutes for lunch.

In 1805, Charles Bulfinch, leading architect of his day, doubled the width and height of Faneuil Hall without changing its basic design, increasing the number of stalls from three to seven. The "Bulfinch interior," installed on the second floor, has hardly changed since. The third floor holds the museum and armory of the Ancient and Honorable Artillery Company of Massachusetts, an outfit dating back to 1638, their memorabilia, their charters, their weapons, mementoes of the rabble-rousing days when the oratory spread from the hall to the streets and fanned revolutionary flames.

Due to the unfortunate groundwater backup, the Patriot's Day forum had been postponed, rescheduled. I thought I might attend, occupy a dark wooden bench, listen for echoes of the ancient fire-breathing speeches.

A group of schoolchildren, fourth-graders, maybe fifth, streamed in, unbuttoning their coats, dropping gloves and hats, giggling as their harried teacher ordered them to sit. A uniformed Park Ranger approached to begin the half-hourly historical talk, and I stood.

"Hey, I don't mean to chase you away." The ranger, a gap-toothed twenty-year-old, smiled.

"I'll come back another time."

I had kind of a date. I'd been offered a tour of the still-draining tunnel by Leonard Wells, alias Leland Walsh. There were rats, he'd promised.

**Keep Reading for an Excerpt
from Linda Barnes's Next Mystery:**

DEEP POCKETS

**Coming Soon in Hardcover
from St. Martin's Minotaur!**

I hate running errands. I put them off and put them off, and then one morning the cat's got no food, there are zero stamps on the roll, and I realize I own no underwear without holes. I understand some people actually like to shop for clothes, do it for pure pleasure and entertainment, but I count it as one more damned errand; I'm too cheap to enjoy spending money. When I can't put it off any longer, I make a list and set forth to Harvard Square. I could go to a less pricey area, granted, but the Square has its own post office and is within spitting distance of my house.

I waited in line at the post office till I thought I'd grow roots. I bought panties on sale at the Gap. I mourned the passing of Sage's, where they always carried tons of my cat's favorite Fancy Feast, bought a few cans of an off-price substitute at the CVS instead.

I noticed him as I was waiting, along with thirty-five other assorted students, panhandlers, and shoppers, for the scramble light at the intersection of Brattle and Mass. Ave. His gaze lingered a moment too long and

I wondered briefly whether I'd met him at a party or exchanged small talk with the man at a bar. He wasn't especially noticeable, a middle-aged, light-skinned black man in a well-cut tweed jacket and charcoal slacks. Didn't hold a candle fashion-wise to the young guy nearby wearing buckskin fringe. Still, I had the feeling I'd seen him before, and I thought it might have been at the post office, behind me in line, or across the room at one of the writing tables, scribbling on the back of an envelope. Then the traffic light changed. The herd charged across the street and dispersed, some heading for the subway, some the shops, some disappearing through the gates to Harvard Yard. I stopped at the Out of Town News Stand, and gazed at the covers of foreign magazines. So did the black man.

The next time I saw him, he was standing outside the Cambridgeport Savings Bank while I was considering a bite to eat at Finagle a Bagel. He'd added a tan raincoat and a battered hat to his attire, and if I had to describe what he was doing, I'd have to say he was doing zip, simply loitering, which made him stand out from the crush of hurrying pedestrians. When I walked past, he fell into step thirty paces behind me.

Now, Cambridge is a crowded city, and Harvard Square is its hub. Teenagers cruise the streets, parading their finery, hoping someone will admire their most recent tattoo or pierced body part, but this guy hadn't been a teen in twenty years easy. I crossed Mass. Ave. again, turned right, then left on Church Street. I hurried past the movie theater and the Globe Corner Bookstore, hung a quick left on Palmer, a glorified alley, slowed down, and kept watch in the plate glass windows of the Coop, purveyor of all things Harvard. Sure enough, there he came, hurtling around the corner, hurrying to catch up. I tried to get a better glimpse of his face, but it was shadowed under the brim of the hat. I feigned interest in the fine art posters displayed in the front window, then sauntered on.

I'd just finished working a case in which I'd managed to frustrate a bunch of survivalists cum terrorists. The Feebies, no less, had warned me to be on the lookout for revenge-crazed looneytunes. But the group supposedly out for my blood was the sort that wouldn't associate with black people, much less admit them as prized members and give them the choice assignment of taking out the half-Jewish bitch who'd foiled their finest scheme.

I used to be a cop, across the river in Boston. I worked Major Crimes and I worked Homicide, and there are no doubt former and future felons who hold a grudge. But I was pretty sure most of them would do a better job of shadowing. Truly, this guy was not good at his work. If he was an accomplished felon, I was Queen of the Junior Prom.

He stayed too close, and then he stayed too far. He didn't know the basics, like walking on the opposite side of the street. He didn't use a shiner, a small mirror, so when he wanted to check where I was he had to turn, risk a full stare, and look straight at me. He was strictly an amateur but bird-dog stubborn, and extremely patient while I visited HMV and sorted through stacks of bargain CDs.

The gent also looked prosperous. If I'd sent him away and he'd come out of jail dressing the way he did, he owed me thanks. I considered strolling over to a beat cop, informing him that the elegant black man was tailing me, but I knew too many Cambridge cops to relish the horselaugh that would follow. Plus, I take pride in handling my own problems. My shadow didn't seem like much of a threat so far, but I wasn't about to lead him home or walk solo down some dark alley where he'd feel free to pull a gun if such was his intent. I could have lost him easily, could have hailed a cab or jumped a bus. Instead, I marched him around the Square while considering my options, then entered the Coop at the Mass. Ave. door, quickly stepped to the right into an open elevator, and pressed the button for the third floor.

As the doors narrowed, I saw my man rush inside and take note of the departing elevator. I figured he'd wait for the next trip, and wait a while, too, since there's only the single car. I had plenty of time to turn left twice and secrete myself in an alcove surrounded by books on medicine and a handy fire extinguisher. Hidden from view, I stuffed my parcels into my backpack, turned my reversible jacket inside-out, blue to gray, and yanked a knitted cap over my red hair. I try to be prepared. Me and the Boy Scouts. It took him four minutes to elbow his way off the elevator and start tracking me down.

I stayed behind him, veering from extreme left to far right, shielded by high bookcases, feeling like a crafty fox who'd turned the table on the hounds. The guy was tenacious, I'll give him that. He didn't approach the information desk or ask any Coop shoppers if they'd seen me. Instead, he walked to the back of the store, glanced down the curving staircase, decided I hadn't taken it, and charged across the third-floor pedestrian bridge, past the restrooms and the phones into the connected Palmer Street Coop. There, he checked out the aisles of the textbook department, then worked his way down the floors of the Palmer Street building. Dorm furnishings, greeting cards, Harvard insignia bears and chairs, sweatshirts and baby booties.

He took the seven steps down into the Brattle Street building, exited, did a brief survey of pedestrian traffic before stopping to consult a Rastafarian street musician who commanded a view of the door. I stayed put behind a circular rack of crimson insignia bathrobes. The guitar player shook his head slowly, dreadlocks wriggling like snakes, and accepted a cash donation. The black man re-entered the Coop, passing within ten feet of my hiding place. I followed him back up the stairs, across Palmer Street, and into the Mass. Ave. building again, where he took the elevator to the third floor and started working his way down through the huge bookstore, philosophy to periodicals to fiction.

He'd reached non-fiction before I grew impatient and approached. When he saw me, a look of relief washed over his face and crinkled the corners of his dark eyes. Then, when he realized I was walking straight towards him, the relief was replaced by panic. He grabbed a book off a pile and buried his nose in it. He was holding *The New Joy of Sex* upside down.

Maybe if he'd picked another book, or if a crease of anxiety hadn't furrowed his brow, or if he hadn't been quite so good-looking, I'd have shoved him against a wall, demanded ID, and threatened him with the cops.

As it was, I made do with a firm hand on his arm.

"Store Security," I said. "Come along—"

"*You are not.*" His low voice was indignant.

"*Gotcha.* How do you know?"

He pursed his lips and thought about fleeing. He was my height, maybe an inch shorter. Six feet, narrow frame. With the shoes he had on, I didn't think he could outrun me.

"Miss Carlyle," he said. "May I buy you a drink?"

"Isn't it a little early?" I didn't return his smile. He knew my name and I didn't know his, which upset my sense of balance.

"Coffee? Tea?"

"If following me around is your idea of a cool pick-up ploy—"

"This is, um, a professional matter." His fingers discovered he was still clasping the book and replaced it automatically on the table. "It's just I'd rather no one— I'd rather not be seen at the places I usually—places where I'm known—"

The Square is always crowded, the tables in the cafés jammed too close for private conversation. I considered and rejected several convenient spots. *A professional matter.* My home doubles as my office, but like I said before, I wasn't about to guide a stalker, even an in-adequate amateur, to my front door. It was chilly for early May, the hard winter refusing to release its grip, but warm enough to camp on a park bench or stroll by the river. I discarded both venues. If the man didn't want to risk being seen with me, neither fit the bill.

I considered simply walking away. Curiosity won out. "Come with me," I said.

Passim is a music club on Palmer Street, the alley-like stretch between Church and Brattle. It's famous as the reincarnation of the old Club 47, where Dylan and Baez used to play, even though the actual club was in a storefront on Mount Auburn. It's open for lunch, but secluded and sparsely populated in the afternoon. The small stage and tightly packed basement tables are approached by an outside staircase. The staff knows me, because I'm a semi-regular. I can leave the folky stuff alone, but if somebody's playing the blues, especially the old Delta blues, I'm usually in the audience. They don't sell alcohol or let you smoke, but where else can you hear the Nields one night, Paul Rishell and Little Annie Raines the next?

Skinny Sharon, on the desk, gave me a nod. I huddled with her briefly, and then my pursuer and I zigzagged past the kitchen, down the narrow hall near the bathrooms, and turned right into the back room where the talent hangs between sets. I've used it before; it's nothing much—a couch, a couple of chairs, yellowed posters on the walls. Two hard-shell guitar cases were propped haphazardly against the sofa and the place smelled of cigarettes and stale beer, indicating that the talent indulged in vices forbidden to the audience.

I flipped on the overhead light and blinked in the harsh glare. "You want coffee?"

He gave his surroundings a careful once-over. "Actually, no. You?"

"I don't know your name."

He gazed around the small room like he was searching for the hidden videocam. "Can we leave it like that for a while?"

"A short while."

I lowered myself into a folding chair and he did the same, both of us avoiding the enforced intimacy of the sprung sofa. The room was so tiny that our knees almost touched. If you could wipe some of the worry off his face, he'd be better than good-looking, I thought. His face was narrow, his forehead high, his nose broad. Angular cheekbones and a strong chin. I'd deliberately brushed against him in the narrow hallway, to ensure that he wasn't carrying in a clip at his waist. He smelled of spicy after-shave, and his tailor hadn't allowed room for a shoulder holster.

"Something I can do for you?" I asked.

He took a deep breath, the kind a man might take before plunging over a cliff into a cold lake of uncertain depth. "Before I say anything, please tell me about your ties to Harvard."

My eyebrows rose. "You've been tailing the wrong person."

"Seriously, you don't have *any*?"

More than one local newspaper columnist snidely refers to Harvard as "WGU," the "World's Greatest University." Some tourists seem to think Harvard and Cambridge are interchangeable, one and the same, with MIT tossed in as a bonus. The students certainly think they own the place, and the Harvard Corporation actually does own a considerable chunk of the city to which I pay property taxes. Red-brick buildings and ivy-covered walls line both the narrow streets and the major thoroughfares. A constant influx of students keeps the stores humming, the rents astronomical, and the foreign language bookstores in business.

"I walk on their sidewalks. I cross the quadrangle, so I guess I walk on their grass, too. I've used a book or two from Widener, but I swear I returned them."

"You didn't go there?"

I'd worked nights as a cabbie to afford down-scale UMass–Boston. "Nope."

"What about your house? Harvard owns property all over that area."

Bastard knows where I live. He must have picked me up there this morning. I didn't like that. I'd seen him for the first time at the post office.

"Not *my* property," I said.

"Ever do any work for them? Ever take a class there?"

I run a one-person private eye outfit, and I doubt Harvard has taken notice even though I'm perched in their back yard. I don't have a sign on my front door. The neighbors would never approve of such a thing, some of them having graduated from the hallowed halls of the WGU.

The extent of my Harvard connection . . . Let's see; I used to park illegally behind the Ed School before they put in the raised-arm sentry system. I figured he didn't need to know that, so I simply shook my head no.

"Good. Excellent. Next, I need to know about confidentiality. I've never consulted a private investigator before, and I need to know to what degree I can be frank about my requirements."

"I'm a private citizen, not an officer of the court. If I'm working for an attorney, then his privileges can extend to cover me as well."

I wasn't sure what this guy did for a living, but whatever it was it paid. His understated clothes were expensive, his hands well kept, the fingernails manicured. His hands were ringless and very pale, the palms paler than my own.

I've been going out with an African-American, an FBI agent temporarily on assignment in Boston, and the paleness of Leon's palms was nowhere near as pronounced.

My stalker bit his lip. "Therefore you could be compelled to testify in a court of law."

"Yes."

"Damn." He worried his lips some more and seemed at a loss as to how to continue. He had faint lines at the corners of his drooping eyes. I placed him at forty to forty-five, give or take a couple years.

"Are you ready to tell me your name?" I asked.

"Not yet."

A clatter of dishes and silverware penetrated the soundproofing, reminded me that people were finishing up lunch not fifteen feet away. Sounded like a hapless waiter had dropped a tray in the kitchen.

I said, "Often prospective clients consult me about hypothetical matters. Or they might talk about something that's happened to a friend."

"I have a friend," he said, leaning forward eagerly, "who is being blackmailed. He is—he doesn't know what to do."

"Your friend could pay up," I said sharply. Then I took a deep breath and decided I wasn't behaving in a manner likely to produce paid employment. I was behaving more like a pissed-off woman who didn't enjoy being followed around. "Sorry. I was thinking that your 'friend' could have made an appointment to see me."

"I was—I should have—I didn't mean to alarm you."

"You *didn't* alarm me. Go on."

"About the blackmail. My friend *has* paid. He thought it was over, but . . . it's more than that . . . It's the threat. I find—my friend finds he can no longer live with the constant threat of exposure."

I don't know what I'd expected—police harassment, a missing friend, an unfaithful wife—but blackmail took me by surprise. Blackmail is an unusual complaint. Blackmail isn't what it used to be. Secrets aren't what they used to be. What with confessional TV, and talk-radio jocks hosting gay cross-dressers and their second wives, and internet chat rooms devoted to perversion, it takes a certain type of deed to provoke modern blackmail, and more importantly, a certain type of person to attract it.

"Tell me more about your friend," I said.

"He is in a position of trust."

"Working with money?"

"Working with young people."

"Very young people, or people the age you might encounter at Harvard?"

The mention of Harvard was enough to make his hands clench. "Do you know how few tenured faculty positions exist? Tenured positions at fine universities?"

"I can see where your friend might want to keep his job."

"He does, believe me. He does."

The man probably looked familiar because I'd seen

him around the Square. A Harvard professor. Not one of the famous ones, not a local celebrity like Henry Louis Gates. Still, the quality of my prospective clientele was on the rise.

"Was your friend's action illegal?" I asked.

"What action?"

"I assume your friend is being blackmailed for a reason."

A fine sheen of sweat was visible on the man's forehead and I wondered if he was going to balk at detailing his imaginary friend's offense.

"No, not illegal. I—my friend, upon consideration, would call it immoral—although considerations of morality—I don't know, times changed, didn't they? The rules changed, somewhere along the line. Sex was—is—always about power, but we—we deluded ourselves, told ourselves how irresistible we were, told ourselves bullshit stories. I deluded myself. I thought of myself as an individual, a man, myself, not some powerful god-like professor."

I didn't interrupt, but I didn't like the way the conversation was going.

"She was of age, and in fact, she initiated the, er, contact." He looked me directly in the eye. "I should say, the affair, the relationship. What the hell do you call it without sounding like an idiot or a cad? Understand that my friend is not proud of his behavior."

"I don't understand," I said. "Your friend, is he the Master of a House?"

"No."

"Is he some whoop-de-do professor of Ethics?"

"No."

"What I hear, his behavior is absolutely normal, par for the course, unexceptional." I was understating the case; from what I'd heard, Harvard profs could sleep with assorted students of both sexes, not to mention barnyard animals, pay for prostitutes, call it research, and get away with a polite slap on the wrist if caught with their pants around their ankles.

"Times have changed," he said. "And my own particular circumstances make me vulnerable."

"Tell me about them. Beginning with your name."

"Please try to understand. I find myself unable to concentrate, unable to contemplate the future. I had everything, but I didn't know I had it, and now that I could lose it, I find myself behaving irrationally."

Irrational was right. A Harvard professor chasing an ex-cop through the Square.

He went on. "I find myself making foolish promises, going to church more often than I have since I was a child, begging forgiveness of some supreme being I'm not even certain I believe in. I feel out of control, in a way I can only compare to a mental illness—Excuse me. This is beside the point."

"The point being—"

"Leonard Wells mentioned you."

Ah. Leonard Wells is the FBI agent I'm dating. When I met him, he was calling himself Lee and I was pretending to be Carla, both of us working undercover on the Dig. "You asked Leon for help?"

"No, but he mentioned a connection to an investigator and I thought of it as a possibility, a place to begin. I was taken aback when—"

"What?"

"I assumed you would be a black woman. When I followed you—I—I suppose I was trying to decide whether it made a difference."

"Does it?"

"Doesn't it always?"

His tone held me. It wasn't bitter, more flat and certain. Matter-of-fact. I let his words fade. It didn't seem there was anything I could say in response.

"Leon trusts you," he said. "Could you find out who this blackmailer is? I need to find out who's doing this to—to my friend."

"Then what? You planning to go to the police and have your blackmailer arrested?"

"Of course not. I'll talk to him, to her. I'll explain myself. Surely there must be some way I can stop this person from ruining my life."

"I have a feeling blackmailers aren't big on chit-chat."

"I'm an academic, a talker by profession. I'm a very persuasive man. Don't you think so?"

I almost smiled. I found his earnestness and naïveté touching, and I wondered how he'd come to know Leon. "You're telling me you have no idea who the blackmailer is?"

"I don't. I—my friend was discretion itself. He told no one, he never met the woman on campus."

"Told, met. You're speaking in the past tense."

"The affair is over."

"Because of the blackmail."

"It ended before the blackmail began."

"If your friend was discretion itself, we have to assume that the woman—his student?"

"His student. Yes, but she seemed so much older, so mature for her years, so intriguing. I can't explain or excuse—" He studied his hands and adjusted his posture in the rickety chair. "My friend could never explain his infatuation satisfactorily to me."

"If I took on the investigation, I'd start with the woman. Would she be doing this, as a kind of revenge? Was it a bad breakup?"

"The woman in question is dead."

"Dead," I repeated.

"Yes."

"How?"

He moistened his lips with his tongue and swallowed. "A fire. She was killed in a fire."

"An accident? What kind of fire? What happened?"

"I was out of town, at a conference. I don't really—I have tried to avoid the details of the disaster." He closed his eyes, his face a mask. "Understand that my friend had ended the affair with Denal—with the woman over a month before her death."

He waited for me to say something. I waited for him. It's a trick I learned when I was a cop: Don't be eager to fill the silence. You learn more by listening than by talking.

The silence in the room was absolute. Outside, the clatter of dishes was interrupted by the hum of the espresso machine.

"Perhaps you would not be interested in representing my friend after all," he said.

"Look, if the girl is dead, all you have to do is deny the story. Unless there are photographs."

"There are no photos. I was careful—"

"Then why did you pay?"

"There are—were—letters. Are you interested in the case? If you don't agree to—I feel I've left my friend open to a new situation, a new peril—"

"I'm not a blackmailer."

"I'm sorry. I didn't mean to imply that you were. Trusting people is not easy for me, and trusting a white person with this . . . It makes me uneasy to the depths of my soul. I'm not some showcase professor. I don't have a named chair or a university designation, not yet, anyway, but I am a Harvard professor, and if this gets out, my whole life, my career, everything I've worked for is held by a perilous thread. God, I wish he could have held off, that this complication could have held off for another six months, another year—"

"The blackmailer's been in touch again."

"How did you know?"

"You wouldn't be talking to me if he hadn't been."

He nodded and stared into his lap. "I thought it was a one-shot deal, that it would be over."

"What does he want this time?"

"He's offering to sell me another of my letters."

"How many did you write?"

"I don't—no more than ten."

"Emails or actual letters?"

"Letters. Handwritten. I know, it seems old fashioned, stupid somehow. I never—I believed she had destroyed them."

"Does he want the same amount?"

"More. Five times what he asked before."

The blackmailer was a quick learner, I thought. And

a greedy son of a bitch. A phone rang in the hallway, three times, five times, six.

I said, "You—your friend has a couple of options."

"What are they?"

"I already mentioned one: paying up. If you do, you're in it for the long haul. Don't kid yourself that it's one more time and you're out of the woods."

"There must be something I—he can do."

"I would suggest your pal tell all, to his department chair and anyone else at the university with power over him, his wife as well, if he has one—"

"His wife would not be understanding."

"Limit it to people at the university then. Tell them that he has a regrettable incident in his past that he would like to divulge in the hope that it will inspire other members of the faculty to err in other ways and not his own."

"Hah," he said. "Understand that this was an undergraduate with whom my friend had an affair, and a light-skinned one at that. My department chair would have my friend's head on a plate."

"No love lost."

"None."

"Could he be the blackmailer?"

"Frankly, I can't imagine it."

"Well, then, you could hire me to retrieve your indiscreet letters. Technically, it wouldn't be stealing. Letters belong to the recipient. In the event of the recipient's death, the sender has as strong a claim as anyone. I might be able to bargain with the blackmailer, convince him he ought to take what he's gotten so far and leave well enough alone."

"But you said you thought a blackmailer wouldn't listen to reason."

"Put it like this: Everyone has something to lose. You could hire me to find out how to blackmail your blackmailer."

A slow-spreading smile widened his mouth and lit his eyes. It wiped the creases off his forehead and took years off his age. "I like that. My friend would—I like the idea of that, the symmetry. You would find something in his life to hold over his head."

"I charge by the hour, plus expenses. I usually get a retainer. You'd need to sign a contract."

"But—"

"It wouldn't have to specify precise details. I'd need to know your name."

He opened his mouth and sucked in a shallow breath. His hands were clenched so hard his knuckles stood out like shards of white bone. "I think I—I need to think it over."

I got to my feet. "You're not ready." The action moved him off the dime.

"I am ready. Dammit, my life is intolerable." He stood too, and then he stared into my eyes like it was a contest of wills, like he was memorizing their color and shape, trying to see behind them into my mind.

After five seconds that felt like five minutes, he extended his right hand. "My name is Wilson Chaney, Professor Wilson Chaney."

Considering what I knew about him, I could have discovered his name in no time. I didn't tell him that. I accepted his declaration as a leap of faith and shook his hand.

Don't get me wrong: Profs who boff students are not perched at the top of my favorites list. But I doubted this guy's livelihood was imperiled due to an amorous misstep. My demon curiosity had been aroused, not allayed by his tale.